I Mu

Obsess

Amber. R. Cotterell

Lilymoore Publishing

I Must Not Obsess is dedicated to those suffering from OCD, or anyone else who can relate to this book in anyway. Don't suffer in silence.

I must not obsess is a fictional book however the topics involved are very much real. OCD affects around three quarters of a million people in the UK.

Obsessive Compulsive disorder as stated by the OCDUK.ORG website is an "anxiety-related condition where a person experiences frequent intrusive and unwelcome obsessional thoughts."

OCD can be incredibly distressing and significantly interfere with every aspect of your life, but treatment including medications and therapy can help to keep it under control. With this book I have tried my best to research as much as possible in order to bring awareness of the seriousness of OCD, and to help people be more aware that the phrase "I'm so OCD because I like to keep my house clean" creates a significant misrepresentation for people dealing with the genuine effects of OCD.

If you want to find out more about OCD or talk to someone about it, these services can offer a safe and understanding space.

OCD action – All ages – 0300 636 5478 (9:30am-8pm Weekdays)

OCD UK – All ages – 01332 588112 (9am-Midnight – Weekdays)

If you or anyone you know is suffering with mental health problems and/or want to talk to someone you can contact the people below to receive the help you may need.

Samaritans – All ages – 116 123 (free 24-hour helpline)

Childline – Aged 18 & under – 0800 1111 (7:30am-3:30am daily)

CALM – Men aged 15-35 – 0800 58 58 58 (5pm-Midnight daily)

MIND – All ages – 0300 123 3393 (9am-6pm Weekdays)

Crisis Text Line – All ages – Text SHOUT to 85258 (24-hour text line)

Don't suffer in silence

Chapter One

Hi, I'm Tom, I'm 24, and I suffer from a mental health condition called obsessive-compulsive disorder, or OCD for short. I first started noticing my obsessions when I was 18 years old. Which also happened to be the time my twin sisters were born, and my dad left home. The obsessive thoughts started slowly, I would have to check all the doors were locked exactly 13 times a night, just to ensure no one would break in.

According to Dr. Sanford my dad leaving caused me to feel like I had to take on his role and look after the girls. Their safety quickly became a priority, it was a lot to put on young shoulders, and I took it all on myself.

Checking all the doors quickly developed into me repeatedly checking the oven and stoves were off, then the obsessive hand washing began; I had to wash them 13 times before I would allow myself to pick one of the twins up. I was terrified at the thought that they might get sick, I would constantly check their temperature, and worry over even the smallest sniffle.

If you don't know what OCD is, let me try to explain it in the best way possible. OCD is a mental health condition that creates unwanted and horrible thoughts, which then go hand in hand with an unnecessary action or behaviour. OCD makes you believe that if you do not follow its instructions, something terrible will happen.

For example, it sets up habits in which the person suffering feels the need to follow, or else the worst may happen. With hand washing for instance, you may find that you must do things in a certain way, like there is an order to things, you have to rinse for 30 seconds, scrub with soap for 40 seconds, rinse again for another 30, dry for 60 seconds, and then if anything were to go out of that routine you will have to start the whole process again. You may find yourself in an endless loop of handwashing, until you feel the job has been done correctly. That's my experience of OCD, doing things repeatedly, it's agonising, but that thought in your head is telling you that you must or someone you love will get hurt.

Every person suffering with OCD will have a different experience of it. The driving force behind OCD is the fear of someone you love becoming hurt or unwell. OCD thrives off the fear that you may hurt yourself of someone you care about whether that is deliberately, or accidentally. To make it clear, no one with OCD wants to hurt another person, but the OCD makes us believe we may be capable of such things. The important thing to remember is that having thoughts does not mean you will act on them.

The compulsive behaviour side of OCD starts as a way to try and control the anxiety we feel due to obsessive thoughts, the behaviour is always obsessive and in reality, has no connection to the thoughts we are having.

My OCD manifested in hand washing, and checking, it was my way of controlling the anxiety that I may inadvertently hurt my family. Logically, people with OCD know that the thoughts are only thoughts, but our anxiety takes over making it impossible to separate the two. It's the chance that our OCD is telling the truth that keeps driving us. It's the idea that if we ignore it even once it may win. Fear is what keeps the disease thriving.

OCD to me was like living in an internal hell, I allowed these thoughts to consume me, and take over my whole world. Following the rituals, I had set out for myself helped me to keep the intrusive thoughts at bay for a time. I would wash my hands so much that my skin would start to peel and crack, leaving them covered in painful scabs. It hurt like hell, but in my mind, I would rather put up with the pain than allow something bad to happen to my loved ones. It's an endless cycle of agonising thoughts and unintentional self-harm.

Just over a year ago, I was held under Section 4 of the Mental Health Act and was put in hospital for 30 days. I would have been released earlier had I not spiralled when my mum told me that the girls were ill with a cold. I truly believed I had made them unwell. That was the lowest point of my life. If you could have seen me them, you would be astounded by how far I have come. These days, I'm doing okay. I still live with OCD, but it is something that I control, it no longer controls me.

It was a very different story back when I was leaving The Cotswold Psychiatric Hospital...

* * *

"Do you feel ready to go out into the world?" Dr. Sanford asked.

I was sat across from him playing with the squishy ball that I received when I boosted up a level at the hospital.

"I feel good. I want to go home." I grinned.

"Do you feel ready? It's good that you want to go home, but are you prepared for what that means?" He asked again, knowing that I was unsure of the answer.

"Honestly, I don't know." I eventually said. "I am excited and ready to go but I don't want to revert back to how I was before."

Dr. Sanford understood. "It makes sense that you would feel that way, you have been in here a month, it's going to be a massive change, but I think you are ready.

9

You'll be back twice a week for our one-on-one sessions, and there is always support at the end of the phone should you need it."

I stayed silent, I was nervous, truth be told I was absolutely shitting myself.

"Trust me, you're ready Tom. I wouldn't have approved this if I believed any different."

Dr. Sanford stood and walked me to the door. I headed to the door, my mouth was dry, and my palms were sweating, this was the first time I would see the real world in other a month.

Dr. Sanford is the head psychiatrist at Cotswolds. He looked after me while I was in the hospital, he made sure my diagnosis was correct, that I had the proper medication, and then he helped me to open up about the reasons I suffered from OCD.

Dr. Sanford is an unusual man, his reactions to things always seemed so strange to me. I could say things that to anyone else would sound completely insane, something so extreme that I would find myself thinking *'maybe I should stay in the hospital permanently'* but Dr. Sanford wouldn't react at all, not even a flinch, he would simply ask me where I believed the thoughts came from, and then he would pick them apart bit by bit. I always thought he would probably be good at poker, his face never changed, no matter the circumstance. He never smiled, he never frowned, his face was a constant blank canvas, completely free of any emotion.

Dr. Sanford was 50 years old, he had magnificent locks of grey hair, enough to make most men his age jealous. He easily looked ten years younger than he was, the only reason I knew he was 50 was because he had commented on it in sessions a few times. He wore glasses, which came off the second a situation we were discussing seemed particularly concerning, and his big bushy eyebrows and brown eyes would suddenly become obvious.

10

Dr. Sanford always wore a similar shirt each day, trousers, a tie and a knit cardigan. His tie would be the one thing that changed every day, but was always a variation of blue, purple or green. I asked him one day why he never wore a red tie, he told me it wasn't important, but of course my OCD could never accept that. I made up multiple theories and went to him with each one. He found it so annoying that eventually he told me it was simply because most of his patients didn't like the colour and associated it with gore.

I noticed that when I would ask an uneasy question, his glasses would end up on the table in front of him. He would cross his hands in his lap and listen intently. He did this when I asked why my dad left, or why I blamed myself for my sisters getting ill, or why I had to deal with OCD. He didn't always have the answer, but he would help me to work out for myself why these things might be linked. Dr. Sanford never gave me the answers, he always helped me to find them myself.

* * *

As I left the hospital, I said goodbye to the friends I had made during my stay. It's a rule that once you leave the hospital, you leave everything behind, including the friends you had made. That meant that saying goodbye to them really meant goodbye forever. If you had told me when I first entered the Cotswolds that I would be hesitant to leave, I would have thought that you needed a place there too. However, as I stood at the doors waiting for the security guard to let me out, I felt terrified. I had no idea what to expect from the next few days and weeks, my future was unknown.

I stepped outside, into the real world, and as I breathed in my first breath of freedom, I felt dazed. My mum was stood next to the car, a huge smile on her face, she was so happy that I was coming home. I wish I shared her joy.

I walked over to her, duffle bag full of my clothes in hand, my stomach turned with each step.

"Hey!" Mum exclaimed. "It's so good to see you." Tears brimmed her eyes.

"You saw me three days ago, mum."

"I know. I know. But I mean...Well you know what I mean." She placed her hands on my cheeks.

I knew what she meant, it was good to see me out of the hospital, I just wished that right then I shared her enthusiasm.

My mum is amazing. That's one thing I cannot deny. She is a single mother, raising three children alone, whilst also maintaining a full-time job. She has been a mother for almost all her adult life, she was just 18 when I was born, and although my dad was around, he didn't ever help much. Dad was always either at work or planted in front of the TV. He and I never spoke much, we had nothing in common. The only time he would acknowledge me was to say something along the lines of, "You can watch TV with me but don't talk otherwise you can piss off upstairs."

To be honest, I preferred staying upstairs anyway. Most of the time mum would join me. She was always happy to sit and play with my K'nex or Action Man toys. That was until dad came upstairs to demand that mum spend time with him. "Leave the boy to play alone. It builds character."

Mum would kiss me on the head and follow him downstairs to save any arguments.

I don't think he ever really wanted to be a dad, so when mum announced that she was pregnant with the twins, his world crumbled. He suddenly got angrier, he would throw things, and shout all the time. He never physically hit us, but the verbal abuse was more than we could bear.

I will never forget when mum was around 6 months pregnant, dad had gone out drinking with his mates and came crawling home in the early hours. He woke me and mum up, and when she confronted him, he threatened to punch the twins out of her stomach. I could hear it all from my room, I climbed out of bed and burst into their room. Dad was startled when I squared up to him, he had never had anyone stand up to him before, he was so drunk that when he took a swing for me, he completely missed and hit the wall. That didn't stop him from trying again though. Mum was so worried that she called the police, they took him in, and he spent the night in a cell. He woke up full of apologies, he came home with gifts for mum and took us both out for lunch. Mum smiled and accepted his apologies, but I wasn't buying any of it. I still don't know what would've happened if I didn't burst in there when I did. I'm not sure how far he would go.

He ended up leaving a couple month after the girls were born. All he left was a single note with something along the lines of, *"Keep the house, I don't want any of this."* written on it.

I can't say that I was mad that he left, even now I don't hold a grudge, it was the best thing for all of us, He was never truly a father to me anyway, and the girls are so much better without him. Dad technically owned half of the house, but when he took off, mum decided to borrow the money from my grandparents to make the whole thing legally hers. It's been very hard on mum trying to maintain bills, and groceries on her own, but I have tried to help in any way I can, along with my grandparents.

I work full time at a DIY shop and give almost all the money I make to mum to help with household costs. I didn't mind, after dad left, I felt that it was my responsibility. The last thing I wanted was for mum to struggle, especially around Christmas time. I wanted the girls to have everything their friends did. I couldn't stand the idea of them opening their Pound shop toys and wondering why their friends at school got Ipads.

I believe that dad leaving, and the fact that he had never been a real father to me, made me want to take on a fatherly role with the girls. Yes, I was still young myself, I was just 18, but none if the "typical" 18-year-old things really appealed to me. I've never taken an interest in going to clubs or drinking, the thought of being in a smelly, dirty, greasy club, around drunken idiots never appealed to me. I just know that one foot inside a bar or nightclub and my OCD would be in a frenzy. I would probably have a breakdown on the spot. I think the fact that my dad would drink so much put me off ever wanting to do it myself. Seeing someone waste their life down a bottle kind of does something to you. My best friend Mikey has tried multiple times to get me to go out drinking with him, but I have always turned them down. He mostly goes to gay bars, and says they are totally different from typical clubs, but I would rather avoid any type of club.

* * *

Once mum stopped hugging me, I climbed into the car, and we headed home.

I had my phone ready just in case mum got confused with any of the directions. Sure, she had done the route a few times now, but she was never good with finding her way around.

Mum used to have a short temper; I don't think dad helped with that. But when I started to become really unwell, she mellowed out. I think she realised that I couldn't take much more stress. Honestly, I think she blames herself for my OCD, I think she believes she put too much on me. I would explain that she wasn't the problem, but of course she would never accept that, she was the ultimate worrier (sometimes she was even worse than me).

As mum was driving home, I had chance to have a good look at her, in the hospital I found it hard to make eye contact, or even to look at anyone for too long. I thought that I had failed her, that I was a disappointment because I had been committed to the hospital. No matter how many times she tried to tell me that she wasn't disappointed, I wouldn't believe her. While I blamed myself, she blamed herself just as much.

As I watched my mum driving home, I realised just how much the stress of the last few years had aged her. I knew that things hadn't been easy, but it was only as I stared at her that I realised what a toll that had taken on her. Mum had naturally blonde hair, but the grey was creeping through in her roots, her eyes, which were glued to the road, had bags sat under them, it was clear that she hadn't been sleeping well. I glanced over her hands gripping the steering wheel and could see where she had bitten her nails down, the skin around them rough and ripped. This was her go to habit when she was worried.

She had tried to put herself together this morning, hoping to appear completely fine, even if she was breaking inside, she had on a short grey dress, and a smart blazer. Her hair was pulled together in a low pony, held together in a clip. My mum was beautiful, no one could argue with that, but as I watched her today, I could see how tightly she was trying to hold it together.

She caught me glancing a few times and smiled, but it was obviously forced. We didn't talk, just exchanged awkward smiles every so often. I was thankful that the drive was short.

When we got home, the girls were waiting outside with my grandparents, they were holding up a sign that they had made with stuck together A4 paper and scribbled on with felt tips. As I looked at them from the car, they were jumping up and down with joy that I was finally home. I tried to smile and match their energy, but honestly, I was terrified. The tablets I'd been taking to help control my OCD had helped with the thoughts but did nothing for the guilt of being away for a month. I was supposed to be the man of the house, but the man of the house doesn't end up on a psych ward. I felt like a failure.

I took a breath, grabbed my bag, and got out of the car. Before I even had chance to slam the door, the girls were running towards me, completely abandoning the signs they had made. The girls weren't exactly strong, but with both running at me, they nearly knocked me off my feet.

"Hey girls! It's only been a month but look how big you are."

The girls didn't seem to want to let go of me. It took a lot of convincing to pry them off so that we could go inside.

"How are you doing son?" Grandad patted me on the back.

"I'm doing better."

My grandma pulled me into a massive hug, the kind only grandmas could give.

"It's good to see you love." She kissed me on the cheek.

"Good to see you too, grandma."

My grandparents were exactly what you would expect when you think of grandparents. My grandma had white hair, had a small frame, much smaller than when I was younger, and a smile made completely from dentures. She would randomly chuck me a tenner when I went to see her with a "treat yourself." I tried to refuse every time, but she wouldn't have it. Anytime we would visit her house she would bombard us with biscuits, sweets, cakes and any other treats she had tucked in the cupboard. I never saw her eat much of it herself, but she loved to feed us up.

Grandad was had wispy grey hair, and a tall, thin frame. He always wore the same rectangular glasses; despite being told he needed to replace them. Grandad never spoke much, not to me at least. He loved his time with the girls and was happy to have them style his hair with clips and God knows what else.

My grandad and I did share a love for all things Science Fiction and Football, so when we did talk it was always about either of those. He was an Arsenal fan, whereas I loved Liverpool, so we would banter over whose team was better.

When they lived closer to us, I used to go over every single Saturday to watch Doctor Who with him. We watched in almost silence, apart from when grandad disliked something the Doctor did. "He'll regret that." He would say under his breath, and then, "I told you you'd regret it."

The thing is I love my grandparents to bits. Most of the time they are amazing, but when it comes to my OCD and mental health in general, they just don't understand.

* * *

"I'm just going to sort my stuff out." I shouted while heading towards the stairs. I needed a moment to take a breather, the morning had been overwhelming, to say the least.

I peeked inside the girl's room on the way past, it was its usual mess with discarded toys thrown everywhere. There were more pictures hung up on the wall, I loved to look at their latest artwork. They were mainly superheroes and princesses, but there was one photo they had drawn of the family. It was me, mum, the girls and grandma and grandad. It had both their names at the bottom, so I think it was a team effort, it made me smile.

I left their room and headed to mine. It was exactly as I had left it. Mum knew that I would struggle with any changes that I couldn't control in my own space.

I would call my room "hospital clean", nobody is allowed inside except for me. I didn't have anything sentimental on the walls, they were just a plain blue, and I had plain blue bedding to match. Apart from the bed, was a desk with my computer and notepads on it, and a wardrobe, nothing more, nothing less.

My wardrobe had next to nothing in it, apart from the same few tops and bottoms I wore. I never felt the need to hold onto things once they were no longer useful, so close I hardly wore were binned. Inside my wardrobe was the one sentimental thing I always held onto, my memory box. I took it out and opened it. Inside was a small teddy from when I was a baby, some photos of my family and some with me and my best friend Mikey, and concert tickets from all the gigs I had been to. I looked at my wrist that still had the hospital band on it, ripped it off and placed it inside of the box. Sure, my stay at the hospital might not have always been good, but it was an important memory to keep.

I popped the box back and started to clear out my bag. There was nothing much in it, just a few clothes, toothbrush, wash stuff and a book. We weren't allowed phones on the ward so that was inside the bag and turned off. It was given back to me before I left. I placed my book "To Kill a Mockingbird." on the desk, and grabbed my clothes, they had been washed at the hospital, but I wanted to wash them again. The hospital wash had a way of making everything itchy.

I headed downstairs and put them straight into the washing machine. Mum saw me on the stairs and followed me into the kitchen.

"Do you want a cup of tea love?" She asked.

"Um yeah, sure, thanks mum."

"You could have saved that for later hunnie, your grandparents were looking forward to seeing you."

"Sorry." I said. I hadn't really thought of it like that. I just wanted to get everything in order.

In the living room the girls were sat on the carpet playing with the dolls I had bought them for Christmas. I sat on the sofa opposite my grandparents.

"How are you both?" I asked, attempting small talk.

"We're fine love. The new routine has taken some getting used to. But we can't complain. How are you feeling?" Grandma asked with a warm smile on her face.

"Yeah, I'm okay." I smile back, trying to keep conversation to a minimum. I never liked talking about myself, and this was no exception.

"How was it staying at the hospital?"

"It was okay I guess; it was a bit like school, except I wasn't allowed to leave." I joked.

Grandma chuckled.

"At least it was more like school and less like prison." Grandad chimed in. "In my day if you were sectioned you weren't coming back out."

Grandad always seemed so cold sometimes. He had thought in World War Two, so he had a thick skin. He always meant well, but he never truly understood my struggles. He couldn't understand how at my age he was fighting a physical war, whereas my war was going on inside my head. He would say things like, "Kids these days don't understand how easy they have it. We had nothing and we were always happy."

I think grandma had spoken to him about being more sensitive.

They didn't stay long in the end. As they were leaving grandad did his typical goodbye with the girls. He would put his hat on sideways and say, "Is this how you wear it?" They would laugh and say, "No gramps!"

"How about this?" He would say and put it on his shoulder. "No!" They would shout,

Finally, he would put it on his head the right way. "How about now?"

"Yes gramps." They would chuckle.

He used to do it with me until I grew out of it. Now all I got was a pat on the back. Grandad got a kick out of having grandkids, it meant he could be a big kid for a little while.

Once they left there was nothing else for me to do. I sat on the sofa and watched all the rubbish daytime TV that was on. I had only been out for 5 minutes and already I was bored out of my mind. Dr. Sanford wouldn't let me go back to work until he decided that I was ready, so there really was nothing for me to do. I am desperate to return to work. I want to be able to go back to helping mum out.

My job at the DIY shop was just a sales assistant role, but I liked it enough, it paid the bills. Basically, I ran around after customers all day for a measly £9.50 an hour. It suited me well enough. Sure, I wasn't big on DIY, but I was happy restocking the shelves and serving customers.

I have to see Dr. Sanford every Tuesday and Thursday until he gives me the all clear, I'm hoping it's not very long until he decides I'm ready.

The girls however were ecstatic to see that I was home every day, they wanted me to play games with them all day, they wanted me to read them a bedtime story and they were hanging around me all the time. I couldn't believe how much they had changed in the space of a month.

Elise is the first-born twin, which she likes to tell everyone "I'm five minutes older than Callie" she tells everyone she meets. Elise has long, blonde hair that she likes to put into plaits, she is loud, she always has been even when she was a baby, she would be the first to cry and she'd make sure her cry was the loudest. She loves playing dress-up and drawing. She has an amazing imagination, and I can't think of any other six-year-old that has her head screwed on straight. She is intelligent for her age; she was walking at seven months. She talks like a posh girl, like she was brought up in an estate home, I blame Peppa Pig for that. If I was going to argue with one of the girls it would be Elise, she always has something to say, and she even talks in her sleep!

Callie has shorter, blonde hair that she likes to accessorise with a different headband, she is the quieter one, she's more reserved. She's happy to do whatever Elise wanted and is down to earth. She's happy to watch TV and talk to me about what's happening, as if I don't know but she's also happy to watch TV and say nothing for the entire episode. Callie was a slower learner to begin with she walked at ten months and when she would talk it was normally in sections rather than whole sentences. Now she's a great artist for a six-year-old and every drawing has a story to it. I hope she pursues it when she's older because she could easily be a cartoonist. I get on with Callie a lot more than I do Elise but that's just because she's easier to get on with. If you wanted her to put away toys, she does it whereas Elise thinks of seven different reasons why she shouldn't do it.

I love both the twins equally but for different reasons, and yeah, they might have been one of the reasons as to why my OCD got bad, but I'd never blame them for that, I was just wanting to keep them safe. I didn't want anything to go wrong with them, I didn't want them to get ill or hurt. I would sacrifice myself if I knew it meant they'd never get hurt in their whole life, and that's how my OCD started getting bad but now I'm better. I don't feel the urge to wash my hands 13 times, I don't need to turn the tv or oven on and off 13 times. I don't need to do anything 13 times. I wish I didn't in the first place, I wished for a normal family, with a mum and a dad, and the dad was a dad. I wish now and then I could be a normal person who could hang out with friends at the last minute but I'm not. I'm not complaining, I wouldn't swap the family I have for a million years but I can have a dream. If I ever had kids, I wouldn't do what my dad did to us.

I always look forward to bedtime stories, the girls always told me I was the best at them. They loved how I changed my voices and how I left suspense. I always must read two stories before they go to bed, one in my reading style and one that calms them down a bit. They're reading James and the Giant Peach and Peter Pan. I loved reading these books as a kid so it gives me so much joy when I can read them to the girls, and they love them too. When the girls get into a book, they really get into it, and then they enjoy it so much that I end up having to read it every night for two weeks before they decide on a new book, they also like to let me know when my voice is different from the previous night and how they specifically wanted the same voice, which gets difficult because I don't know what that voice was.

Despite just getting back from the hospital that night was no different and it was even more special for them because mum no longer needed to read them a story. Mum likes to read the story the whole way through in a monotone voice which puts the girls to sleep sooner but mainly because they get bored. I think it's hilarious, she would always say 'well it works' while walking away. Mum's more analytical whereas I'm more creative. They were wanting me to read them the story and they wouldn't stop asking until I did. It took the usual two books and then they were out of it. I headed downstairs and when I got to the front room, I found mum asleep on the sofa. I decided to go upstairs and leave her to it, she clearly needed the sleep. I went into my room and sat in my chair. Looking at my room, now there's not much difference from my room and the room at the ward, although I was looking forward to not getting woken up every couple of hours by a flashlight being shone into my room and having to wake up at 7am for meds.

I went to my wardrobe and checked my bag. In there my small notepad still remained, it was the one that Dr Sanford had given me from my first day on the ward. He told me to use it as a journal of sorts. I laughed when he first told me to do it because I wasn't a journaling type, which I told him. He would talk about my love of writing and how journaling is writing but in a different form. Instead of writing stories about wizards or kid's stories for the girls, I would write about my feelings. He told me it would be good, even if I didn't write about my feelings, writing in general was a good way of expressing myself. He wanted me to find good ways of spending my time as well as finding some joy in something I love doing. I used to write all the time. When the girls were two, they were always making these drawings and with the drawings there was a story. I liked the stories so much that I would make a book out of them. I used to staple pages together, I would have a box for the girls to do a drawing and then I would write the book. We must have spent an entire summer holiday making these books, I think in the end we had about 30. The girls didn't get bored of it, and I loved writing the stories based on the girls' ideas. I just loved spending time with them, I knew they wouldn't stay like that forever, they'd already grown so much in six years, and it was only going to get faster. I always wondered what the girls would be like when they became teenagers, it scared me. It scared me more than when they were babies.

I always dreamt about having my own family one day, I liked the idea of living in the middle of nowhere, maybe by a lake, there would be a village not too far away so I could walk or cycle and get the necessities I need, and the shops wouldn't be big corporate shops, it would be small businesses owned by the same family for generations. The village would win village of the year for the 40th year in a row, they would have hanging baskets outside every shop, and nobody would litter. It would be the perfect village; everyone would be friendly, and they'd all be polite to each other and the customers who went into shops wouldn't be rude because they all stuck up for each other. They all had respect for each other. My house would be small, but it wouldn't be cramped, it would have a tiny balcony where I would be able to sit and write my books all day long. My kids would play in the forest, making tree houses or swings, and they would go swimming in the lake. They wouldn't play on their Ipad or watch TV because they wouldn't want to, they'd have so much to explore all the time that they'd grow up like I did. It would be complete bliss; they wouldn't be worried about how many likes they were getting on Instagram or if they'd get a load of Facebook notifications. They wouldn't care because they wouldn't be interested in that kind of thing. The misses and I would meet at 24, we would find ourselves loving every moment of being with each other, she would understand my history, but she wouldn't care if I was happy, and I wouldn't care about her history as long as she was the one. We would be grateful for each other, and we would live each day like that was the most important day ever. I would hold her like it was the last time I would ever hold her, and I would love her more than anyone could ever love something. That would be my dream family, but it's just a dream. Truth is, I've spent so much time looking after the girls and mum that I don't think I'll find the girl of my dreams. I wouldn't change my life for the world, I liked to think that everything happens for a reason, I wouldn't be the person I am today if my dad didn't walk out, and I didn't have OCD. I'm me because those things happened, I learnt from others' mistakes, I've battled my demons and I've come out victorious and I'm the person I am today because of that.

Whenever you think that your life isn't going great, or you think there's nowhere else to turn, just remember that everything happens for a reason. No matter how terrible that thing is now, one day it won't seem as big. One day you'll be able to look back and be proud of who you've become because of what happened. You can think 'hey this terrible thing happened to me when I was younger, but I survived it, I lived to tell the tale and no matter what anyone says that's the main thing. Your body is atoms, those atoms could have formed into anything, you could have become a tree or an ant, but you became a human. You were brought into the world as one of the most powerful sources, use that power. I don't mean create an empire and be the evil leader, but if you have to use all of your power to simply stay alive, do it.

One day you will look back and you will be the greatest human to ever live because you did it. You survived.

I waited for mum to go to bed, she never checks on me because of the one rule of not coming into my room. I heard her footsteps coming up the stairs, she stopped for a second outside my room but proceeded into hers and shut the door. I waited another 20 minutes before I left my room and headed downstairs. It was my first proper day of freedom, and I didn't want to be stuck in my room the entire day. I quietly put my shoes on and headed out, it was a brisk night, it wasn't too chilly, but the wind made it obvious it was autumn. I walked and walked and about 30 minutes later I arrived at my destination, I called it the lookout. It was the highest point of our city and allowed you to see the entire city from one specific spot.

I loved coming up here and watching the fireworks when I was younger. Dad didn't care for it, but mum loved it just as much as me, she would bring me up here for the day, leaving dad at home so he could have a couple of hours on his own. I remembered the times mum would bring up a blanket and she would wrap me up like a burrito and we'd just watch the city, we'd look at the cars going past, and I'd point out how tiny they looked from all the way up here. We'd look at the buildings that were once huge, 30-foot looming structures and were now just silhouettes. Mum and I would stay up there for ages, she loved spending time with me, and she loved spending time away from dad. She once told me that "not all teen romances are worth it, that's why they're called teen romances, you're supposed to move on." I don't think she met the right person, she thought she met the right one but as soon as she got pregnant with me, dad's mum said he had to stay, he had to give her a ring because it wasn't right to get her pregnant and walk away.

My dad's mum was actually the one who helped my parents with money for the house, she sold her house and with the remaining money she gave it to dad to put on the house, she told him it would make everything easier if they weren't in so much debt. Mum thought she would be right, but she wasn't, money didn't solve the problem, if anything it made it easier for him to leave knowing she would survive without him. It still took him another 16 years after his mum gave him the money to then leave. I remember the week after he left, his mum rang us up, she explained how sorry she was about what had happened and how she didn't know him anymore, she explained how she wanted to still see us kids and wanted to be part of our life even if he didn't but funnily enough, she never came round. She never visited us, she never got us a birthday present or a card, she never rang again after that. I think she was trying to make herself feel better, she didn't want to be the guilty one but if anything, she was worse than him. He left and never contacted us again, but she contacted us just to make herself feel better. It's why I don't say she's my grandma or nan, because she isn't. She wouldn't do half the stuff that my actual grandparents do. That side of the family didn't exist anymore and yet despite all the terrible things he's done I'm still in the habit of calling him dad. I guess despite everything he was still in my life for 18 years, I had called him dad for 18 years, it's just muscle memory.

Sitting at the lookout I notice there's something different compared to the last time I was there. The city looked quieter, the buildings looked dimmer, there weren't as many cars on the road, it was quiet, but it wasn't tranquil. It was like there was a reason for the silence, but I didn't know what. It felt eerie to be up here by myself, but it didn't mean I was scared, I don't think I could be scared of anything anymore. I stayed at the lookout for about an hour, but time was getting on and I knew if I stayed out any longer mum would notice I was missing, and I didn't want her to think that I was losing it when I had just gotten out of the ward. I didn't want to make her worry, so I checked my phone to make sure she hadn't texted or called. Nothing, that's a good sign. I headed home, the trip back seemed shorter despite it being the same distance and taking the same amount of time.

It's weird how when you're leaving somewhere it always seems to take less time. It's called the return-trip effect. It's when the journey to somewhere seems to take longer than the return trip, this is normally because the initial trip takes longer than expected (because of traffic or stopping at the services) so when returning the expected time is lengthened and therefore the trip seems shorter.

As I entered my house, I made sure to be extra quiet, I didn't want to wake anyone up, I didn't want to wake the girls in case they thought someone was breaking in and got scared, I didn't want to wake mum in case she found out I had gone walkabouts in the middle of the night. I didn't know which one I would rather have if one had to happen. Luckily it was all clear, I was able to head upstairs and into my room with no issues, nobody got up, nobody was scared. The house was as quiet as it could be, you could hear a pin drop. When I got into bed, I had forgotten how comfortable my bed was. For the first time in a month, I wasn't sleeping on a thin single mattress that had no springs in in case we broke it open and used them as a weapon. For some reason despite my bed being incredibly comfortable I couldn't sleep, I had gotten used to the hard bed that squeaked every time I turned over, I had gotten used to a light being shone into my room every hour and I had gotten used to the screams in the night from other patients who were having nightmares.

I must have fallen asleep because I woke up to banging on my door. "Yeah?" I groaned. "I have work, can you look after the girls for an hour until granddad comes round?" Mum shouted through the door. "Yeah." I replied and got up. When I got up, I had a shooting pain through my back, I must have slept awkwardly. I put on some joggers and a black t-shirt from my wardrobe and headed out of my room. Sitting on the landing was Callie, as I scooted past her, I noticed she wasn't following me. "You alright Callie?" I asked her, kneeling on one of the stairs to meet her eye level.

"Yeah." She mumbled.

"Are you sure? You look sad." I always tried to talk to the girls about feelings and emotions, I wanted them to be able to articulate their emotions and I wanted them to know they could come to me if they were ever feeling down. "I feel sad." She mumbled again.

"Do know why you feel sad?"

I had learnt this from Dr Sanford, if we admitted a feeling or emotion he would always ask "do you have a reason" rather than "why do you feel like that." There was a massive difference between the two, as Dr Sanford once said, we don't always have reasons for the feeling or emotions we're having and that's fine, we can have down days for no reason just like we can have good days for no reason.

Callie shook her head.

"Well, do you wanna watch Sesame Street or you can watch Dora the Explorer."

"Dora!" she exclaimed, and with that she was running down the stairs and into the front room. I walked in the front room and put it on for her, Elise was already downstairs, but she was playing with her dolls. That's something I love about the girls, they don't do the same thing all the time, they can easily be on their own doing their own thing, and then now and then play together. They were the complete opposite despite being twins. I was surprised Elise wasn't making a fuss about having to watch Dora, she didn't like Dora the Explorer. She was more of a Teletubbies fan, but she didn't even care about it. A lot has changed since I was gone.

I went into the kitchen to make some cereal for the girls when the doorbell went off. It was too early for granddad to be coming round, so I headed to the door and opened it. It was Mikey.

"Alright mate, I thought I heard you'd come out the loony bin. You coming out today?"

Mikey was alright for a mate, I mean he was an asshole, he would try to have banter, but it would just be him taking the mick out of you, but he was a good mate. If I was bored or wanted something to do or someone to see, he'd always be up for it.

"Na sorry mate, I gotta look after the girls." I told him while looking back to check the girls were okay.

"That's sound mate, just drop me a text when you wanna meet." He answered and then walked away. Just beyond my front garden on the path stood Sammy. Sammy is Mikey's boyfriend, they met about two years ago at a rave, Mikey and Sammy became friends quickly, but I was hesitant, I found out about three months later that they started hooking up. I didn't care about that, but I didn't get to see Mikey as much as I would have liked, they wanted to spend time together without me. I started spending most of my days at home, looking after the girls and doing not much else. I didn't spend enough time with Sammy to be friends with him, from what I know he's intelligent, not someone I would imagine Mikey with,

When Mikey walked away, I shut the door, I checked in the living room to make sure everything was alright and then headed into the kitchen to put the milk in the cereal.

"I don't want cereal" Elise shouted, which scared me half to death and almost made me spill milk everywhere.

"Don't shout, use your inside voice please. What do you want then?" I asked her, I was trying to teach her to not shout when she wants attention.

"I don't want anything." She whispered.

"Okay you don't have to have anything; I'll have it instead." I poked my tongue out. She seemed to get frustrated with that and then changed her mind.

"Actually, I do want it."

Reverse psychology. If she knew what that was, she wouldn't have taken the bait. Elise always likes to say she didn't want something to get attention, we learnt to say 'ok' and then take the thing and suddenly, she then changes her mind. It worked though, I took both bowls into the front room and placed them on the coffee table. Both girls sat on the floor, legs crossed and ate their cereal. Once they were done, they continued what they were doing originally.

I cleaned the kitchen and washed all the dirty plates and bowls that were on the side. I then tidied up and did some vacuuming, it was the least I could do seeing as I wasn't bringing home a wage at the moment. I was hoping that would change in a week or two, because the saving funds wouldn't last forever. Just as I finished cleaning the bathroom there was a knock on the door, I walked downstairs to open the door and Elise had already done it. Granddad was standing at the bottom of the stairs. "Not cleaning again." He muttered to me. "I was doing the bathroom for mum." I told him. Granddad didn't understand why I was like I was, he thought cleaning was a woman's job and working was a man's job.

He didn't get my generation where both men and women have to work and do chores. He walked into the front room with the girls and started chatting to them. I sat on the stairs for a bit.

It felt weird being out of the hospital, it felt like I should still be there. I liked how everything was in a routine and you had to eat in a certain place and at certain times, how you had art class at 4:00 on Mondays and Wednesdays and group therapy on Friday mornings for two hours. If certain things weren't done, you'd be marked down a point and potentially a level if you didn't improve. Every small thing was marked, it was their way of seeing if we were improving with day-to-day activities and if we could handle the outside world but, it was nothing like the outside world. I enjoyed the scheduled days, I knew what I was doing and when, I had no reason to be anxious over the unknown.

I stayed upstairs for most of the day. I came down to ask Grandad if he wanted a drink or anything to eat but he had already gotten himself a cup of tea. I asked the girls if they wanted anything, but granddad had also sorted them out. I sorted myself out with a diet coke and a sandwich then headed back upstairs. It seemed like granddad had it all sorted, he had taken up my role since I was gone, and he was doing a great job. I hope there will be a day where he didn't need to come around and help. I feel like an alien not being trusted with the girls. I know it's only the first day but it's embarrassing that my granddad has to come round to look after the girls when I'm more than capable of doing it myself. I'm being treated like I'm 8 years old, and it's completely demoralising, hopefully soon it will go back to normal. I am so much better now.

Mum came home about 5:30pm and granddad left five minutes after. I had made some pasta for tea, so as mum was coming in the door, the girls had just sat down to eat.

"You made tea?" mum asked me, shocked that I had done something.

"Yeah, I thought seeing as I'm home I should." Mum smiled in answer. I ate some of the pasta, helped clean up the plates and then headed into the front room. I sat next to Callie who was still watching tv. I know it's not good for kids to watch tv for long amounts of time, but Callie will go through phases of watching non-stop tv and then won't watch it at all, it's strange because she won't just watch an hour a day it's one extreme or the next. I went to change the channel and put on something more for my age range, but I started watching the kids tv shows with Callie and I have to say it's interesting, they were talking about the sea and how there are over 228,000 creatures in the sea. They would also talk about how dinosaurs would live between 20 & 30 years. I couldn't believe how factual a kids tv show was. Mum came into the front room still in her work clothes and slouched down on the other sofa.

"How was work?" I asked her.

"Stressful but fine" she answered, mums never liked talking about work. I'm not 100% sure what she does as a job. I know she works in a call centre, but I don't know what she does. I think she works in customer service but she's higher up than the others. I'll be honest I'm not too sure and she's been doing that job for two years already, I don't really want to ask her now. She works five days a week and has Sunday and Monday off, she works hard and often brings her work home.

When I started getting bad mum would work from home to look after the girls and she thought it might reduce the thoughts and obsessions. It also meant she could keep an eye on me, she would often work in the front room so the girls could play and do their own thing and every now and then she would come upstairs to check on me to make sure I wasn't doing anything she didn't want me doing. Like cleaning my desk 13 times to make sure there weren't any germs or remaking my bed 13 times. I have to say OCD sucks, it sucks more than a high-grade vacuum. You can't do anything, if I wanted to leave the house, I would have to spend two hours doing all my rituals before leaving the house. Otherwise, I thought someone in my house or the person I was going out with (normally Mikey) would get seriously hurt or killed. It was the worst time of my life, before getting admitted I would spend a lot of my time in my room doing everything 13 times. I would get up at 4:00am just so by the time I did everything I was ready to leave for work. At work they hated me, I had to check stock 13 times. They ended up putting me on the customer service desk, so I had as little to do as possible. So, when people turn around and say something like 'oh I'm so OCD because I like my pens in a line' I wanted to punch said person in the face. That's not OCD that's being organised. If you said, 'I have to keep my pens in a straight line and make sure not a single pen is out of place otherwise the tiny voice in my head tells me something will go terribly wrong.' Then yes you have signs of OCD but don't turn my mental health disorder into your organisational or cleaning love. If you like cleaning, you don't have OCD. If you like being organised, you don't have OCD. If you have to do one or the other because you think someone's going to die or get injured then go see a professional because those are signs of OCD and if left untreated can become life-threatening, not for others but for you.

* * *

I tried talking to mum about how grandad didn't need to come over, but she insisted that until Dr Sanford clears me to go back to work, she would feel better, and it would take the strain off me to look after them. She also said that granddad liked spending time with the girls, he didn't mind it at all.

He told mum that he enjoyed watching films with them, one of the films was called UP. It's a Disney movie about an old man attaching a load of balloons to his house in order to fly to Paradise. He loved that movie. It reminded me of him. He was a grumpy, old man whose main obsession was his wife, my grandma, who he adored completely. He would always tell me "You'll know when you meet the one as soon as you see them. This wave of warmth engulfs you and all you wanted to do is spend every second of every day with them." My granddad would always tell me that, he always mentioned how grandma was his one and only, I thought it was romantic.

They met when they used to go ballroom dancing, they would go with their friends in the city, and they started dancing together. They recognised each other but didn't know where from, they danced all night the first night they met, and it wasn't until they got the bus together and were walking home that they realised they lived six houses away from each other. I always thought it was a romantic story, they spent their whole lives in the same street, six houses away and it's only when they're grown up that they get together. They officially got together a month afterwards, married 8 months after and have been together ever since. When my great grandparents passed away, my grandparents brought the house my grandma had lived in her whole life. They wanted to keep the house in the family like a tradition. It meant my grandma was born in the house, my mum was born in the house, and I grew up in the house. It's been in the house for three generations. I wanted to buy it off them one day, I wanted to keep that tradition going because unfortunately I don't think my sisters will be old enough to buy it off my grandparents.

The next day, I had my first counselling session after being in the ward. It was two days into me being allowed to leave and I was going back, only for an hour but still. Mum drove me there before heading to work, which I made sure to thank her for. I had to get the bus back, but I didn't mind. We headed through the gate, and I got out of the car "I'll see you later." Mum smiled at me and then drove away. I put my bag on my back and headed into the hospital. When you're visiting or going for counselling you only must go through one door whereas if you're there as a patient you have to go through three. I headed down the corridor, I knew the hospital like the back of my hand, I knew where every secret hiding spot was and where all the kids would go to smoke when they were too young to smoke. I knew where the corridors were to all the rooms, and I knew where each fire alarm was. I had a map inside my head, and I didn't need any help to find Dr Sanford's office. I waited a couple of seconds and then knocked.

"Come in." Dr Sanford bellowed. I pushed the door open and entered. "Ah Tom, come on in. Take a seat." He gestured towards the seat in front of him. I sat down and placed my bag beside the chair. Nothing had changed since I was here last. "So how was your first day or two outside of the hospital? How have you adjusted?"

"Yeah, I'm doing well, I mean I just wanted to go back to work." I told him. Dr Sanford didn't give away any emotions or feelings, he didn't show what he was thinking like some of the nurses on the ward would.

"Why is it important for you to go back to work?" He asked.

"I want normality, I wanted to go back to work and act like me being here didn't happen. I wanted to live a normal life and mum needs help with the house. I wanted to help her."

When I first came to the hospital, I wouldn't talk about my feelings or emotions or just about anything going on in my head but that didn't help. If you wanted to get out of the hospital you need to want to get better, you need to talk about what's going on in your head.

"I know it's tough but until I'm a hundred percent certain you're ready, you have to stay home, you can help your mum in other ways rather than financially, like cooking dinner." Dr Sanford was a tough doctor but under the exterior he really did mean well for his patients, he was the tough dad a lot of us in the ward didn't have.

"I did some cleaning and cooking yesterday to help. I didn't over clean either, which is good progress." I told Dr Sanford trying to convince him that I was ready to go back to work, but he didn't take it.

"I'm not going to give you all clear, you know that right Tom? You haven't even been out of the ward for a week. You need time to adjust." Dr Sanford told me. Once our session was finished, I picked my bag up and left. Dr Sanford had asked me to keep writing in the diary and to bring it next time in case I wanted to speak about anything I wrote in there. He told me he didn't want to read it but if I wanted to speak about anything in there then I was able to do so. I could tell he was wanting me to be free to speak of anything I wanted to. I could tell he was wanting me to be as honest as possible, he wanted me to be in the clear just as much as I did but he had to make sure that I was able to deal with any triggers I might have. I took the bus home and made sure I didn't touch too much, buses were filled with germs and bacteria, the amount of people that put their dirty hands on the handles is unbelievable, I heard that they're dirtier than toilet seats. When I needed to press the button I used my elbow, and I know what you're thinking but I know many people who don't have OCD that do the same. It's a common rule, buses are filthy, that's why they have the funky pattern on the seats, it's to hide the amount of dirt and stains that are residing on them.

When I got home, I headed upstairs, the girls were in the front room with granddad and they didn't even bat an eyelid when I came in, which shows how they're already used to me being home because they don't run up and hug me. I put my bag in my wardrobe, took out my diary and sat on my desk. I opened it and took a long look at each page. Some of the pages were doodles, some were scribbles. Some pages were filled with writing, and some had a sentence or two. Some even had writing scribbled out, where I had written what I wanted to say and then scribbled over it so no one else could read it. I opened a new page and started writing. I was only writing for half an hour, but it felt good to be able to write again. I wrote about how happy I was about being home but how nervous I was in case I got bad again and had to go back to the ward. When I finished, I went and had some lunch downstairs, I made sure to take my pills and then headed back upstairs. That day was just like the day prior, granddad left when mum came home, we ate tea and then I went upstairs into my room until the girls wanted a bedtime story. After reading them a bedtime story I headed into my room and stayed there until I eventually fell asleep.

Chapter Two

A month after being allowed out of the ward I was still
unable to work. Dr Sanford said I was getting close to
being allowed back to work, but he wanted to do some
exposure therapy before giving me the all clear. I had
group therapy with people back at the ward, where Dr
Thomas would oversee the group therapy sessions. Dr
Thomas was the loveliest lady, she acted like a
grandmother to so many of the patients. She would ask
people questions that are difficult to answer but she asked
them in such a way that it was easy to answer. She would
ask something that would be easy 'put your hand up if...'
it would start with easy ones that basically everyone who
was at the hospital would raise their hand too. Then she
would ask more and more questions, each one harder
than the last but because so many people put their hands
up previously you didn't feel as awkward for putting yours
up. What I liked about Dr Thomas is that she would put
her hand up as well if she agreed with the statement which
made everyone feel that little bit more normal. If we felt
weird, we could look at Dr Thomas who straight away
had her hand up. That would normally take up the first
twenty minutes of the session, for the other 40 minutes we
would talk in a circle about our weeks, both good and bad
things that happened, how we felt and how we got past it.
If we had a bad day, how did we battle it? What did we
do? Did something trigger us? We'd be asked a lot of
questions, but it was nice because we didn't have a lot of
time to answer, we didn't need to make it go on like a

therapy session because there were six other people waiting to talk about their struggles or victories.

I thought I would have finished my sessions with Dr Sanford two weeks ago, I thought I would already be back to work and almost getting my first paycheck again however it didn't happen. I know Dr Sanford is a professional, but I was so annoyed. If I had known how long it was going to be I would have asked for benefits at least then mum would be getting some financial help, and I wouldn't be sitting at home all day thinking that I had done nothing. I was supposed to be the man of the house but it's a struggle when I couldn't even be trusted to look after the girls. I thought about trying to do small things to help, like all the DIY that mum needed done, she had stuff in the garage that was waiting to be done. Then I thought about the fact that mum was quite fussy with the house so if I did it, she'd probably go back and do it herself. I couldn't think of anything that I could do to help her out that I wasn't already doing. I was just begging for the day that I could go back to work, and I never thought I would say something like that. I didn't think I could ever be excited about going back to work especially when work hates me.

I would try to explain to mum about how I was ready to look after the girls on my own, that it had been a month since the hospital and I was feeling a lot better, but she was insistent that I could only do it once Dr Sanford had given me all clear to go back to work. I was starting to resent Dr Sanford, it seemed like he was taking his time about figuring out how long I would be out of work, and he would only tell me I wasn't ready yet.

Yet I knew I was, I knew I was prepared. I was nervous but I think in this day and age a lot of people get nervous about leaving the house especially if they haven't in a long time. I felt more normal, like I could go out and not have to do my rituals, despite what people would say about it, therapy worked. I know it didn't work for everyone, but it worked for me. I liked to think it's less about therapy as a whole and more to do with the therapist. If you have a therapist, you don't like or that didn't quite understand you, then it can be easy for you to be put off by the idea of therapy as a whole. You might have tried it once and that one time was terrible, or just didn't work and that could be down to the therapist. Therapists have their own way of doing therapy, they might be specialised in Behavioural Activation (which aims to give you motivation for small, positive changes), or they could be specialised in Mindfulness-based cognitive therapy (which uses meditation and breathing exercises as well as therapy to help you work through your problems). You might find that you don't like therapy because your therapist is making you shut your eyes and breath in through your nose and out through your mouth while also making you listen to whale music. Not every therapist will do that, you might have to research the type of therapy you'd prefer to have and then find a therapist that suits your therapy style.

Luckily Dr Sanford didn't do mindfulness, I couldn't think of anything more awkward than closing my eyes and imagining an ocean, but I knew people in the ward that did like that. Each to their own, I guess.

I found myself trying to do anything to get Dr Sanford to approve my clearance but he wasn't having it, I even tried joking around with him telling him "I'm completely fine, I could lick a seat if you wanted me to to prove it" but Dr Sanford didn't laugh, he was a very stern man, some might even say scary, he would look at me and say something like "do you use humour to deflect from conversation?" I would try to explain to Dr Sanford that me using humour wasn't a deflection but in fact a coping mechanism, if you can joke about something that's serious to you isn't that a good way of coping with it. It means you can look at the situation and see the funny side of it, however I don't think Dr Sanford joked around, I don't think I'd ever seen him even laugh. The other patients and I would talk about it like it was an old man's tale. Someone would say that they saw him laugh once with the nurses, but we wouldn't believe them because we didn't see it. I had never seen him laugh, which I guess is why he has so little wrinkles for such an old man. I would try to get him to laugh on several occasions, but he wouldn't budge, he either takes his job way too seriously, he didn't know how to laugh (like he is unable to) or he just thinks my jokes aren't funny. I knew it wasn't the last one because everyone on the ward found them hilarious even if they were either depressed, anxious or schizophrenic, they would always laugh at my jokes. I didn't give up trying to tell him jokes, I would even go in at the start of each session and I would tell him a joke that I had thought of especially for him, he would either ignore the jokes completely or ask me something about the joke as if the joke had context towards my OCD. I thought for a while it was his way of stopping me from telling jokes, but I didn't stop. It became a competition; would I stop telling jokes first or would he laugh at one of my jokes, but I wouldn't give up that easily.

I wanted my life back to normal; I didn't want him to prolong my life any more than it already had been. I wanted to get back to work and to bring in an income and look after the girls without my granddad being there. I felt less of a man than I did when I was in the ward, and when I was there, I had to stick to a schedule and I had to do things otherwise I would get marked down, sure it was degrading but everyone there had to do it, so it didn't feel unnatural.

Now I don't need to do those things and yet I'm finding myself more useless. I wanted normality. I wanted to be able to be a normal person and do normal person things. I wanted to go to the mall with my mates, I wanted to go cycling with them, I wanted to go to the cinema. I wanted to get a car. There're so many things I wanted to do but I'm unable to because I'm not leading a normal life. That didn't mean I wanted to be one of those normal people, I didn't want to be the wannabe, I didn't want to like what everyone else liked and be the person everyone else wanted to be. I still wanted to be me but that didn't mean I didn't want to do what everyone else does.

I would spend most of my time upstairs when granddad was home, it wasn't that we had a bad relationship, we used to be close, but I felt like he didn't like me at that moment. He had to visit the girls because of me, I know he would much rather spend seven hours a day at home doing some occasional gardening and reading the newspaper. He didn't want to be looking after two six-year-old girls and watching Peppa pig for seven hours a day. Although I'm sure he would deny any of that if you asked him because he's too polite to say the truth. He is still an old man though and back in his day, he wouldn't do stuff like that. The only reason grandma didn't come round is because she volunteers at a charity shop so she wouldn't be able to spend all day with the girls. It's easier if grandad comes round.

I always found it awkward trying to do the housework when someone else was in the house, it felt rude to start vacuuming or do the dishwasher if a guest was here but at the same time it was my granddad, and he was here every day at the moment. I would interact with him a small amount. I would ask if he wanted anything, I would talk to him about football, even though I wasn't as interested in it as I used to be. I would make small talk basically and once that was over with, I would do the housework and then go upstairs. Sometimes I would write in my diary, a lot of the time I would watch films on my tv, and all the time I would spend thinking about the day where I could go back to normality.

Every time mum came home from work, we would have small talk, she would ask me what I did today, and I would respond "same as yesterday" and she would automatically try to say something positive like "you're a day closer to being given the clear."

It was rubbish. I wanted freedom. I can't imagine being stuck in it day after day. I mean the girls were stuck in but that's because it was school holidays and they enjoyed staying in, they had a best friend in the house, they had each other. So of course, they wouldn't mind spending everyday with each other.

I decided to go out with Mikey and Sammy, I thought that was the one normal thing that I was able to control. That was the normality I had, mum was hesitant, but I told her that I couldn't live a normal life if I wasn't even allowed out with my friends and besides Dr Sanford might like that I'm interacting with 'normal' human beings. Well, I'll put normal in quotations because these two are the least normal people you'll ever meet. They don't like watching Love Island, getting a Cold Brewski with the Dudes and going on an all-inclusive holiday to Maga just to find six randomers to have sex with (one for each night, of course). They would be the opposite of that. They enjoyed watching Supernatural (both the show and the genre), they enjoyed listening to rock music at 85

43

decibels. They enjoyed blacking out their windows and using UV painting to make their rooms look like a nightclub. They would stay in their rooms blasting out rock music while also getting insanely high. They would wait for one of their parents to leave for work and then they would go round each other and make out. I always thought it was bad that they had never told their parents they were together. I know parents hide their true self in front of guests, but I thought they might have told at least one of their parents. They can't both be true hard Christians and hate gay people that much. Although I know what I was like when I first found out.

Mikey and I were in year 11, we were both 16 filled with this pubescent angst, I had never known anyone that was gay before. I knew my dad didn't like it, he always thought I was gay, and I knew I wasn't because I liked girls, I wanted to have sex with girls (not that I did, I was too self-conscious for that). When Mikey told me, I overreacted. I was an absolute asshole about the whole situation. I embarrassed Mikey and myself, I just shouted for no reason "You're a fag?! Are you serious?" and walked away, leaving Mikey in a hallway full of teens.

I didn't speak to him for three days because I was angry, but I wasn't angry at him being gay. I guess in the whole grand scheme of things I thought he would have told me sooner, we'd been friends for years and there was no inkling. He wasn't into anything a stereotypical gay person was into, he didn't watch Drag race or wear a rainbow flag. He was still Mikey. I guess I reacted the way my dad had always taught me, he would see gay people on TV and say something like "they wouldn't be gay if they had decent pussy" and I would look at him so confused. He always thought it was a choice and for a second my reaction was because of my dad. It didn't make it any better, I was 16 years old. I could think for myself. So, when I saw a group of year 11 boys pushing him around in the corridor, I went straight up to them and beat the crap out of them. I honestly didn't think I had it in me but in the moment of madness I blacked out. I only remembered what happened as the head teacher was running down the corridor and all the boys were on the floor holding their noses. I got a week suspension and Mikey and I started talking again. I apologised to him all the time and he said it was fine but for a while I think it stuck with him. He wouldn't bring anything up that he thought would be considered gay, he definitely didn't talk about his love life. I didn't pry. I didn't want him to think I was going to take a cheap shot. It took six months to build up something that I broke with one sentence. Even now I think he gets a bit nervous to kiss Sammy in front of me, I try to tell him it's not because it's guys kissing, I just find PDA (public displays of affection) awkward because I'm always the third wheel.

Mikey and I go long back, and even though I don't know massive amounts about Sammy, those two together, they are the happiest people I ever met in my life. The only parents who know that Mikey and Sammy are together is my mum and that's because she didn't care. When Mikey told her, she said "Mikey you're like a son, I don't care who you are, what you do, as long as you are happy and not doing anything illegal in this country, I don't care." I think that was enough for Mikey, I think I even saw him shed a tear, but he would have said it was hayfever. He's a hard man, which is why his family hadn't guessed yet.

When Mikey first introduced my mum to Sammy, he thought my mum was Mikey's mum. Mikey told him he could wish for it, but it still wouldn't be true.

He always loved my mum, anytime there was a problem he had the couch. He could come in and eat out food if he wanted, although he was too polite to ever do that (seriously this a note to those that think just because your best friend is your best friend it means you can help yourself to their things. Don't take food without asking first even if they say don't ask, still ask, it's the polite thing to do, you don't know their financial situation, that packet of crisps you just took could have been the last packet they had. Be polite, have manners.)

Mikey and I met up at the skatepark, I didn't skate and neither did Mikey, but Sammy did, so we would meet up there while Sammy was skating and that would be our free time together. We met up for the first time since I'd been out the ward, I walked up to him, he was sitting on a bench with bags surrounding him.

"Hey man" I said, getting close enough for him to hear me.

"Hey, I didn't think you'd actually come as I ain't seen you in two months now." He laughed while rolling a zoot.

"Well, you saw me on my first day out." I told him, laughing at the awful way he was rolling.

"Yeah, for like, two minutes I don't count it. How's it hanging man? Or can't I say that?" He laughed.

He always enjoyed making jokes and most of the time it would be out of me, I didn't care. It kind of helped in a weird way.

"You're rolling is still terrible I see." I took it out of his hands and finished rolling.

"Well, you would have had loads of practice to do that in the nuthouse." Mikey chuckled.

I looked at him disappointed. "You know medicinal marijuana isn't legal in the UK, right? It's

46

important to me you know at least one tiny fact about weed if you're going to smoke it."

Mikey looked at me stunned then started smiling "what about CBD oil, that's cannabis?"

"Technically CBD is a Cannabidiol, which is a natural compound in cannabis or hemp. It didn't get you high though because it didn't have THC in it." I was winning, I was waiting for him to think of something but all he could say was, "fucking nerd." Game. Set. Match. I won that one. Actually, if it involved anything to do with facts and fictional shows or books I would always win.

"I'd rather be a 'fucking nerd' than a bumbling idiot."

I'm not a huge fan of swearing, dad used to do it all the time and I don't really like it. I think there's so many other beautiful words in the English dictionary to use, why choose the nasty ones? I only swear if I'm quoting someone's words or if I'm really, mad. I don't think that will change. Mikey and I sat down, smoked and talked about life. He told me that his mum and dad kicked him out because they found him and Sammy in bed doing it. He said as he was packing his dad turned around and shouted, 'couldn't you at least be on top?' which I thought at first was a joke but when I saw Mikey wasn't laughing, I stopped. I realised the whole situation was a lot worse than I first anticipated. Normally Mikey over exaggerated a situation and when we talked about it he would at least look back on it and have a laugh but not this time. This time I knew he wasn't in a good place. He told me that Sammy's family were letting him stay on the floor.

Sammy told his mum about him, and Mikey and she wasn't fussed but she told him not to tell his dad especially while Mikey was staying because then two people would be out on the streets. I told him that he could stay with me anytime, he didn't need to ask anyone else if he needed it, he could have it. He thanked me and told me I was a good mate; he did apologise for always taking the mick out of me and my OCD. I knew he only meant to joke around with me, he knew if I would get upset about it, he wouldn't joke around just like I don't take the mick out of him being gay. I know it's the one personal thing he gets upset about, now his brains I can take the mick out of all day every day. He knew he wasn't the most intelligent person, and he didn't care, he'll try to prove me wrong now and again, but he ends up still being the stupid one. You'd think he'd learn by now.

When Sammy finished skating, we walked to the shops, Mikey needed to pick up some food. He didn't want to eat all the food in Sammy's house because he knew they already had three mouths to feed. Mikey was an understanding bloke, that was a good quality about him, he didn't need telling or asking, he observed, he understood, and he tried to help. He was a good guy, but I think people misunderstood him, they really did. He had a hard exterior but break it down and he's just as sensitive or soft as everybody else. Sammy knew the true Mikey, Mikey trusted Sammy enough. It was nice to see him happy, after everything all I wanted was for Mikey to be happy.

I left Mikey and Sammy when they were turning off Sammy's street, Sammy's house is only four streets away from mine, so we walked most of the way together and then split off at Sammy's Street. I walked the rest of my way home, it's only an extra five minutes to my house but it felt weird walking by myself, even after a month, I felt a bit vulnerable to be honest. I'm not a strong person and I would feel intimidated if a group of kids came along, no matter the age. I don't like trouble so while I was walking home, I was checking to make sure no one was in front of me, I didn't want to bump into anyone. I realised that I had gone from walking home to speed walking home. I suddenly wanted to get home, I didn't feel comfortable, I felt like someone was watching me, waiting for me.

When I stepped my foot through my door, I felt a lot more comfortable. Mum was sitting on the sofa watching tv, I took my shoes off and joined her in the front room.

"How was Mikey?" She asked as I joined her on the sofa.

"He got kicked out, he finally told his family and they told him to leave."

Mum jolted up looking at me with concern "oh no, is he okay? Does he have somewhere to stay? He can stay here if he needs."

"He's fine, he's with Sammy at his, Sammy told his mum and she's fine with it." I told her which calmed her down.

"What's he going to do in the long run? I mean it's nice for Sammy to let him stay but eventually he'll have to find his own place." Mum asked.

I looked at her knowing she was right.

"I think he hopes his parents will talk to him and allow him back."

Mum looked at me with worry in her eyes "Is that a good thing though? His parents are nice to me, but I know what they're like, you don't think it will be more harmful for him to go back? He's just a kid."

I sat up and looked at mum "Mum, listen, Mikey is not a kid, he's 22 years of age. He's a grown adult, he has some savings, I think he wanted to travel the world, but it looks like he'll have to rent somewhere for now. He'll be fine."

Mum patted my shoulder; it was like she knew I was just as nervous as she was about him going back.

"I wouldn't tell Mikey's family about you being in hospital let along about their only son being gay."

I looked at her both stunned and confused. "Why would you tell anyone about me in the hospital anyway? It's no-one else's business." I paused for a second and then asked mum "Wait... Who have you told about me being in the hospital?" Mum stayed a little too quiet for my liking "For God sake! People don't need to know my business mum!" I raised my voice, stood up and walked away.

"Why are you embarrassed? It's...It's normal."

"Normal? You think everyone on this earth has gone into a psych ward? This isn't summer camp, and anyway, let's say theoretically everyone on the earth did go to a psych ward, do you know how many people are affected by OCD? 1%, that's it, 1% of the population of the UK. So, if you keep turning around and telling me it's normal it's not... IT'S NOT NORMAL."

I hadn't realised until I stopped speaking that I was in fact shouting, I calmed down, composed myself. "I just don't want people to treat me differently. I want to be normal." Mum looked at me, I don't think she was sure about what to say so she said "Normal's boring."

"Maybe I wanted to be boring," and with that I walked upstairs.

I peeked into the girl's room, it seems they missed my story, but they were asleep, so I didn't mind. I headed into my room, shut my door and opened my diary. I thought about writing everything that I had just said but I was so angry, I had already forgotten it. Instead,

I placed my pen on the paper and started scribbling away, the page was getting ripped, and the pen was going on the page underneath, but I didn't care.

This sudden rage filled me, I clenched my jaw, pieces of paper were being ripped from the page by the pen, I suddenly threw the pen across the room and punched my table, I tried the breathing exercises that Dr Sanford had suggested to me for when I got angry or annoyed. The simple breath in through the nose and out through the mouth. It helped me to calm down, and once I was calm, I still couldn't understand why mum felt the need to tell everyone about my personal life, I didn't tell her she could. She didn't even ask.

* * *

I told this to Dr Sanford on my next visit, I think he understood what I meant but it felt like he was siding with mum, asking me why it was such a big deal that people knew. I tried to explain to him in the best way possible, but he basically told me that what's done is done, and to embrace what happened. I think he wanted me to suffer. He did tell me that he wanted to sign me off, which I jumped up in my seat with excitement. I couldn't believe he was going to finally let me go back to work, he did however want me to do an exposure therapy thing before he signed me off, he wanted to make sure I was able to control myself. So, he took me out of the ward and waited at the bus station.

"When the bus comes, you're going to pay for you and me to go into town with this cash" He held out coins which had been in his pocket for God knows how long. It took me a couple of minutes to pick the coins up, my brain was telling me how dirty they were, but I needed to go back to work, once I had picked the coins up, we got on the bus. Now I normally get a single ride, so I don't take tickets from the driver but because we wanted a return, I did need to pick them up. That would have been another issue previously, but I was feeling brave, so I picked them up. Now the seating, it's always good to choose the least popular seating because it means the least amount of people have sat on it, but I didn't want Dr Sanford to catch on to my thoughts, so I sat right at the back where all the dirty, youths of today sit. I tried to blow away the thoughts of what could have happened on the seats.

"How are you feeling?" Dr Sanford asked.

"I get the bus all the time so I'm fine."

We sat in silence for the 10-minute trip it took to get into town.

"So, we're going to get off the next stop, if you could press the button with your finger that would be great."

See now he got me, I struggled to press the button with my finger,

"I'm not the only one that doesn't use my finger, it's normal."

He looked at me, raising an eyebrow. I knew the look, I was basically telling him I wasn't ready, which I was, I just had to get out of my head long enough to press the button. I looked away from him.

"Okay. okay. I'll try." I sat there until the bus got close to the stop we needed. I held my finger a couple of centimetres away from the button, as I was hyping myself up to press the button, the bell went off. It wasn't me who pressed it. Dr Sanford looked at me "well we have a chance on the way back." I had just gotten away with it, and even though I was happy that I didn't have to touch it, I was worried that me touching it was the only way I

52

would get the all clear. I would have to press the button on the way back to make sure that I got the all clear.

We walked through town talking, it was one of the easier sessions I had. I always found it easier to talk while I was doing something, it meant my body was busy doing something else, so it wasn't overthinking. I hoped we would just walk around and then go back to the hospital where he would say something like

"Well done. you've passed. You are now cured and can go back to living a normal life" but he wanted to go into a shop. I thought it was weird, it was not a shop he would shop in from the looks of his outfit. It soon came clear he was testing me in natural environments.

"Okay this shop has two floors, you can either use the elevator and press the buttons, or you can use the stairs, but you have to hold the handle."

"Are you serious?" I asked nervously.

He looked at me dead in the eyes, "yeah, look one day you might be shopping with your mates, you use the lift and press the buttons, or take the stairs and hold the handle, I don't want you to then think about it afterwards. To think I'll have to go wash my hands, oh I touched my clothes, they'll have to go in the wash. That cycle that you've been trying to stop for almost three months now, I don't want you going back to it. If we can do exposure therapy and it helps or it shows improvement, then we know that you're ready. I'm pushing you because I think you're ready and I know you think you're ready."

I looked at Dr Sanford. For the first time since I met him, it was the most he's ever talked in one sitting, and the nicest thing he's ever said. It almost sounded like he wanted what was best for me (I just thought he was in it for the money). We headed towards the lifts, I knew pressing buttons was easier, so I'm guessing he had a trick up his sleeve.

As I got to the lift, I looked it up and down, and then I fixated my eyes on the button. I knew Dr Sanford wouldn't be impressed if I pressed into it with my elbow, I knew I was going to have to touch it with my finger. I know I can do it but all I can think of is how dirty the buttons are. I know for a fact that the buttons don't get cleaned by the cleaners, they're paid to just vacuum and clean the toilets, but elevator buttons are something they don't go near. While my brain was going through every single disease I could think of, Dr Sanford asked me to express my thoughts, which I did. Dr Sanford was able to use certain words and breathing exercises that helped me to calm down. Once I had calmed myself down, I closed my eyes and concentrated on breathing, I started to rock my arm forward and backward slightly. I was hoping that I would press the button at an unknown time, so the thoughts aren't as bad, but Dr Sanford asked me to open my eyes and look directly at it. He wanted me to know that nothing bad would happen if I pressed the button on purpose.

I stood there for five minutes, luckily no one was in the shop, so I wasn't blocking anyone. As my breathing began to get better and I wasn't as panicked, I repeated *'nothing bad will happen. no -one will get ill. Nothing bad will happen. No-one will get ill'* in my head until I finally pressed the button.

"Well done. Now let's go" he said as he walked into the elevator. I got in as well waiting for him to say something, the doors shut, and we waited there. "Level two please" he asked me as he waited patiently. I looked at him in shock, I had to do it again. I focused my breathing and continued repeating what I had previously told myself. This time it only took three minutes for me to push the button with my slightly shaken hands. It went up slowly, at the top, the lift opened. We got out. "Well done, you did that one so much faster. You're doing great." I smiled. I had just done it. I thought that meant the hard part was over, however Dr Sanford started walking away. I followed him and we ended up at the stairs. Great. "Okay, we're going down the stairs, I want you to hold the handle the entire way down." I thought he would end up doing something like this, either way we would have done the other thing on the way down. I should have guessed it was too easy for Dr Sanford.

This time it took longer than expected. I knew I had to hold on for longer, the only thing that wasn't making me have a complete meltdown is because cleaners normally do clean these handles, however it means the handles would have been dirty for five hours already. After 15 minutes of standing at the top of the stairs, I grabbed onto the handle, I thought about how our session was almost up and I wanted to get signed. I walked down the stairs quickly, I didn't want to hold onto the handle for a long amount of time. Once I got to the bottom of the stairs, I literally jumped and shouted. I couldn't believe I had done it. I was so happy and relieved and then tears came out. I couldn't believe I had done it; I was too excited to think about how many germs were on my hands.

Dr. Sanford patted me on the back. "Well done. Now our sessions are almost over so we need to head back." We started walking back to the bus stop, while we were waiting for the bus, I asked Doc, "so am I done? Can I start work?"

He looked at me with an eyebrow raised. "We'll discuss it back at the hospital." We 10 minutes for the next bus. We got on the bus no problem, it was quiet, and the bus went off straight away, the roads were quiet too and I knew my moment of pressing the button was coming. As I went to press it the button went off, I looked around and Dr Sanford had pressed it instead. "You've already done plenty today" he told me while getting up off the seat to walk off the bus. I waited for it to stop and then got off without touching the bars. I needed to take baby steps rather than jump straight in.

"So, you've done really well today, Tom. I've seen a lot of improvement through exposure therapy, and I think you're ready to go back to work. However, I still want to see you once a week." Dr. Sanford said once back in his office.

I couldn't stop smiling when he told me that I would finally be able to go back to work. I thought about all the money I would be able to bring back in. I thought about being able to live a more normal life and despite having counselling once a week it's more normal than being in the ward. I'm on the right path. I wasn't even listening to the rest of what the Doc was saying because I was too busy thinking about ringing work as soon as I was finished from here.

"So, Tom. You need to start on part-time work for two weeks and then you can go full time." I looked at him utterly confused. "Wait, why? You're signing me off. I'm ready to work." I would be earning but not enough to help mum properly. "I know it must be annoying but for your best interests, this is the only way I will sign it off." I reluctantly agreed, I thought I've been wanting to go back to work for so long and I can't ruin this chance I have. I can do part time for two weeks, it's not even a whole month and then as soon as I know it, I'll be back doing full time hours, looking after the girls and living my normal life. I wondered whether or not Dr Sanford would know if I did more than part-time, like if I told my manager I could stay on or do an extra day because I'm free but knowing the Doc he is probably friends with my manager and has him keeping an eye on me.

Once we finished our sessions, I headed out to the bus stop. I was so excited to be able to work, it's what I've been waiting for, for a whole month. The bus was due in 10 minutes so while I was waiting, I decided to call work and let them know. The manager Steve answered straight away.

"Hey Steve, it's Tom. I'm just ringing because I'm allowed back to work, so I'll see you on Monday."

Steve didn't sound that thrilled on the phone, it was like he was putting it on, but he said he was happy I was coming back and that he was glad I was better.

Steve was a funny bloke, but I got along with him most of the time (until my OCD got bad and I became a liability). I hopped on the bus and when it was coming to my stop, I decided to try the exercise that Doc had asked me to do today. I knew I could do it now. I held my finger by the button and pressed it. I thought 'nothing bad will happen' and it didn't. I didn't get ill. I didn't contract any deadly disease. I was fine. I basically ran home to tell granddad that I was in the all-clear but when I got home, he wasn't there, and neither were the girls. I assumed he took them to the park to let off some steam. He liked going to the park with them because they acted like kids, they weren't arguing or watching tv. They were kids playing in a park, it bought him happiness, and the girls got ice-cream.

I sat down and watched tv, I flicked through tv shows not really knowing what I wanted to watch. About an hour later the girls came running in

"Tom! You're back!" the girls shouted as they jumped onto me. I let out a yelp and when they wouldn't get off me, I decided to start tickling them. It seemed to work because in a minute or, so they were on the floor laughing. I looked up and granddad was standing by the door. "

The Doc gave me the all clear today" Grandad didn't answer, he just smiled, which I found odd. In another 20 minutes mum came home, without exchanging words grandad left and mum came and sat on the sofa.

"Is granddad annoyed at me?" I asked mum.

"No, I think he's just a bit miserable today."

I looked at mum who was slouched down on the sofa, watching tv. "Mum, I got the all clear from Dr Sanford today. He told me to do part time work for a couple of weeks and then go full-time."

Mum looked at me and smiled "See I told you it wouldn't be too long before you'd be back at work. It's great news. It means Granddad don't have to come around as much now, only a couple of hours a day." This made me smile, it meant that she was starting to trust me to look after the girls again. She did say that if I got cleared then I could look after the girls and now it was finally happening after all this time.

I was able to hide my happiness on the inside, I didn't want to show that I was too happy with being released. I did talk to mum about looking after the girls, I wanted to be clear.

"I still have therapy sessions with Dr Sanford for now, but it's only once a week, so can I look after the girls now when I'm not working?"

Mum hesitated for a second, looked at the girls and then looked at me "Sure but if you ever get those thoughts, call me."

I agreed. I thought it was the least I could do, now that I was allowed to look after my own siblings. We would be able to do so much together and hopefully I would get to take them out to the park as well. I loved seeing them at the park enjoying the outside world rather than being stuck inside playing with toys or watching tv.

I went upstairs after talking to mum and wrote in my diary. I still don't like the fact that it's a diary, I would prefer calling it a journal, log, memoir or even chronicle but nope it's a diary and it has been helpful to write stuff in. I wrote about how happy I was with my sessions and how excited I was to be able to do things with the girls again. It gave me the little bit of serotonin that I needed to push myself. I can't tell you how boring and depressing it was staying in, day after day, not being able to make money for the family or even look after my family. It was horrible but now, now I can start living life the way it was before.

Chapter Three

I had been at work for a couple of weeks and life was going back to the way it was. I was still only working part time but that was less to do with Dr Sanford's advice and more to do with the fact that the girls weren't back at school until next week and I needed to be home to look after them. I told my manager that I could come back full-time next week, and he didn't seem fussed by it. However, something weird happened since I'd been back at work, everyone treated me like I was a bomb about to explode, they were all treading lightly and it was weird.

I guess I didn't expect to be treated normally straight away but I thought people would come up and talk to me about anything, to be honest. The sales assistants would talk but then when they joke about something, they'd apologise and say they shouldn't have said it. They think if they joke around, I'm going to break again and end up in the psych ward. The manager is just as bad. He would ask me if I'm "able" to do a task, he thinks that because I was in a ward everything, I learnt beforehand I have forgotten, or I can't do anymore. The stigma around mental hospitals is incredibly bad especially there, and if there was a chance I went back there, it wouldn't be because of the jokes or my inability to do something, it would be because they were treating me like I was a psychopath. It's like they think I have a knife in my pocket and I'm ready to kill them if they say anything wrong.

I tried to act normal and pretend like nothing was wrong but when they're treating me like I'm an alien from outer space, it was hard to feel normal at all. My favourite time was when it was time to leave and go home. I lived close to my work so I walked home, most of the time I would stop in the shops and get some food for the girls when I was home. Granddad wasn't as bad as he was as he only had to spend half the time at our house. He even indulged in conversation with me, I mean it was about work and whether or not we sold a certain size screwdriver but still it was a conversation that we hadn't had for months.

When granddad left, the girls would always come up to me and give me a massive hug, they would talk to me about what they had done that day and show me any drawings they had done. I would always let them know that their drawings were amazing and that one day they could be the most famous twin artists the world has ever seen. They would always get excited and would then proceed to put on an art show. They would make me buy their art, which I thought was hilarious and adorable at the same time. I would give them my shrapnel, 10p's, 20p's that kind of thing and they would always act as if I had just given them a million pounds. They would then go and put it in their piggy bank and save it. I wondered about how much money they had saved in there by now, they were always finding money under the sofa or doing chores for money, and I never saw them spend it, they always put it in the piggy bank. I enjoyed spending time with the girls, it was nice to be a child for a while, I never had siblings when I was young, the girls weren't born so I always played on my own. I didn't have someone like they did so I enjoyed playing games with them when they wanted to.

I would make sure that all the housework was done and completed before mum came home from work, I was still working part time so I thought the least I could do would be to help around the house. Mum was working even when she was home, her work was busy, but instead of staying on in work, she would bring work home. It meant she could get into her pyjamas and have a glass of wine while finishing her work. I always tried to see if she wanted my help with anything, but she never did, she always said, "it shouldn't be much longer, I only have a few things left to do" and then she would still be there a couple of hours later. I admired her determination. I couldn't work somewhere where I was overworked and underpaid, I have too much of an attitude problem to work somewhere like that. I would be fired within the first week, my ethos is I do the work for the hours I get paid. That's it, as simple as that. I don't want to work for free, I need the money too much to do anything for free.

* * *

Mikey called me and asked me to hang out, I thought about it for a while, and I decided I would go out to see him. I haven't seen him in a couple of weeks, and I was wanting to find out what was happening with him and his family. I wondered if they had made up and had finally gotten over Mikey being gay. I mean I really don't understand how it's a big deal, he was born like it, it wasn't like he decided to do it because he wanted his family to hate him... Nobody likes to be kicked out by the family that's supposed to love them. I told him I wouldn't be able to come out until 6pm because mum didn't get home much before 5:30pm and I didn't want to leave her straight away to feed the girls.

When mum got home, she was home later than usual, I didn't mind because she did an important job.

"Hey mum I'm going out with Mikey for a bit." I told her while packing my bag and putting my shoes on.

"Oh, I have a load of work to do but it's fine, the girls can just watch tv," she complained. I guessed she was moody about me going out and making plans before talking to her about it, but I didn't care right now. I know it might seem bad, but I have spent so much time sat at home that I just wanted one day where I could go out with my mates and have a normal life. I knew mum was moody, but I decided to ignore it, I didn't want to give up my one night out in weeks.

I met up with Mikey, he looked a lot skinnier and completely down with life. His eyes had bags under them like he hadn't slept in weeks, his eyes were bloodshot, and his breath stank. Infact, his whole body stank.

"Mate, what happened?" I asked, shocked.

"A lot of stuff has happened in the last couple of weeks." He took a seat on a bench and started opening his bag, inside there were different zip lock bags which I assumed had drugs in. He took a bag out which had some bud in it and started to roll a joint.

"Mikey, I thought you were staying with Sammy, why do you look like you've been sleeping in the park?" I asked him to try to make a joke out of it but Mikey wasn't laughing.

"When my parents kicked me out, I went to stay with Sammy, for a while, it was fine. I would sleep on the floor, so his dad didn't catch us out." He finished rolling the spliff and gave it to me, he always allowed me to have the first half because he knew I didn't like having it after someone else had. I started smoking it and then Mikey continued his story "Anyway one day when everyone was out, we were in bed together, we were making out and shit like that and then his dad came in. He went fucking mental, you wouldn't believe, he started beating the shit out of Sammy and told me to get out the house. I picked my stuff up and I left."

I was gobsmacked, I couldn't believe that some people were so homophobic.

"What did Sammy do?" I asked him "I did try to help him, but his dad was too angry, he stayed there and took the beating. I tried ringing him and calling him, but he wouldn't answer and anytime I went to his house his dad was there." Mikey did something that wasn't like him at all, for the first time since I've known him, he started crying. I didn't know what to do, I didn't know how to react, so I just put my arm around him and let him cry. He must have been there for 20 minutes, and he was just crying. I knew that me saying anything wouldn't help at all, so I didn't.

I thought about how everyone reacted when I had my breakdown and I wish I had someone who reacted the way I did right now. I wish I could have been there for me when I needed someone to just sit there and hold me. When Mikey got himself together, I asked him "where are you staying?"

He looked at me and waved his hand around "when you said about me sleeping in a park, you weren't lying. I've been here for a week. I smell like shit. I haven't washed in a week. I spent the last of my money on drugs. I just wanted something to do, life is so shit without them."

I put my head down, I couldn't believe it.

"I'll call my mum, I'm sure she'll let you stay but you need to get a job."

Mikey smiled. "I do have a job, I forgot to mention. I work on the docks. Shit job but great pay and they don't notice if you smell like crap because they also smell like crap."

Oh wow, I didn't realise that Mikey would be adult enough to get a job. I thought he would rely on Sammy for most of his life or would become a drug dealer (although that still isn't off the cards).

"Also, if you're coming to mine, you can't be doing the drugs mate, mum hates that I smoke weed, she wouldn't let you in if she thought you were doing something worse."

Mikey agreed that he wouldn't do any hard drugs while staying with me.

I rang mum who instantly said he could stay, she just wanted to make sure that he stuck with our routine as well, which I told her wouldn't be a problem because he would be at work for most of the day. Mikey added that when he got paid, he would help with some money. I was happy that he would have a place to stay but I did have a few suspicions. I knew what kind of person he was; I knew his history and I hoped he wouldn't let me down. We headed back to mine talking about Sammy and how much he missed him, he wanted to reconcile so badly but didn't want to get him into even more trouble. I asked him if he thought about calling the police, but he told me that his dad was close with the officers around the area and would pass it off as him being mad.

Once we got home, I got him a blanket and he slept on the sofa. I headed upstairs and despite feeling like I had done something good for a mate I also had a bad feeling about it. I know what it's like to be obsessed with something, you don't just stop it because someone wanted you to, you would do anything to get that fix. I waited for a couple of hours before I headed back downstairs, I opened the front room door slightly and looked in, Mikey was fast asleep. The room was completely normal, and nothing seemed different. I went into the kitchen and got a glass of water. When I was back in my room, I opened my diary and started writing. I wrote about Mikey and everything that happened. I also wrote openly about my feelings. I then placed it in my wardrobe and went to bed.

I suddenly awoke to the girls screaming "Mikey."

I headed downstairs and saw Mikey watching tv with the girls

"I just don't understand why he would do that," he said looking quizzically at Fireman Sam. The girls them went into full geek mode explaining the plot. I always thought that Mikey would be a good dad, he seems to get along with the girls great and talks to them like their adults. He didn't ask them stupid questions like a lot of people do when they first meet the girls, they assume the girls are younger than they are and don't realise how intelligent they are.

"What do you want for breakfast girls?"

"Coco Pops!" "Frosties!" The girls shouted in unison.

"What about you Mikey?" I asked him, sticking my head back in

"I'm alright mate." I raised my eyebrow, I thought it was strange that he didn't want anything to eat. I knew Mikey, and I knew him well, in the time that I've known him he has never denied breakfast. If anything, he would eat us out of house and home. I thought it was strange, but I didn't want to ask him about it. I thought maybe he was just being polite because he needed a place to stay but the thought continued to linger. I wanted to be polite, I knew that I was Mikey's last option so small things like him not wanting breakfast when he normally would, didn't seem too farfetched.

I headed into the front room with the girl's breakfast and placed it down on the coffee table, while they were scoffing down their cereal I sat next to Mikey

"not like you to decline breakfast" I commented, while watching the tv. "I'm just not hungry that's all" He brushed me off. It seemed like he was being careful with what he said. I wondered whether Mikey had taken drugs last night, but then I thought about how he promised me that he wouldn't do it and Mikey always kept his promises, in our entire friendship he's never once broken a promise that he kept. He would always say, "no point keeping a promise if you know you can't keep it".

When mum got up, she was already dressed and ready to leave the house. I'm guessing she had done work in bed and had very little sleep because she was rushing around like there was no tomorrow. By the time she had come downstairs she was basically leaving the house, she rushed in to kiss the girl's goodbye and told me to wait for granddad. I wasn't working because I had to see Dr Sanford, I left Mikey downstairs with the girls while I got myself ready. I came downstairs to the girls in the same position continuing talking to Mikey about Peppa Pig now.

"Dude, Peppa Pig is awesome," Mikey told me while laughing. I knew some kids' shows could be pretty good, but he seemed to be really enjoying it. Like he was enjoying it too much for a 23-year-old. "Yeah, it's a pretty savage show." I told him.

"Don't you have work today?" I asked him.

"Oh yeah I have today and tomorrow off" he answered, still totally engrossed with the kids show.

"Look mate I have to go out, so you'll have to leave for a couple of hours", I waited a couple of seconds for a response.

"Yeah, that's fine mate" he answered. Mikey didn't seem to mind, I guess he knew that it would only be a couple of hours and then he would be able to come back.

When granddad turned up for the girls, Mikey and I headed outside, I left him at the bus stop. I assumed he was going to go and sit at the park for a couple of hours, he would probably try to ring Sammy for a while and then he'd give up and probably smoke a spliff. I hoped that would be the only drug that he would be taking. I know I told him not to do it while in the house, but I didn't want to bring him home when he's high on drugs. It's not a good environment for the girls to live in and I didn't want mum to become more stressed than usual. She would hate it if someone she allowed to live in the house was a drug addict, I mean she already had a nut case in the house she didn't need a drug addict to add to that, otherwise she could start her own mental hospital right in the home.

Going to the hospital was a strange experience, the bus was mega packed until it dropped the college students off and then the remaining route to the hospital was quiet, there was one or two other people there and it seemed like they would be visiting family members. I was the only one going there for therapy, I was hoping to transfer my counselling to someone outside of the hospital. Somewhere closer to me, that I don't have to get a 30-minute bus ride too. I knew there was a councillor a 20-minute walk away from my house, but I have to wait until Dr Sanford tells me his sessions are finished. I might try convincing him that I wanted counselling from this other person, I think his name was Dr Goodall.

When I got to the hospital, Dr Sanford wasn't in his office. I was told I could wait inside, and he would be any minute. 10 minutes later he eventually showed up, he apologised and told me a patient needed him immediately. I started by telling him, "I don't think I need these sessions anymore, I don't mind continuing counselling, there's a councillor by me that I could see." But when I told him, he didn't seem pleased.

"I would be more comfortable if we continued these sessions for another month, at a minimum."

I was gutted that he didn't just allow me to go straight away, I mean all my information is on the NHS system so my new counsellor could find it out for himself and then be prepared but Dr Sanford seemed to want to do it the hard way.

"Why? We've been doing this for four months now outside, what can you give me that another therapist couldn't? It's not like you're special" As soon as it came out my mouth, I knew I was out of line "I'm sorry... I didn't mean it like that...I...I just"

"I know what you mean Tom, it's fine. I can see your frustration, from my experience for up to six months from leaving a psychiatric facility a patient is most vulnerable. I just want to know that I'm doing everything I can in that period of time or until I'm completely satisfied with a patient's recovery. I think you're doing well Tom, but you have experienced trauma that you have not spoken about, trauma related to your OCD and that could be a potential trigger. I worry about you, as I do all my patients. I want what's best for you and I believe I'm doing that." He explained. "How have you been this week?"

I thought about it for a second. "I'm doing okay I guess; the thoughts aren't nearly as bad as they used to be and if an obsessive thought comes to me, I'm able to ignore it." I told him. This was true, it was like the exercise in town with Dr Sanford had cured me.

"How are you finding exposure therapy? Are you pushing yourself?" I thought about it for a second and I realised that I hadn't really done any of my own exposure therapy.

Last week Dr Sanford wanted me to do three exposure therapies by myself, he wanted me to be able to find something I would normally obsess over and then try to overcome said obsession. The trouble was I didn't have any time to find an exposure therapy. I mean work would have been the only time that I could have done it, but my manager has left me to do customer service, and nobody has returned anything, so I can't even say I did exposure therapy by touching a box somebody had just touched. I hadn't done anything.

I looked at Dr Sanford who had a stern look on his face.

"You see the thing is, I haven't really had any obsessive thoughts that needed me to do exposure therapy on myself."

Dr Sanford wrote something down in his notepad and then looked up at me. "It's important to try and find them, you don't need to wait for moments to arise, make some situations yourself. You have two sisters who touch a lot of their toys when they play with them. Kids are renowned for being dirty."

I looked at Dr Sanford and automatically said, "no, their toys get cleaned once a week...not by me... no

70

mum does it. So that wouldn't work" and as I got to the end of my sentence, he looked at me with a raised eyebrow.

"It's not because of my obsessive thoughts, she just does it because some of their dolls have gum in them, which is weird because they're not allowed gum..or...or they spill juice over them by accident... and sometimes on purpose... But my point is it's not because of my obsessions." I was babbling but Dr Sanford kept looking at me, I couldn't quite figure out what he was thinking, he was too neutral.

"Say something. I have no idea what you're thinking." I eventually blurted out when he just kept looking at me. I was digging myself a hole and wanted him to change the subject.

"What would you like me to say?" He asked me, as if I was supposed to know.

I scoffed and then started my rant "I don't know..I don't know, maybe ask me how work is going for me, maybe allow me to go to work full time seeing as it's been a month and I'm still working part time. Maybe talk to me about your life, seeing as I don't know anything about yours. Maybe make small talk, talk to me about the weather. Maybe ask me what kind of obsessive thoughts I had this week.. Well you couldn't because I didn't really have any except for the fact that my mate is staying round mine and I'm pretty sure he's doing crack or heroin and I don't want the girls to find him, but that's not an obsessive thought. That's just me worrying about whether or not he'll get them addicted to drugs at six years old by showing them drugs. But again not an obsessive thought just a brother worrying about his sisters and there is a difference, it's not an obsessive thought and if it was it's not like I've done anything about it except ask him to not do drugs at my house which I feel like is a pretty normal standard when you stay round someone's house. I mean it's not like having shoes off in the house where 50% of people wear shoes and 50% don't, this is like 99% of homes don't allow Type A drugs into homes especially someone else's."

I stopped and saw that Dr Sanford had shut his book and was now looking at me. We sat in silence for five minutes before he chose to talk.

"Tom, I can't let you go full time at work until I'm convinced you can manage, it doesn't mean I don't think you can manage, I just think we still need to work on certain things. My life is boring, I'm not married, never have been, never will be, I have a cat and being a therapist is my entire life. Sometimes I'm at work for 14 hours out of the day. I think what you're experiencing with your sisters is an obsessive thought, their six years old they wouldn't know what it is, however the fact you haven't done anything is a good sign, it means the thoughts are there, but the obsessive action isn't present."

"I didn't think you'd remember everything, I guess that's why you get paid the big bucks" I told him with a smile. I was surprised at how good his memory was and how he was able to answer the questions without forgetting the original question. Dr Sanford and I didn't really discuss anything afterwards, I felt a bit uncomfortable going off at him in a therapy session but it kind of helped. I left his office feeling a lot better, maybe opening up and ranting about things does help.

I got the bus home and no I didn't touch the buttons, I didn't need to. There was a really annoying kid at the front of the bus pressing the button at every stop. It was a bad thing for the bus driver who had to pull over at every stop in case but a good thing for me who didn't need to touch the grimy buttons that similar kids have touched with their dirty fingers.

I headed to collect Mikey; I knew he would be at the park as there was nowhere else for him to be but when I got there he was nowhere to be found. I tried ringing him, but his phone was dead. I decided to not think too much of it and headed home to see the girls and relieve granddad of his granddad duties. As I got to my house, I heard the girls screaming and a deep voice, as I headed inside, I saw Mikey was already in my house. He was chasing the girls around the house, he was pretending to be the big, bad wolf. "Mikey, what are you doing here?" I asked him as I shut the door.

"Oh, hey Tom, I'm just playing with the girls, your granddad is in the kitchen" he answered while continuing to chase the girls around the front room.

I headed into the kitchen, granddad was sitting on one of the dining room chairs reading a newspaper and drinking a cup of tea.

"Hey granddad, who let Mikey in?" I asked.

"I did, he knocked on the door and asked to use the bathroom, he said he was your mate. So, I let him in, and when the girls saw him, they got excited." He told me while chuckling. I looked at granddad with rage in my eyes. You see, when granddad was younger, they used to leave the doors open, they didn't have to worry about Paedophiles or Murderers coming into the house. They would leave the door open, and anyone would walk in. Nowadays it's not like that but granddad seems to forget that.

"Granddad you can't just let people in the house if they say they're my friend. They could be dangerous." I tried telling him, but he wasn't having any of it.

"Oh, stop. That boy in there is fine. He's great with the girls and I'm in the next room. You need to stop worrying." Granddad spoke with little empathy because even if Mikey was a weirdo he was looking after the girls. That's all Granddad could think about, he just wanted his life to be back to normal and he wasn't fussed about how it would happen.

"Granddad in the future, ring me before you let anyone in." I tried cleaning up the kitchen as it was in a mess from granddad trying to make lunch for the girls.

"You need to stop worrying. You should be like that boy in there. He's happy playing with the girls. You should play with them more often." I tried to ignore Granddad's nasty words and put it down to being a grumpy, old man. If granddad knew Mikey like I did, then he wouldn't allow the girls and him to be in the same room.

I walked into the living room and found Mikey underneath the coffee table. "What are you doing?" I sighed.

"I'm playing hide and seek with the girls, but I can't find them." I looked around and saw the girls hiding behind the curtains, their usual place of hiding. I coughed to get Mikey's attention and then pointed to the curtains, he whispered "I know" before going round the living room and loudly explaining everywhere he was checking.

"Are they under the sofa? No. Are they behind the sofa? No." He kept going on and on until he checked the curtains. "I found you!" he shouted, and the girls screamed and ran away. I knew Mikey wasn't a nasty person, he was however an addict and the worst thing to do to an addict is to tell them they can't take drugs. I didn't want to rule Mikey's life, but I didn't want him to be a danger to himself or more specifically the girls. I didn't want him to get as high as a skunk and then do something he might regret. I needed to keep an eye on him around the girls, they might be rowdy, but they are still only six years old, they can get injured easily.

* * *

When mum got home, Mikey and I went out for a bit. I wanted mum to be able to have some down time and I wanted to talk to Mikey. We walked to the playground and as we were walking to the playground, I was trying to think of the right words to say. I didn't want Mikey to think I was accusing him of something, but I also didn't want him to take over my house.

"Mikey, I got to talk to you about something." Mikey continued walking so I continued talking.

"Look, you can't come round when I'm not home. Mum said you could stay when I'm here, but we thought you'd be at work when we were out as well, it wasn't really part of the deal." I was trying to explain it in a way that didn't sound like I didn't want him there. I also didn't want to accuse him of taking drugs in my house because I didn't have concrete evidence.

"It's sound man, I only wanted to come in earlier cause I really needed the toilet." Mikey replied but there was something in his tone that made me feel like it wasn't fine.

"You sure? Cause you sound off?" I asked him.

"Yeah man, I just thought we were friends."

I looked at him funny. "We are mates, what you talking about?" I asked him this time looking straight at him. I was getting angry at the thought that he wanted more from me.

"I got nowhere to go in the day, I just don't see what the problem is." I stopped walking and just stared at him

"What. You want more from me? My mum was nice enough to let you stay at night, in fact she said you can help yourself to whatever you want but when I go then so do you. That was her only rule. The one thing she wasn't okay with was you being in the house when I'm not there. I think it's pretty fair." I told him while raising my voice.

"What does she think I'm going to do?" He asked, raising his voice.

"I don't know but it's her house and her rules and if you don't like it Mikey, then you can leave. You're ungrateful for what you have." I shouted at him. This was the first time Mikey and I have ever fought; we've had mini arguments but they're more heated discussions than anything else.

"So, you're gonna leave your best mate to live in a park?" Mikey shouted. I looked at him, my face was scowling, I looked like a dog ready to attack.

"No, I told you, you can stay but you have to leave when I do, I don't see what your issue is."

He stood up from the bench that we had been sitting on. I stood directly in front of him.

"We've known each other longer than we haven't, and you don't trust me to stay at your house, what do you think I'm going to do? I ain't gonna steal shit from you, it's not like you own a lot anyway, it would be like taking off a fucking charity." It was at that moment I knew Mikey was on drugs, he said a lot of hurtful things to me, about me but never about my family, never about the situation we were in, he wasn't like that. In that moment this anger built up inside of me.

"FUCK YOU!" I shouted at him, and I started walking away when I heard footsteps behind me, I turned around and Mikey was running after me, before I could do anything he tackled me to the ground and started hitting me. I put my arms up against my head to defend myself from the blows. Whatever he had taken meant his swinging was nowhere near as good as I knew he was. I was able to get him off me by rolling myself around. Mikey didn't weigh a lot, so I was able to switch. Once he was on the ground, I quickly got up and looked at him

"What is wrong with you? I knew you were on something more than weed, but you need help before you lose everyone around you." I told him. I touched my hand to my face and when I looked my hand had some blood on it.

Mikey got up and seemed like he wanted round two, but I wasn't giving it to him.

"Walk away Mikey before you do something you regret." I didn't want to fight, I just wanted to go home.

"What you going to do about it? You won't hit me; you're probably too scared you'll get germs and die."

Mikey started laughing. I didn't want to scoop down to his level, but he was pushing his luck. In one swift punch Mikey was on the floor with a bloody nose.

"You're dead to me." I told him and walked away, Mikey continued laughing on the floor, clearly too high to fully comprehend what was happening.

When I got home mum immediately asked me what happened. I looked in the mirror to see what state my face was in, luckily, I only had a bloody nose and cut lip. He didn't do any other damage but enough for mum to know I got into a fight.

"I thought you weren't going to fight anyone anymore." She told me with a glum look on her face.

"I didn't start the fight mum, Mikey did."

Mum's look went from disappointed to confused. "Why did Mikey hit you?" She asked.

"Because I told him he couldn't come here when I wasn't here."

Mum looked confused again. "Why did you say that? You know he could have stayed; it would have saved granddad coming round." I thought about whether or not to tell her the whole story. I didn't want her to think that I was doing what Mikey was doing.

"I didn't want him in the house without me there because he's taking drugs, and no I don't mean weed. I found some drugs in his bag when he first came round. I didn't want him to go crazy when I wasn't here and harm the girls in any way so I told him that he couldn't stay. Well specifically I told him you didn't want him to come round when I wasn't here."

"Oh god. Okay... I see why you did it but not everyone is going to try and hurt the girls you must remember that."

I looked at her confused, I didn't know why she was being so chill about it. "Wait what?" I asked.

"Has your OCD gotten bad again?" She asked and for a moment I just stared at her.

"This isn't about my OCD mum. I'm serious. One bad trip and that's it the girls are in danger, the drugs he's taking are serious, they have seriously bad side effects."

Mum looked at me again as if I was the crazy one.

"Oh wow, seriously. Okay just allow any Tom, Dick or Harry into the house then. See if I care." I turned walked upstairs.

I did care but that didn't mean it was my OCD. It was nothing like that. I was just being cautious of a drug addict coming into my house. It's like mum didn't know me or my OCD at all. How is me kicking out a smackhead from our house in any way related to my OCD? I went upstairs and the first thing I did was write in my diary. I really need to call it something else, something cooler. Diary sounds like something a girl would write in to express her feelings and emotions, which is also what I'm doing but I'm not a girl. As I was writing a soft knock came from my door, I went over and opened it, and standing there was Callie. "Can you read me a story please." She asked me. I smiled at her and headed into her bedroom. Elise was already in the bedroom waiting with her favourite book Dr Suess' Green Eggs and Ham. I took the book from the girls, sat on the floor between their beds and read them their book. At that moment, I knew why I did what I did with Mikey, I was protecting these girls not from germs or illness but from the nasty people in the world.

* * *

I headed to work the next day, well aware of the fact that Mikey was still around. I didn't want to be the first person to contact him, I didn't want to give in like I always do. Unlike how Mikey lost Sammy and got kicked out of his own home, this was his fault. He didn't need to react so badly to me telling him the news.

When I got into work my boss took me to one side. "Tom, I was wondering if you'd be able to move the garden furniture around outside, because corporations wanted it to look like this instead." He told me and handed me a piece of paper. I looked at the photo, which was completely different from what we had it like, but I knew I could do it. "Do you think you're able to do it?" He asked me but in such a way that sounded like he didn't think I could do it. "Yeah, I think I'm fully capable." I simply told him. I went out into the garden that we have and started looking at what to start with. The job itself only took me two hours to do, and that was me taking my time with it. I thought if I'm out there nobody will bother me, and they didn't, which was great, I ended up redoing it like six times just to try and waste even more time. When I finished that the manager wanted me on the customer service counter. It was a Tuesday and not many people come in on a Tuesday, especially a week before payday. I was excited to know that my first full paycheck would be coming in next week. I already knew I was going to get the girls and mum a little present, I just didn't know what.

Something I've noticed since coming back from work is how little everyone talks to me now. It's not a great place to work when you get people who are talking and then you come along, and they disperse. I felt like I was being judged for having OCD and I didn't like it at all. I don't think anyone likes being left out for something they have no control over. I would try to spark up conversation with other colleagues, but they would reply with the most basic replies and then walk away. I had decided on my first week back that if it continued, I would try to find a job somewhere else but when I spoke to Dr Sanford about it, he was wanting me to stick with it until I could go back full-time and then I could look for another job. He didn't want too much change to make me unwell again, which I thought was strange. Surely me working in a negative environment would worsen my mental state?

I would always leave before lunch as I was still on the half day work schedule, which meant I didn't have to worry about eating lunch on my own, which I know will be a problem when I work full time. I wasn't massively fussed about eating lunch by myself because most companies did that so there were always people on the shop floor, and they didn't have to close. I preferred to eat lunch alone so I could watch whatever I wanted. What bothered me was being left out of jokes or even possibly being one of the jokes they're talking about but not knowing about it because they don't talk about me. I wasn't fussed if they wanted to joke about my OCD like Mikey did, but I knew they were not making jokes they were just being mean and not even being direct about it.

So, let's just say when it was time for me to leave, I was happy too. I was glad to get out of that place for the day and not have to go back until tomorrow. While I headed home, I took a detour to the park to see if Mikey was there, but he was nowhere to be found. This did have me a bit concerned because I knew that Mikey knew my hours and knew I would be at work, and I didn't want him to have tried coming to the house while I wasn't there and for granddad to have let him in. I thought about all the bad things that could happen if he was let in, he might even try to hurt the girls just to get to me.

I got outside my house expecting to hear a load of noise but there was nothing, I headed inside and there was some giggling coming from upstairs. I looked in the living room and grandad was sat there reading a paper. He looked at me and as calm as he could be said "your friends upstairs, the girls wanted to show him their new dolls." I looked at him with rage, chucked my bag on the floor and ran upstairs. I opened the girl's door.

"What are you doing here Sammy?" I asked him, surprised that it was Sammy and not Mikey. Sammy stopped looking at the girls' dolls, stood up and walked over to me.

"Mikey's in hospital. They rang me last night saying he overdosed on Methadone. Apparently, he was found in the middle of the village acting strange."
I stared at Sammy in shock as the guilt set it.

"Oh god. I think it might be my fault." I told him. "We got into an argument yesterday." Sammy didn't say anything.

"Wait, why did they call you and not me?"
I asked him.

"Apparently, he kept saying my name while he was out of it, and when they went through his phone and found my number, it was an obvious first choice. They did also try ringing his parents first, but they didn't answer, obviously." Sammy looked different than he did before. He looked straight, he was wearing jeans and a t-shirt, but he looked different, and he looked unhappy.

"Well thanks for letting me know."

"Are you not going to come and visit him?" I thought about it for a second.

"Look, if I was one of the reasons for it, he wouldn't want to see me. We had an argument yesterday, a bad one and he's in the hospital today. Last person he wants to see is me." I sighed.

"I think you're wrong and stupid Tom. Course he wants to see you, he's still your mate." I looked down at my feet

"I told him he was dead to me."

Sammy half smiled. "We all say and do stupid things when we're angry."

Unfortunately, no matter how hard Sammy tried, I didn't go, because I didn't want to see Mikey. It's not that I hated him or that he was somewhere that I was in for so long it's because he disrespected me. He spoke about my OCD like I was crazy, he joked about my family's financial situation, he wasn't joking around about it, he was wanting to hurt me, and maybe deep inside there's a part of me that wanted him to end up there. A part of me thinks he deserves it, like an instant karma.

* * *

It was three days since Sammy told me that Mikey was in the hospital. Sammy came round again that night to let me know that Mikey had been admitted into rehab and told me that Mikey wanted to see me. I couldn't handle going to see him, the longer I didn't see him the harder it became, what would I say? Rehab is also in the same part of the hospital as Dr Sanford's office, so I thought next time I had a session I could always go see him then. I wanted to go and see him, but it was left on such a raw note, even if he wanted to see me, I'm not entirely sure I still wanted to see him. I would love to go in there and take the mick out of him. I wanted to joke about his drug addiction but I'm not that kind of person. I would never intentionally say words that might hurt someone's feelings. I don't like it when someone jokes about something I've been through. Mikey was in the wrong, but he was also high on drugs. My brain was in two mindsets, and I didn't know what to do.

I thought about writing how it made me feel in my diary and explaining it to Dr Sanford and maybe even Mikey when I saw him next, but I didn't see a point. Me talking about my feelings and emotions wasn't going to help Mikey whatsoever. He was a selfish person who liked the world revolving around himself, which is why when his only friend let him down, he did what he did. I know one thing, I'm not going to apologise for the way I behaved before he does, but I'm also not going to be horrible and say things that will make him worse.

I spoke to Sammy about what happened with him and Mikey, and it turns out that not only did Sammy's dad catch them at it, but Mikey did try to defend Sammy. Apparently when Sammy was getting hit, Mikey started punching Sammy's dad but didn't have any luck and with one swift push, Mikey was outside of Sammy's room and escorted out of the house. Sammy told me that he was watching him from his room and saw his dad push him out of the house so hard that Mikey fell straight on his ass. Then Sammy's dad came upstairs and continued beating the crap out of Sammy. He took his phone and locked it away in his bedside cabinet and then locked him in his room for three days so he couldn't get out, his dad went as far as to put a bucket in his room for Sammy to go to the bathroom. I couldn't believe what I was hearing. I knew Sammy's dad beat him, but I didn't realise he locked him up as well. His dad found out about him being gay and he thought the best thing to do about Sammy being gay was to lock him away like a prisoner or an animal. Just from hearing Sammy talking about his dad made me infuriated. It made me want to go round and try something, but I knew I would end up like Mikey, on the floor.

* * *

Sammy was able to convince me to go with him to see Mikey at the hospital. He told me he would pick me up and we'd go in together to see Mikey. I thought I may as well go even if I do only see him for 10 minutes at

84

least I've been. I thought about how little he came to see me, and I realised that no, I didn't want to be the same, I should see him. It is semi my fault for scooping low enough and getting into a fight with him.

We headed to the hospital after mum came home from work and I knew the girls had been fed. Sammy had a Corsa, one of those cars that normally 17-year-old boys zoom around in trying to pick up 13-year-old girls. He had an insane sound system and moved the car when it was stationary because of how good the bass was. We rolled up to the hospital and while Sammy was paying for parking, I went to reception to find out where Mikey was. I knew the rehab centre was near the psych ward, but I was unsure of what room he was in and if we were even allowed in to see him.

"Hi, I'm wondering where my friend Mikey Lewis is, he was admitted into the rehab ward a couple of days ago but I'm not sure what room." The receptionist did some tapping on the computer and then told me I would have to go to the rehab reception for them to be able to help me out further. Sammy and I headed straight there, we made small talk, but we were both just focused on getting there and getting into the ward to see Mikey.

We eventually got to the ward and for a moment I had to stop and relax, I knew the feeling of being somewhere like this. Both Mikey and I have an addiction, his was to Opioids and mine was germs. We all have battles, and we all have ways of coping with them.

"Hi, we're here to see Mikey Lewis." Sammy told the rehab receptionist, again she tapped away and told us that he was currently in a meeting but would be available in an hour. We stood around wondering what to do, should we go and come back another day? Should we wait around for an hour? We decided to wait, we got ourselves a coffee and sat down. We didn't have much to say to each other and sitting here in silence next to the psych ward made me uncomfortable.

It reminded me of when I first got admitted here and had to wait with two policemen outside the doors until a doctor let us in. The police officers didn't speak to me either, I always thought it was because they thought they were better than me, but it turns out it was just because they couldn't say anything in case it made my thoughts worse. They had to stand guard in case I tried running, which I admit they were only called to in the first place because I did try running out of the hospital. I ran out of the hospital in the gown that opens at the back and no socks or shoes on. It didn't take long to find me; I was pretty hard to miss. If they find the ass, they found me. They had to try and convince me to go back into the hospital, and it was only when I started going blue that I thought it might be a good idea. I'm honestly surprised I lasted if I did without dropping down and getting hypothermia, I mean it was cold and I was out there for a couple of hours. I can see looking back now that I did need that help but at the time, I was adamant there was nothing wrong with me. I was adamant that all these thoughts were going to come true, that if I didn't clean the house that the girls were going to die. That's the thing with mental illness, because it's in your head you truly believe it and it's not until you get help that you realise the mental illness is playing games with you, that it's dragging you along by some string and telling you how to act and what to do.

Once it was time to head in, a nurse came to escort us to the room that Mikey was in, when Sammy and I entered the room, we were shocked at what we saw. Mikey was in his bed covered in sick, the room had a

horrible smell that I could only describe as death. "Mikey
" Sammy quietly spoke, nudging himself into the room
ever so slowly, as if a lion were in the room and it was the
lion's dinnertime. Mikey mumbled something but neither
Sammy nor I understood what he said. Sammy walked
into the room, I stood by the doorway tapping it six
times for good luck.

"Mikey it's Sammy and Tom " Sammy spoke
again, this time Mikey got out from under the sheets and
edged towards us with this grimace look on his face.

"I know, why are you here?" Mikey was face to
face with Sammy, looking him up and down.

"We came to see you." I answered knowing that
whatever we said wouldn't help the situation.

"Why?" He asked, neither of us knew what to
say, what the right answer was.

"Because we're your mates' ' I eventually said.
Mikey's attention went from Sammy onto me.
"Oh really? I don't think a mate would lock their mate
up, would they?" Mikey snarled and before Sammy and
I could say anything else Mikey pounced on top of me.
He swung for my face with each fist clenched as hard as
they could be. I was able to put my hands up in defence,
but it didn't stop all of the punches.

"YOU'RE A PRICK. YOU'RE SELFISH. I
HATE YOU. YOU'RE NOT MY MATE, MY MATE
WOULDN'T LOCK ME UP!" He screamed and
shouted while continuously punching me. Sammy was
shouting for help while also trying to get Mikey off of
me, but despite Mikey weighing only 80 pounds, Sammy
couldn't get him off. Mikey was out for revenge, not
realising it wasn't my fault.

Eventually the nurses came in and gave him a
sedative to calm him down, which gave me enough time

to get off the floor and run out of the room. I wasn't too badly injured, he managed to suckerpunch me in the eye, which already started going blue by the time I got to the bathroom to access my injuries. My top lip had been cut open but in general I wasn't too bad. I expected my arms to bruise up later as they took most of the damage. My face had just healed from Mikey's previous punches and now it was going to be battered and bruised again.

I sat on the chair outside of the room, the nurses wanted to check on me in a separate room, but I insisted I was okay and didn't want any help. Sammy came out to see me "why did he say it was your fault?" I looked up at Sammy who had his arms crossed. "I don't know, all I told him was that he couldn't do drugs in my house." I looked at Sammy who looked tired and sad. He looked like he hadn't slept since the night his dad beat him up. He looks like all of the life has been drained out of him. "Have you slept much?" I asked him, knowing that the answer would be no but wanting to change the subject quickly. "No, I don't think I've properly slept since that night." Sammy replied, I knew what night he meant. It was obvious. I didn't want to intrude or ask too many questions, I didn't know him well enough to be that close and personal, and yet I wanted to bring him into a massive hug. In that moment I wanted to do exactly what I would do with my sisters. I wanted to wrap my arms around him and tell him I would protect him no matter what, but I didn't.

We walked slowly back to Sammy's car and Sammy got inside but I hovered at the door not wanting to get into the car with him. I didn't want to go home; I didn't want to stay at the hospital. I didn't want to be anywhere. I just wanted to disappear.

"Are you getting in?" Sammy asked me as he rolled down the window.

"No, I'm gonna go for a walk." I told him and started walking in the opposite direction of the car.

"Tom!" Sammy shouted out of the window, but I was already too far to turn back. I needed to think. I needed to go somewhere that I could think straight.

I started walking, I had a few places in mind but I let my legs take me to where they wanted to go. With each step I thought about Mikey, I thought about what was going to happen to him if his parents found out, or if they even cared. I thought about Sammy and how miserable he must be to not be allowed to be himself in his own house, otherwise he gets beat up. I thought about the girls and how much they have grown up from when I was inside. I think about granddad and how disappointed he must be in me. How I'm the only son and grandson and how I ended up in the loony bin. I thought about my mum and how on earth she's managed for so long. Thinking didn't help. Obviously.

I then tried thinking of songs to sing in my head, something I would always do when I wanted to escape from my thoughts. I tried humming 'Don't stop me now' by Queen (classic banger), then I tried humming "Staying Alive" by the Bee Gees, the choruses were easy, but I couldn't remember the exact words, so I ended up making some of them up.

I eventually stopped walking when I came to the lookout. It's not actually called the lookout; I just call it that because if you stand on the rocks, you can see the entire town below. It's beautiful at night. I've always thought how nice it would be to share this place with someone, for the lookout to turn into our thing and for the both of us to love going there. I've always thought it would be a romantic place to go and just watch the town below, maybe find someone who enjoys smoking just as much as me and we can just smoke and watch the world go by in our own little place. I've never found anyone to do that with, most of the girls at my work are either gay or are taken (isn't it always the way), maybe I should broaden my horizons, maybe I should do online dating.

I don't think Dr Sanford would approve; he would tell me that I need to focus on myself. That I need to get myself better before worrying about new problems, relationship problems. He would tell me that it's a bad idea, because what if I fixated on them instead of the girls this time and it became worse.

That's another thing with me, I fixate on people. Once I become close to someone, I fixate on them. I see them everywhere; I think about them constantly and I want to protect them all the time. I always thought it was a good thing but it's not, not when it turns into an obsession. In fact, I created my own checklist to figure out if I was fixating on someone or if what was happening was normal.

Have you started dreaming about them?
Have you started seeing them in public and realised it's someone else?
Have you started writing about them in your diary?
Are they as interested as you are?
Are you finding it's always you messaging?
Are you planning to do things with them without proper consultation?
Do you get angry when they cancel plans?

I go through the checklist, and I make sure that

I'm not doing more than two of them, if I am then I completely stop contact with the person. I know it's not the best way to do it, but the alternative is worse. I wanted to make it clear that I would never hurt someone, I would never do any harm to another person or animal. The problem is normally the opposite, that's why I didn't do anything with Sammy because I didn't want to become fixated on helping him and for that to end badly.

I know it sounds like I'm a creep and I follow people around and things like that but that couldn't be farther from the truth. I'm not a stalker, in fact fixating on people is completely different from stalking them. I fixate on the relationship as well as making sure they don't end up in harm's way, the last thing I wanted is for them to come to harm. I cover up my fixation well, I have a small group of friends, I see them a couple of days a week and I make sure that it's a double-sided relationship. If there are any signs that it's me bothering more than them, I would cut them off before I made myself look stupid.

I think it's another sign of OCD, but I can't be too certain. My anxiety keeps me up thinking about them like it does with the girls. I didn't want them to harm themselves or others, so I would wrap them up in bubble wrap and protect them. Dr Sanford told me that I shouldn't do that because everyone is their own person, and they need to learn things by themselves. He told me that unless they ask, I shouldn't get involved in other people's personal lives. I remember when he told me the first time because I laughed out loud, and he looked at me concerned. He asked me what I thought was so funny and I remember replying "well, I talk to my mates about life, and they talk to me about theirs so when do I know if they want me to interfere or not?" I remember Dr Sanford sitting there with his clipboard resting on his knee and for a second, I think he was a bit stumped. I don't think he really knew how to answer. "Sometimes they'll ask and sometimes they won't but there's a difference between giving advice and getting involved." I'll always remember it because I think it was the first time that something he had said made no sense to me whatsoever. In the sessions that followed I would ask him hypotheticals and he would tell me how I'm now fixating over the question.

I think after a while I understood what he meant. I always felt wrong thinking about people too often, I felt like a stalker but talking through it with Dr Sanford helped me realise that it's part of the disease. It's part of the monster that's growing inside of me and the monster is never going away, so I must deal with sharing the monster.

Anyway, back to reality, I stayed at the lookout, long enough for my mum to call me and ask where I was. She knew that I was seeing Mikey and that I didn't have work and that visiting hours in a place like that are restricted so she knew I should have been home by now. I answer the phone.

"Where are you?" She asks as soon as I pick up. She sounds angry.

"I took a detour; I'll be home soon." I told her, I tried thinking for a moment, trying to remember if there was anything important about today but I couldn't think of anything. Why would mum be so mad at me? It's not like it was someone's birthday.

"Well how long is soon? You told me you would come home and look after the girls."

Did I? I couldn't remember that at all.

Maybe she asked me when I was super high. That would make sense. Nobody remembers anything when they're super baked.

"I'm sorry I'll be home as soon as I can"

I could tell mum was disappointed by the sigh at the other end of the phone, but I could also tell she didn't want to argue with me either. I started jogging home but thought a fast sprint would be better. I knew the longer mum was waiting for me the worse the repercussions were going to be. If I was 10 minutes late, it would be a slapped wrist. If I was 20 minutes late, it would be a lecture, and so on and so forth.

I remember when she tried grounding me when I was 19. Mikey and I went out clubbing and she told me to be home by 3am latest, as she had work and I had to look after the girls. Mikey and I ended up not going clubbing but sitting in a park, getting absolutely wasted and smoking the heavens. We were screwed and I was even more when it came to 6am and mum called me asking where I was. I had to lie and tell her I was at Mikeys, and that I went there because I left my keys at home. Of course, my dumbass didn't think she would still be home when I got home so as I walked through the door, with my unlost keys and she stood at the end of the stairs with smoke coming out her ears. "WHERE HAVE YOU BEEN?" She screamed. "YOU PROMISED TO BE HOME AT 3" I think I could have gotten away with just some shouting until I opened my hammered mouth

"Technically, you asked me to be home by 3am. I didn't say I would or not." That was it, mum was throwing shoes at me. Telling me how selfish I was and how much like dad I was. When she mentioned dad, I sobered up quickly and shouted back at her. She told me I was grounded and couldn't leave the house and that was how it ended, well until she left for work. I dropped the girls off at Nursery and headed straight over to Mikey's to get wasted again.

That whole ordeal lasted two weeks. Two weeks of mum and I arguing, me leaving the house and getting high with Mikey. It only stopped when mum called me to let me know that Elise had fallen down the stairs and hurt her arm. I remember the night well; I ran back to mine to see Elise being put into her car seat. Her face was red raw from crying.

"I'm sorry mum, okay. I'm sorry" I told mum, but she was too busy sorting Elise out

"We'll talk about it later, just go in and look after Callie would you." Mum told me rather than asked me. She still wasn't happy with me, and I'm honestly not surprised, looking back, I was an absolute terror. I was horrible, the worst I've ever been in my life.

I know I said my OCD started getting bad after dad left but I think this was the "traumatic experience" that started the whole thing. After that, I didn't want to leave home. I left for work and to see Mikey but that started growing smaller and smaller, as I wanted to stay home and look after the girls. I didn't want them to get injured again.

* * *

I got home to mum hurrying around the house "shoes...lipstick...purse" she was mumbling to herself. She stopped to look at me as I entered the house for a split second but continued her hurry.

"I'm going out, girls have been fed and watered. They're in their pyjamas and watching tv now." Mum was putting on her heels, which was strange because she never wore those kinds of heels out. She would always leave

94

them as her best shoes for weddings and things like that.

"Going on a date?" I joked but mum didn't laugh.

"Actually yes."

I stood up straight, surprised at her admission.

"Wait. For real?" I asked her, looking her dead in the eyes.

"Yes. I met him at work"

I continued to look at mum in shock, why didn't she tell me? And that's exactly what I ask.

"I didn't tell you because I didn't think you would approve."

I stood closer to her and put my arm on her shoulder. "Of course, I would approve. After all this time you should be happy too." I wrapped into one of my monster hugs. She smiled.

"You look great. Sorry I'm late."

I never thought about the idea of mum going on a date again. I never thought she would be into it after dad. I didn't think she could deal with rejection anymore, but I was wrong. Then again, my OCD told me a lot of things and they were also wrong, which makes me think if anything I think is the right thing or not. I snap myself out of it before I begin an existential crisis that I can't dig myself out of.

Mum leaves about five minutes after I got in, and now it's just me and the girls.

"Are you hungry?" I ask them and they shout out "YES! YES"

I asked them if they wanted to share a pizza with me and they start getting excited, shouting out the toppings they wanted.

"Pepperoni" "No Sausage" "No Pepperoni"

They shout over each other. I ended up getting a

half and half pizza, telling them both they can only have one slice, so they need to pick carefully. I end up getting half Pepperoni and Sausage and half BBQ chicken. That way everyone was happy, when the doorbell went, Elise answered it, the pizza delivery guy looked confused when he asked if the pizza was for her. I went to the door to confirm I had ordered the pizza and not a small child. We sat down and watched Scooby Doo. I told the girls that if we were having pizza then I was picking the show to watch, and they reluctantly agreed. Callie was extremely happy with the choice, which she told me "I'm extremely happy with that choice"

"That's a big word" I told her and she smiled wide.

Once the girls and I finished the pizza and a couple episodes of Scooby Doo, I tucked them into bed.

"Tell us a story," Callie asked.

"What do you want me to read?" I asked her assuming she wanted me to read a story.

"No, I wanted one of your stories. They're the best." She told me with half her mouth covered by her duvet. Elise stared at me in excitement, she always liked my bedtime stories, but I didn't know Callie loved them just as much.

"Okay so this is the story of the Octopus with only six tentacles."

"But they normally have 8," Callie told me.

I laughed "I know but this one is special. It only has 6" and I told them the story. I'm not going to repeat the whole thing because to be honest I can't remember the whole thing. I forgot it as soon as it came out my mouth, but the girls loved it.

Once the girls were in bed, I went into my room and rolled a spliff. I made sure to add more weed than normal as I couldn't seem to shake off what happened with Mikey. I took out my phone and texted mum.

'If you need help, I'll help just SOS.' I knew she would see the funny side and it would make her laugh. I finished rolling and headed downstairs. I checked the back door was locked and the keys were hidden (Elise likes to go outside at night and look at the stars, which is cute but terrifying) and headed out the front door. I put my key in my pocket just in case the door slammed shut and I needed to get back in. I checked my phone again to see if she replied but she hadn't. Sammy had messaged me though, which I thought was strange because I don't remember saving his number down. He asked me how I was doing after today, I told him I'd be alright and that I knew more than anyone else what Mikey was going through.

I don't think Sammy liked hearing it, but it was true. Out of everyone that Mikey knows, I'm the one that knew what it was truly like to be locked up, to be told when to eat and what medicines to take. For the arrangement of different moods and emotions and not knowing which day was which. I knew what it was like for another patient to start on you for no reason and I knew what it was like starting on somebody else for the littlest of things. I knew what it was like.

I had been in that situation, so I knew. Sammy didn't. Sammy didn't understand what Mikey is going through, which might be why I'm feeling so damn guilty. It might be why I'm feeling like running over to the hospital and breaking him out. It might be why despite not being the one to put Mikey into rehab, I feel like a terrible friend.

Chapter Four

When Mikey got out of rehab, I made sure to contact him, but despite my numerous texts and calls, he never answered. I didn't know where he was living, I didn't know if he and Sammy were back together. I didn't know anything, and it was starting to get to me. I hadn't left the house properly since Mikey got admitted. I would stay at home unless I had to go to work and even that was becoming a struggle. Everyone at work assumed I didn't hear the whispers, but I did. I heard them snicker as I put the stock away, saying things like "I bet he puts them dead straight," or tells a colleague, "do you think he would go mad if I moved them around?" I heard them talk about me, and I would try my hardest not to do anything, but it was so hard for the words to not affect me.

Mum didn't notice that I started checking things before going out again. Dr. Sanford didn't ask me questions like he used to, so he didn't know about how I was getting bad, and I didn't for one moment tell them. It gave me release, it helped me so much, so when I wanted to check the doors were locked and the ovens were off, I didn't see the problem with it. Loads of people did that before leaving the house, I just had to do it six times.

6

The new number. The number of times my brain lets me do something before finally being at peace. I didn't think it was a problem. I thought I was under control until I got to 13. That it wasn't an issue. I thought when I start doing things 13 times then I'll tell someone, but until then I'm not doing anything. I needed this, after everything I needed some peace, and my compulsions helped, they weren't doing me or anyone else harm, so I didn't see the problem.

Everyday started merging into one and I only remembered it was therapy day because mum reminded me. I wish she didn't, the last thing I wanted to do was to go into a room and talk about my feelings. Obviously, I still had to go. It's what mum wanted, and right now I don't think I'm in any position to be having an argument with her. I walked over to the hospital, since Dr Sanford had allowed me to go back to work mum started trusting me to go, to and from therapy on my own. I tried explaining to her that I could be trusted beforehand but until Dr. Sanford cleared me, she didn't want to do anything.

I got to the hospital with 20 minutes to spare, I walked around exploring the outside area. An area that a couple of months ago, I wouldn't have been allowed to go without supervision. I looked at the tulips and daisies that had been perfectly planted so that they would grow into a smiley face. I guess they thought it would cheer up the patients that could look out of their window. I would have thought something like that was completely stupid, how could flowers arranged into a smiley face make someone happy?

Dr Sanford was holding the door open when I arrived at his office.

"You're late," he said as I entered his office.

"By two minutes." I exclaimed as I chucked myself onto the sofa.

"Any particular reason?" He asked me, more stern than usual. "

I was admiring the flowers outside." I replied, looking at him with a smug face.

"If you're not going to answer honestly," he tells me with one eyebrow raised. I laughed knowing that despite it being the truth, he wouldn't believe me. I didn't look at flowers, I had never once shown an interest in flowers or in nature. The closest I would get to nature is the lookout but that's not looking at trees or animals. So, Dr. Sanford's confusion was a correct reaction, but he was in fact wrong this time, I wasn't lying, but I didn't care if he thought I was.

"How have you been this week?" Dr Sanford asks abruptly, which brings me out of my trance.

"Yeah good, I think I'm ready for full-time work now." I lied.

"I don't think we should rush into things' ' he replied, which despite me being relieved, I was also angry.

"When? When can my life go back to normal? I need the money, which I know is something you don't understand but with one income, it's becoming increasingly difficult." I wasn't lying.

Mum had been telling me how difficult it had been with only one full-time income. I told her not to worry and that soon I would be back on my feet, and I would even do extra hours. She would always say, "It's more important that you're well and healthy. We'll just have to struggle for a bit."

I know it wasn't supposed to sound like a dig, but it did. It sounded like she was saying "if only you were healthy, we wouldn't be in this mess."

Mum had been trying her hardest for the last couple of months and I could see how tired she was. I wanted to provide for her. I wanted her to become her old self, she didn't laugh as much anymore. Her frown lines had increased and the bags under her eyes had gotten darker. The job was killing her, but I couldn't tell if it was her work job or the job of looking after three children. Every time I thought about the sacrifices she made, it made me feel horrible inside, I felt disgusted about myself. I was the reason that mum was struggling, I couldn't be a good enough son for her. I couldn't stay well enough for her. I couldn't do the one job I promised her when dad walked out.

I looked at Dr Sanford who was staring at me.

"Sorry what?" I asked him again knowing I must have missed a crucial question.

"What's going on?" He asked and I looked at him clueless.

"What do you mean?"

"Just then when you zoned out. What were you thinking of?"

"I was just thinking about money. Mum's struggling. We're struggling. She didn't want to say anything because she didn't want me to feel bad, but I know she's thinking about it constantly. If our grandparents hadn't helped with the mortgage, we wouldn't have a home right now." I looked down and saw dried blood in the corner of my fingernails. I must have picked them without knowing...

"Tom, your health and wellbeing is more important than money. Money isn't going to make everything better. It might make things easier, but it won't make you better." I looked at Dr. Sanford, who obviously thought he had said something philosophical and laughed.

"You have clearly never struggled with money. Dr. Sanford. I don't mean to be offensive, but you clearly have no idea what it's like to not know where your next meal is coming from or if you can afford nappies for the girls. You don't know what it's like to work 50-hour weeks to try and get extra money just so you can afford some toys for Christmas. You have no idea. So, with all due respect Dr Sanford. Go fuck yourself." I ranted; anger filled in the pit of my stomach. I stood up from the sofa and walked out of the office. I didn't care if we still had half an hour, I wasn't dealing with anymore of his rubbish.

He had no idea.

Nobody had any idea.

I was all alone.

I needed to go for a walk.

I needed to get fresh air.

Breath Tom.

I started walking but there was this surge of electricity going through me. I shook my hands as if doing that would get rid of this strange feeling. It felt like I had become the god of Thunder and I had lightning coming out of my hands. Of course, I could merely dream of being the great Thor, but I would never live up to anything near as good as that. In fact, think of the worst God of all time and I would be worse than them because I was me. I was simply a boy trying to be a man, whatever that is nowadays.

I knew Granddad was disappointed in me. He didn't need to say it because his facial expressions gave it away. When mum told Granddad he didn't need to come round every day because I was now home, he seemed pleased to finally be able to get back to his normal life. Even if that normal life was boring, he wanted his life back and who can blame him. He spent most of his life looking after mum, why would he want to look after more girls? He wanted to enjoy retirement like he should have been able to.

* * *

I found myself at the lookout again, but this time I came prepared. I knew I would need a spliff after Dr Sanford's lesson, the previous week's sessions had been becoming harder to complete. It felt like there was a rock strapped to my chest, I felt like I was being pulled down and I didn't know why. I knew that what Dr Sanford was saying shouldn't have gotten to me, but it did. When dad first left, we really struggled, and I had to quickly become an adult and change my life of partying to focusing on the girls. Dad left and I had to become the replacement male role model. I know mum never officially asked me to do it, but it didn't seem fair leaving her to bring up two kids by herself while I enjoyed being 18. I promised her the day dad left that I would look after the girls. I promised mum I would look after her too, that it was just the four of us and that was all that mattered. I told mum we would never need help again and that we would be fine.

What dad did to her wasn't fair. It wasn't fair on me either, but I volunteered. I'd rather sacrifice some night life for my family. Of course, Dr Sanford told me that I was still entitled to my years and that I could have done what so many did and continued living my life. I never thought about it as an option before, not properly. I had the occasional angry thought when mum and I argued but it never lasted long enough for me to think of it as anything serious. I always thought I was lucky, that at least he didn't leave when I was 10 and that I didn't have to worry about growing up too soon. I was still able to live my life, I was still able to live 18 years of my life, so why shouldn't I grow up and help mum.

A lot of people I knew were underage parents and they did fine, they were able to have a job and a kid and still have a life. I remembered when I told Dr. Sanford this and he just looked at me confused. He simply stated, "But the girls aren't your children" and that was that. Dr Sanford rarely brought up the girls, it was always me bringing them up to him. I think he felt like it was therapy for the twins rather than me, but there was something that Dr Sanford didn't understand. I loved these girls, as if they were my own. I didn't have a typical sibling relationship with them, I basically was the replacement dad. Since they were babies, I would always change their diapers, feed them, and take them to school. I did what a dad should do if not more because then the brother-sister relationship would also happen, so when someone would upset them, I wanted to get involved and mum had to remind me that they were six-year-old children, and I would kill them with one flick.

* * *

The lookout spot was quite spectacular, despite the hectic scenes below, seeing traffic jams from miles away, hearing the distant beeps coming from cars who had no idea why they were being kept waiting. This felt like pure bliss, for a moment I began to feel peace. I felt happy.

"Thought you'd be here" I turned around to find mum staring at me about six feet away, she was still wearing her work uniform. It was the first time I had seen mum like this, she wasn't angry at me. She looked, I don't know, sad. She looked like she wanted to wrap me into a hug.

"I'm guessing Dr Sanford called you" I abruptly asked, moving my attitude from Dr. Sanford to her for no real reason.

"Yeah, straight away. He told me you walked out of sessions but wouldn't say why. He also told me you swore at him." Mum was looking stern now but kept a sympathetic tone. Mum was pretty good at hearing the whole story first before blowing up.

"He told me I needed to focus on getting better rather than working loads of hours for money. He told me money didn't buy happiness and I told him to go fuck himself." I didn't want to tell mum that I mainly had a go at Dr. Sanford because he was insinuating it was mum's fault. Mum walked over to me, and we both looked out at the scene together.

"We used to love coming up here. Do you remember?" Mum asked, clearly feeling too awkward to continue the conversation.

"Yeah, I would make a kite and we would bring it up here to fly" I smiled at the thought of mum and I flying my terrible kites.

"They were awful," I told her while laughing. "But you had fun..." Mum stopped mid-sentence, "WE had fun" Mum placed her hand onto mine.

"You know your father and I were never rich. We struggled just as much as I do now, maybe even more because we had the mortgage, but if you were happy, I didn't care. I loved coming up here and watching you fly your kites, it cost nothing but time, and yet you were so happy. I want that happy child back." I looked at mum who had a tear streaming down her face.

"I'm not a child anymore. I'm a grown adult and I should be able to do what I want. Which is to support my family." I moved my hand and mums along with it and faced her. Mum looked directly at me as if she was staring into my soul.

"I want you to be happy again, Tom. Dr. Sanford is right; money doesn't buy happiness. Okay, it helps but if you asked me would I rather have money or my son, that's a bloody obvious answer." I didn't know what to say, so I didn't say anything. I could argue with mum until we both went blue in the face but both Dr Sanford and Mum agreed that it's better for me to be "100%" before doing too much. It was incredibly annoying, I felt fine. I felt good. I wasn't going to make everything worse by shouting and screaming, behaving like a child and therefore proving their point even more. I just agreed with her.

Mum thought it would be a good idea if I called Dr Sanford and apologised for swearing at him, I told her it wouldn't be necessary as I would see him next week and we'd probably talk about it then, but mum was adamant. "We don't talk to people like that in this family, Thomas" Oooh, the first name, the full first name. That was when I realised how serious mum was. Mum had always tried teaching me ways of expressing my anger without using swear words.

Of course, I called Dr Sanford to apologise for my behaviour to which he asked me to come in.

"I would like to see you before the end of today, my last appointment is 5:25 are you able to get here for half past?"

"Sure" I replied and then hung up. The last thing I needed was for Dr Sanford to turn around and tell me I was regressing and that giving me my job back was a bad decision. I thought about all the bad things I did that he could use against me. Maybe he wanted to see me twice a week again. Maybe he wanted to put me on a report. He might have wanted to take me back to the hospital. I couldn't leave the girls again. What would they do without me? I can't go back.

All the thoughts, trampling me.

My breathing was shaky.

I felt like my head was going to explode.

1 Tap. 2 Tap. 3 Tap. 4 Tap. 5 Tap. 6 Tap.
Breath
1 Tap. 2 Tap. 3 Tap. 4 Tap. 5 Tap. 6 Tap.
Breath
1 Tap. 2 Tap. 3 Tap. 4 Tap. 5 Tap. 6 Tap.
Breath
1 Tap. 2 Tap. 3 Tap. 4 Tap. 5 Tap. 6 Tap.
Breath
1 Tap. 2 Tap. 3 Tap. 4 Tap. 5 Tap. 6 Tap.
Breath
1 Tap. 2 Tap. 3 Tap. 4 Tap. 5 Tap. 6 Tap.
And relax.

Better. My mind was a lot clearer now. I could focus, I didn't feel so hemmed in. The thoughts weren't in a fight with each other trying to get to me the quickest. I felt calm. Until I realised mum had seen the entire thing. She wasn't going to understand that this wasn't the same thing as my old compulsions. She wouldn't understand that this helped me.

"It's not what it looks like, it's a breathing exercise" I told her knowing she wouldn't believe me.

"I thought you were better, we just spoke about it, you said you were better" Mum sighed. She wasn't angry, not at me anyway, she was upset with my brain. The part that no-one can control.

"Mum, it..it's..not what it looks like, okay. I'm fine. It's a breathing exercise" I closed my eyes for a second and when I opened them, mum was now a lot closer to me.

"Tom, all we want is for you to get better and lying to yourself and trying to lie to us isn't going to help."

I knew what mum was trying to say but her words made something inside me boil. It made me angry.

"YOU'RE NOT LISTENING" I shouted, which got the attention of some walkers who were passing by and made mum flinch... I lowered my voice "Now this might be something that you and Dr Sanford find hard to understand. I'm better, this is a breathing exercise and yes, the tapping helps me to focus. I'm so much better than I was before but you don't believe me. You are keeping me locked up. I may as well be back in the Hospital if you're going to treat me like a MENTAL PERSON." I couldn't help it, but my voice raised again.

"You need help Tom. OCD is a serious mental health condition and standing around pretending you no longer have it, isn't helping anyone. It's not helping me, it's not helping your sisters and it's definitely not helping you." Mum is now shouting as well. I try to calm myself but even the tapping isn't helping. I try to do more; I need to be at home. I need to do it at home, that would help. That would make me feel better.

"Tom." I can barely hear mum's words.

"Tom."
"Tom. Breath"

Her voice isn't coming through. All I can hear are the thoughts. They're so loud. I can't think. Mum's trying to hold my hand, but I move it away from her. I

108

feel numb. My whole body feels numb. I can't stay around here; I can't see mum right now. Within a second I decided to leg it. I ran and ran and ran and didn't pay attention to anything around me. I didn't hear mum, so I didn't know if she called my name. I can guarantee she did, but I didn't care, I just needed to run. I needed to get all this energy and all these thoughts out of my head.

I didn't know how long I had been running but I stopped when my lungs felt like they were on fire and my legs felt like jelly. Despite not having a clue where I was going, I ended up at Mikey's house, even my subconscious must be feeling guilty. I stopped and looked outside, it looked quiet, it looked empty. I looked at the front door and after a minute or two I walked up the stone steps. I knocked quickly and took two steps back. I waited for a couple of seconds until Mikey's mum (Pam) opened the door.

"Oh, Hi Tom, Mikey's not here." I nod and smile.

"I know, I don't suppose you know where he is." I looked at Pam who seemed surprised I was still standing at the door.

"No, I don't, I haven't spoken to him for a couple of weeks." Pam looked at me, she was trying to be kind, but you could tell she wanted me gone. I turned around to walk away but before I took a step I looked back, "maybe you should try talking to him. He was in hospital not long ago and despite what your husband thinks, I think it would be good for him to have some support." I walked away without giving Pam a chance to say anything. My statement wasn't supposed to be answered, I wanted her to dwell on it and realise that having a son who was gay was better than having one that was dead.

I didn't want to go home just yet but there was no chance of me going to see Dr. Sanford. I knew mum would have called him by now and he would be giving her pointers on what to do and speak. I didn't want to listen to it, despite what they thought I was getting better. The tapping wasn't a major thing, I mean it wasn't to help my breathing, it was just a blip. That was all. A tiny blip on the system.

I decided to walk from Mikey's to Sammy's. I didn't know exactly where he lived but I had dropped Mikey there a couple of times, so I turned on my photogenic memory and started walking the way I remembered. One left turn, keep going forward by the orchard after the orchard take a right, then it's the 2nd left and the 5th house on the street. I remembered getting there because that's exactly how Mikey would tell me the way. He would use those exact words. When I got up to the house it looked like Mikeys, but it was worn down. The windows looked black from smoke or mould, the curtains were orange stained and the front door had claw marks at the bottom. The garden was in a state, it had old bikes that the grass had grown over, there were some kid's toys which were filthy with mud and just the thought of touching the bell almost gave me a heart attack. I rolled my sleeve up to my finger and pressed it. I didn't want to touch it with my bare skin otherwise I'd be washing it for days.

A fat, bearded man answered the door "What?" He asked with a thick southwest accent.

"Is Sammy here?" I asked him, trying to be polite, I made the educated guess that this was Sammy's dad, and Sammy's dad looked like he could kill you without moving his body.

"Na, that boy don't live 'ere no more." Sammy's dad answered and slammed the door in my face. I turned around and started walking out. If they aren't at Sammy's or Mikey's, then where are they? I couldn't put my finger on it.

I checked my phone, four missed calls and three texts from mum, and a missed call from an unknown caller. I knew the unknown caller was Dr Sanford because it was now 6:15pm and I hadn't shown up, like I said I would. I'm sure that's something that Dr Sanford has already written down for the next week. I was sure he was writing in his book how I should be back in the hospital because I was mental. I tried to calm myself down again, I couldn't physically run, my legs hurt too much for that. Despite being scrawny, I wasn't fast. Infact, I couldn't remember the last time I ran as a sport. I didn't know what to do, should I go home and possibly end up in an argument with my mum or did I stay out and end up getting in more trouble than I was already in. I knew what mum would end up doing, she would call Dr Sanford and they would both exchange words and decide what was best for me, but I had had enough of people deciding my life for me. I wanted to stay out and enjoy my life like I should be able to. I get out my phone and text my dealer. It then made sense why I had been so tense, I hadn't smoked for a couple of hours now and I was needing it.

I met my dealer a 20-minute walk away from my house. I had asked him to roll me one as I didn't have anything, and he was kind enough to do it and not charge me extra. Well, I had been using him now for five years, I bet I had given him enough money that he could buy his own place. I lit up in the park, I knew that nobody would be there because it had started getting dark. I went over to my usual smoking area, hoping that Mikey and Sammy might be there, but when I got to the shelter, no one was there. I was disappointed that I was hopeful I would see Mikey, I had really tried to make things right with him.

Once I finished my smoke, I felt a lot less tense. I felt like I could go home, and that mum and I would be able to talk rather than argue. I headed home expecting a storm. As I got to my house, I noticed a car outside. It wasn't one I had noticed beforehand, and I wondered if it was mum's date. I hoped it would be so I could go straight to bed and forget about what happened earlier on.

Mum told me the date had gone well and that she was seeing him again sometime soon, maybe he came round to support her. I opened the door quietly knowing that if I was too loud the girls would wake up. I closed it and tried tiptoeing up the stairs, a way to avoid having to speak to mum. It didn't work "Tom," mum said from the bottom of the stairs. I looked at her, but I said nothing. I walked down the stairs knowing she wanted to have a chat. As I walked down the stairs, I saw some shoes from the gaps in the railing. The shoes were men's shoes, and they were set perfectly on the floor, but there was something weird about the shoes.

I recognised them.

I recognised the shoes before I recognised the face because I had stared at those shoes for so many weeks. As I entered the front room, I looked up to see Dr. Sanford sitting on the sofa with a cup of tea in his hand.

"Hi Tom" Dr Sanford said.

"What are you doing here?" I asked, shocked to see him in my living room.

"You didn't come to see me."

I looked down, I tried to stop myself from laughing. I'm guessing whatever my dealer gave me was the funny stuff. The stuff that makes you laugh rather than mellow out.

"How are you doing, Tom?" Dr. Sanford asked.

"I'm good." I told him and let out a laugh.

"Really? Tom." Mum asked, knowing that I was currently high.

"Tom, is something funny?" Dr. Sanford asked, while putting the cup of tea on the table and standing up so we were both at eye level.

"I think this whole situation is hilarious, Dr Sanford" I told him, letting out another chuckle after finishing my sentence.

"Can I ask why?"

"Of course, you can, please ask away" I answered him knowing exactly what he was wanting but not giving it to him.

"Jesus Thomas, just answer his question" Mum said sternly in a hushed tone, so she didn't wake the girls.

"Fine."

I direct my gaze to Dr. Sanford

"I think it's hilarious that you wanted me to be independent and yet when I'm trying to be you're pulling me back like I'm a dog on a lead. I think it's hilarious that I can't tap or whistle a tune without people thinking that my OCD is bad again. I think it's hilarious that you are assuming what's best for me but not asking me what I want. I think it's hilarious that you're in our house." I say the last one while literally laughing out loud. Dr. Sanford looks at me and then looks at my mum.

"Tom, your mother and I have had a chat, we think it might be best for you to decrease your work time. We think giving you the extra hours meant that you weren't properly focused on your health and that it's interfering with your therapy."

I looked from mum to Dr Sanford. "Are you serious?" I rave.

"Mum pinch me I think I'm in a terrible nightmare." I told mum. "You're serious. Oh my god! You're not trying to help me! You just want to keep me until mum needs to pay for sessions. You don't want me to get better, you want to drain me dry of cash." I said, fuming. "It's not happening... you're not doing this. I'm done with this. Goodbye Dr Sanford" I walked away.

The thoughts were back, they're going to take me away again and I won't be able to see the girls. They're wanting to get rid of me. I can't do it. I can't be in there without them again.

"Tom, I know this is hard," Dr. Sanford said, but I interrupted,

"Shut up, you have no idea" I told him and before I knew it, I ran upstairs and into my room.

If you touch the switch six times, they won't take you away.

Now if you touch your bed six times, they won't take you away.

If you tidy your desk six times, they will know you're fine and won't take you away.

If you, do it, they won't take you away from the girls.

I cleaned and tidied, I tidied my desk and then chucked it all on the floor, just to put it all back and tidy it again. I hear knocking on the door, but I don't answer it.

They're going to take you away. That's them now.

You're never going to see the girls again.

They're going to take you away unless you do the ritual.

DO THE RITUAL AND THEY WON'T TAKE YOU AWAY.

My breathing was heavy, and I couldn't stop the thoughts, tears were streaming down my face. I couldn't stop the thoughts, they kept coming. Without thinking I grab the scissors from my desk, and I start carving into my arm. The blood started coming out, it wasn't much but it was enough to calm the thoughts, ever so slowly the thoughts stopped. It was enough to calm the pain. The more I saw the blood coming out, the calmer I became, as if the blood were my thoughts and they were being drained from my body. I sat in the corner of my room, my knees up to my head and my arms crossed. I need to stay as calm as possible. I tried to breathe in through my nose and out through my mouth. I looked at my room around me and tried to focus on something, but I didn't have anything to focus on.

"Tom, can I come in" it was Dr Sanford. I looked down at my arms and I didn't know what to do. There wasn't a lot of blood, but it was enough for him to notice the cat-like scratches. I grabbed a jumper from my wardrobe, quickly chucked it over me and I opened the door. The room was somewhat tidy except for the scissors that were still on the floor. I knew he wasn't stupid, but I backed away, edging closer to the scissors to try and make my body hide them. It didn't work. I knew he noticed, and he knew, I knew he noticed.

"Tom, I think it's a good idea to get you checked out." Dr Sanford said, looking at the scissors and back at me. "Did you hurt yourself?" He asked me, picking the scissors up and putting them on the desk. I immediately moved them to their place, exactly one centimetre from the pencil and eraser. Dr Sanford looked at me and I automatically wished I hadn't just moved them. I knew how this went. If I didn't get examined with him then he would call the police and they would escort me to get examined. I knew how this ended so I do as he says.

I walked downstairs, and outside. I didn't say anything to mum. I was still angry that she agreed to this. I waited until Dr Sanford had unlocked his car and then I got into the back, I didn't want to sit in the front with him. As soon as I sat in the back of the car I wondered if Dr Sanford was testing me, whether me sitting in the back of the car was another tick on his checklist of getting me back into the hospital. I needed to get out, I couldn't go back there. As if Dr Sanford has read my mind, he clicks a button, and all the doors lock from the inside.

"Just in case I jump out?" I ask him but Dr Sanford keeps his eyes on the road.

"I'm not crazy Doc, I'm far from it" I tell him, wondering whether I'm trying to convince him or myself.

"Listen Doc, I can't go back there. My family needs me." As if out of a movie he stops at the red lights and turns his head to face me.

"Your family needs you alive... and healthy." Dr Sanford kept his eyes on the road

"I wonder how you became a therapist when you never listen." I looked in the mirror, but Dr Sanford remained silent for the rest of the trip.

We arrived at the hospital about 15 minutes later, the journey seemed to take way longer than expected. Dr Sanford parked in the staff parking, put his badge on display and got out but I couldn't. For a moment I couldn't move my body, my fate was being decided as soon as I stepped into those doors, I wondered if when I got out, I could make a run for it. Dr Sanford walked around the car and opened my door "come on" he said, I couldn't tell what his expression was for it had gotten too dark to see out properly and his tone didn't really give any major hints.

"I can't go in" I told him, my legs had started shaking and I could feel my heart beating. I couldn't do this again, not to mum, not to the girls. I couldn't be locked up again. I felt like my heart was going to come out of my body at any point.

"Tom, breathe" but I couldn't. I felt like my legs were tingling and my whole body felt like it was on fire. My breathing was becoming shorter and each time I tried gasping for breath it felt like more was coming in than going out.

"Tom listen to me" Dr Sanford had kneeled down so that I could see his face in the streetlight. "Tom, you need to breathe," He told me but all I could manage to wheeze out was, "I can't." My eyes were filled with tears, but I couldn't cry in front of Dr Sanford. "Tom, say something you see." I looked at him in confusion.

"Name anything you see, go on."

I looked around still struggling to breathe. "Trees,"

"And another thing."

"Cars."

"And one more thing."

And as I thought of the last thing, I found it easier to breathe. My breathing became steadier.

"Ambulance." And just like that I felt my heart beginning to crawl back into my chest, as if Dr Sanford had just slain it with observations.

"Just keep focusing on your breathing, Tom. Well done." I took a deep breath in, held it for a couple of seconds and then took a deep breath out. I did this a couple of times until Dr Sanford could tell I had calmed down.

"Look Tom, you're an intelligent kid so I'm not going to lie to you and say that everything is fine, but I know you want everything to be fine, so you need to do the work. And it's okay to have days where everything isn't fine. If you can show me someone who has no problems, then that person hasn't lived a life."

I looked at Dr Sanford and I couldn't help it and I don't know where it came from, but I started laughing.

"That Doc was some rubbish advice." Dr. Sanford even manages a smirk. "It was more words of truth rather than advice. Also, a side note taking your medication and smoking Marijuana isn't a good mixture."

I get out of the car "I know Doc, I read the leaflet over and over, but the meds stopped working, I couldn't sleep properly, I just wanted some peace." I shut the door behind me, and we started walking over to the hospital doors but as I'm a foot away from the doors my feet stopped me. "What if they wanted to admit me again? I can't do that to mum or the girls or granddad" I told him.

"Tom, I'm here, I'm with you. I don't think they'll admit you, especially if I say so." Dr Sanford told me. We both looked at each other and I started walking first.

Once we were in the hospital, we were escorted up to A&E. The nurse at reception asked if I felt suicidal, I told her no, because I wasn't despite what it may look like. Dr. Sanford and I sat in the A&E room for about an hour, we barely spoke except when I told him to go home.

"It's fine go, I'm here now. What's the worst that can happen?" I asked him but he remained seated.

"I'm not going to leave you alone. This might be hard to understand but I care about you."

I looked at him in obvious confusion.

"Eww, you care about me... oh my god, Doc. Do you love me? I just want to say that despite how grateful I am, I'm not that way inclined."

Dr. Sanford looked at me sternly, but I couldn't help but laugh.

"You know what I meant" and that was the only real conversation we had while waiting in the emergency room. I kept my eyes to the floor for most of the wait, bringing them up when a nurse would come out and call a name. Each time hoping it was my name that was next. I placed my hands on the edge of my knees tapping them six times, waiting six seconds and then tapping them another six times. I tried to stop the thoughts from happening and the tapping helped.

When my name was finally called, I felt a sudden urge to throw up. Now suddenly, I didn't want to go in, but I knew I had to. Dr Sanford wouldn't let me get away from it now, especially as he should have been at home with his feet up watching the news. I felt a sudden urge of guilt, I realised that I knew nothing about Dr Sanford and despite the obvious lack of a wedding ring, I didn't know if he was in a relationship, if he had kids. I knew nothing about him and yet he knew everything about me.

We walked into the nurses. office and I took a seat on the bed and Dr Sanford took the seat in the corner. "So, Thomas."

"It's Tom, sorry only my mum calls me Thomas" I interrupt her.

"So, Tom, what's happened?" I looked at the nurse and then looked at Dr Sanford. I didn't know what to say.

"Honestly that's a good question." I answered in hopes that Dr Sanford would be able to enlighten the both of us. "

Tom," Dr Sanford said, and then unfolded his legs just to fold them in the other position.

"I don't know what you want me to say. What happened? I don't know. Everyone thinks my OCD is coming back but it isn't. The meds are working, and I feel fine, they're just exaggerating." I told them knowing that the only person in the room I was trying to convince was myself.

"Tom from what your mother has told me and from what I have seen, I believe the medication we've given you isn't enough, you're on a low dosage and we think it's best to up the dosage. You are exhibiting OCD traits, and even though they are not the same as you previously experienced, they're still not good." I looked at Dr Sanford, who was now holding my doctor's notes and flicking through the pages. I didn't know why he needed to know what he already knew, why did he have to go through notes he has access to? Nothing changed since he last looked at it.

"I don't suppose you're going to believe me if I say it's not what you think. Look, can we just up my meds and leave?" I asked him, but he continued talking to the nurse for a few moments.

"Nurse Sharon is going to look at your wounds and will assess the best course of action." I looked at Dr Sanford who was now standing directly in front of the door.

"What does that mean? Best course of action. Just up my meds and let me leave."

When Dr Sanford stayed silent, I repeated myself but louder.

"Tom, you've been tense recently, you've been acting sporadically and it's worrying." I looked at him and then back at Nurse Sharon who was setting up a cleaning station for my wounds.

"No, I haven't. I've been doing exactly what you wanted me to do, and I've been fine. I've taken my meds, I've been taking it slow at work. I haven't been cleaning too much. The thoughts aren't back!" I said, making the last sentence louder.

"Okay so let me ask you this, when did you start doing things by the figure of six?" Dr Sanford asked the question and for a second it felt like I left my body, and I was simply observing from below.

"Or how about when did the panic attacks start again?" Dr Sanford asked.

"I get it" I whispered hoping he would stop but he didn't stop.

"Or how about the outbursts?" "What about the thoughts? When did they start back up? Because they did, I noticed the change in you." "And what about the fight with Mikey? Your best mate of 10 years." He kept asking question after question, but I couldn't concentrate because my brain was on fire with one thought;

They're taking you back
The girls will be alone
They're taking you back
They won't have me to protect them
They're taking you back
They're going to get hurt
They're taking you back
You need to run. NOW!

I found myself jumping off the bed and running towards Dr Sanford. He seemed to be aware of what was going to happen and as I went to push him away from the door, he tackled me to the ground.

"GET OFF ME" I shouted, and despite how weak Dr Sanford looked he was able to hold me down. Out of anger and frustration I started hitting my head against the cold, concrete floor, hoping Dr Sanford might let go of me long enough for me to make a run for it.

"Tom calm down" he kept repeating but I didn't. I couldn't. Everything in my power was keeping me from calming down, I just needed to get out of the room.

"LET ME GO!" I shouted and screamed but he did not let go, in fact he kept hold of me as two more male nurses came in and helped him. I was still hitting my head against the floor so Dr Sanford put his hand under my head so the only damage I could do was to his hand. I looked up to see Nurse Sharon holding a needle. I hated needles and especially because of what was in the needle.

"NO. STOP. PLEASE. DONT." But before I had time to reason with them Nurse Sharon had stuck the needle in my arm.

It took another five minutes of me screaming and shouting before the effects of the drug finally took place and I was placed onto the bed.

"He'll be out for a while, wheel him down to room four and I'll come talk to him when he's awake." Dr. Sanford ordered the nurses, and they did what he said. I tried forcing myself to stay awake, I needed to stay awake and get out. I needed to go home. I didn't belong here, but I couldn't do anything while my whole body felt like jelly. I needed to stay awake. I couldn't let the drugs get into my system and mess with my mind. I must have tried staying awake for 10 minutes but before I knew it, I had succumbed to the sleeping temptress.

When I woke up, I was in a different room, a room that looked familiar, but I couldn't place. I tried standing up, but my legs gave way, the drugs must have still been in my system. I tried standing again this time holding onto the bed for support. I managed a couple of seconds to stand up before I ultimately fell back onto the hard floor. A sudden pain hit my coccis and I let out a sudden scream. I stayed on the floor and pushed my body against the wall.

I knew the drill of this place, they would keep me here until I was calm enough to talk, so shouting didn't do me any favours. I touched the back of my head, a bandage had been wrapped around my entire head, I took it off and felt where the pain was coming from. I could feel a cold piece of metal which I assumed was a staple, as I brought my hand back, I noticed small bits of blood on my hands. Hitting my head against the floor had given me a blinding headache. I tried to close my eyes hoping the headache would ease without the bright white hospital lights shining in my eyes. The floor was about as comfortable as the bed and the drugs were still in my system, so I fell asleep quite quickly.

"Tom"

"Tom"

I heard a calm voice, my brain woke up before my eyes opened but as I gradually opened them, I heard a familiar voice, one that I didn't want to hear. I looked over to the door and standing there was mum. Once I had adjusted my eyes I noticed the red streams down her face, she had been crying.

"Oh Tom, what happened?" Mum asked me, in the same tone that she would ask the girls. She knelt so that she was in my eyeline, she slowly brought her hand up and touched my face. I guessed she already knew about what happened, I'm sure that Dr Sanford told her. I knew she wanted to know why I slammed my head into a concrete floor, why the meds stopped working and why she has a son who's mental. I'm sure she wanted the answers to all these questions, but I was unable to answer them for her.

"I can't leave you and the girls again. Don't make me do this again, please." I looked down at my exposed knees realising that the nurses had changed me when I was asleep. I thought that they weren't allowed to do that but clearly my jeans were a suicide risk.

"Tom, I'm going to give you some tough love that I need you to understand. I would rather struggle with money; I would rather the girls miss you for a month than I would for you to not be around. If you keep going, you're going to get worse than you used to be, and we almost lost you. I don't want to lose you again. So please. Please stop worrying about money and the girls and get better. It's going to be hard, but you will get there. I believe you can...The girls believe you can." I looked down at the floor, for the first time in forever I cried. I sobbed and even after mum left, I continued sobbing. I couldn't contain myself.

All that time I felt like I was filling up with all these emotions ready to explode. I always assumed acting out and getting angry would make them better, but crying was what helped. Once the tears dried up, I felt tired again. I didn't know what was happening to me. I assumed that I was going to be kept in and let go once they realised, I'm not a danger to myself or others.

124

However, once it came to dinnertime and I was being given food from one of the nurses I realised otherwise.

I didn't eat the food at dinner, it looked like dog food and sick put together, maybe it was a dog that had been sick, either way that food was going nowhere near my mouth. The nurses tried to get me to eat but I simply refused and seeing as I didn't suffer from an eating disorder, they couldn't force me.

Dr. Sanford arrived in my room just after the nurses picked up my food. I didn't know what the time was because there weren't any clocks, and they took my phone from me so I couldn't check.

"How are you feeling?" Dr. Sanford asked, dragging a chair in from outside.

"I feel great." I told him, blatantly lying "When can I leave?" I asked him but he didn't answer.

"How are you feeling?" He asked me again while taking a seat. I repeat my question.

"If you answer my question Tom, I will answer yours"

"I feel like crap doc, I shouldn't be here. Okay maybe I need to continue therapy and maybe the meds need to be stronger, but I don't need to be in hospital. I'm not as bad as before, I swear." I told him and for most of it, it was true, well for me anyway.

"Thank you for being honest, not only with me but with yourself as well, it's a hard thing to do, admit you need help." Dr. Sanford started writing in my medical records. I didn't know what he was writing but I knew it was an evaluation of what I said.

Dr Sanford finished writing, dropped the pen onto the clipboard and looked at me "Look despite you knowing you need help, from your behaviour last night we have no choice but to keep you under observation." He could tell I was annoyed so he added "at least until the meds start kicking in, you should be out of here in a couple of days, as long as there are no more outbursts." I nodded and agreed, nothing I would say was going to change his mind. I admitted I needed help and he was keeping me here. I looked up at him and noticed his eye was slightly bruised and his hand was in a bandage. I couldn't have done that could i?

"Did I do that?" I asked him, already aware of what the answer was. Dr Sanford didn't say anything, he stood up and started walking away, dragging his chair with him.

"I'm sorry. I didn't realise I hurt you." I told him. Dr Sanford put the chair outside the room and then walked back in.

"You weren't in the right mindset." He told me. "I don't remember doing it. I remember running to the door and you tackling me. I mean I remember banging my head against the floor but what did I do to your eye?" I asked him. I didn't remember hitting his face.

"Tom, I don't think it's helpful for you to know, it was only an accident." Dr Sanford stopped himself from talking too much.

"Doc, I need to remember. It's important for me to know. I need to know. What did I do?" I looked at the Doc who seemed a bit shook up from the experience.

"Yes, you tried to get out, but you didn't run to the door, you ran to me with your fist. You intentionally hit me. At least your angry state intentionally hit me."

I looked down to the floor, "I'm sorry. I don't remember it like that." I didn't. I remembered going for the door, not for his face. I remembered something completely different happening.

"I know Tom. It's fine. I'll be fine." Dr Sanford said but he didn't seem convinced of his own words.

Dr Sanford left not long after that, he explained that I would be there a minimum of three days just to make sure I was taking my meds and that my moods were improving or at least stabilising. He also told me that I would be going back to two sessions a week with him. I didn't argue with any of it because I knew what would happen if I did. Dr Sanford gave me a new journal, he told me to write whatever I wanted in there. He told me that even if I thought about cheese on toast to write it in the book because it could come in handy at some point during therapy.

As the night drew in the nurses came round with my medication. My new dosage, higher than the one that I had taken previously and some new sleeping tablets that they wanted me to try while I was in hospital. I didn't argue. I took the meds. I did what I was told because if I did then I had a better chance of getting better. I had a better chance of coming home, of seeing the girls again, of mum trusting me.

Chapter Five

I woke up on my first day back at the ward on the floor. The floor was a lot comfier than the bed, so I ended up there halfway through the night. The nurse looked confused when she walked in to find me on the floor.

"Are you okay?" she asked, I don't think she knew what to do. I think she thought I was having a breakdown so when I answered, "It's comfier down here" she laughed and agreed with me.

"Dr Sanford wants to see you after your breakfast" She held the door open and for a moment I was confused. "Are you coming for breakfast? I'm not holding the door open all day" She chuckled. I quickly got up from the floor and scurried out of the door. I needed to get out of the room, and I didn't want to miss the opportunity. The nurses escorted me down the hall, one was small while the other was like the jolly, green giant. I couldn't believe he was a nurse, he looked more like a security guard. He looked like he could tackle the entire ward and not drop a sweat. I walked in between like I was the joker, but it didn't feel cool it felt embarrassing.

We entered the dining hall, the room I had been to so many times before. It was a dining hall mixed with a group therapy hall when the long tables were put up and the chairs bought in. I looked around and luckily there was only one person I noticed.

His name was John, and he was here long before I showed up. He was The Cotswolds longest patient; he must have been in his forties and spent most of it inside. I think he preferred it, he felt safer. He left when I was here the first time but two days later, he came back. He had paranoid schizophrenia and thought the government was spying on his flat; his natural response was to try to blow his flat up, along with 50 other flats in his complex. Luckily his sister came by just in time to find him pouring petrol all over his apartment. People like John are called lifers, they will be in and out of the Cotswolds for the rest of their life. When they leave, they soon come back and that's something that I never wanted to do. I never wanted to be a lifer. John looked up to see me, but he didn't recognise me. The number of drugs he was taking must mess with his mind a little, so it didn't surprise me. It made me relieved somehow. It meant no one would know I was back again.

I took a seat the furthest away from everybody else, I didn't want to get comfortable. I didn't want to get to know people that once I leave, I will never see again. I didn't want to get comfortable. I wanted to leave and be normal. I ate the breakfast as it was buttered toast. We weren't given knives, even plastic ones, so the butter has melted from being under the heater for too long. I manage to eat most of it despite the butter making the bread moist. I knew what I needed to do to get brownie points and even if I didn't have an eating disorder, not eating food at all does not get you those brownie points, and therefore stops you from leaving this place.

Once I finished my breakfast the two nurses escorted me to Dr Sanford's office. I know my way there easily, but I know I have to be kept under surveillance until Dr Sanford says otherwise. I walked into Dr Sanford's office, which despite having been in a couple of days ago looked different. It looked newer.

"Take a seat Tom." Dr. Sanford said. He spoke differently and the bruise around his eye was lighter than yesterdays. I took a seat; in fact, I took the seat that I always took to show him that nothing had changed. I was still the same old Tom.

"I appreciate your cooperation, Tom; it shows not only me but the other members of my team that you want to progress. You want to get better."

I nodded along, it was true, I wanted to get better.

"How are you feeling?" He asked, which was a sudden change of conversation and made me expect bad news.

"I'm better but it may change depending on the bad news you're going to tell me." I looked at Dr Sanford who had put down his pen and had his hands clasped together. I was waiting for bad news; he knew I was waiting for bad news.

"Okay I don't know if I can let you out as early as we spoke about yesterday. We've gone through your tests, and I've spoken to your mum, and I've spoken to my colleagues, and we think it might be important for you to go through some intensive cognitive therapy."

I held my head in my hands. This is what happened last time, and I ended up back here, so it clearly didn't help, which is exactly what I told him.

"Yes, but this time you want to get better, last time you just wanted to get out. So, you weren't fully invested in healing." I looked at Dr Sanford expecting him to be chuffed, but he looked sad. He looked like he didn't want me to be here either, like he thought I'd end up like poor John, a lifer.

"We think it will be beneficial in the long run compared to the other treatment that you've had. Hopefully two weeks of intensive therapy will help you progress, but it may be hard Tom."

I nodded and agreed with him because I knew the best way of getting out of the hospital was by doing exactly what Dr Sanford and the other members of his team wanted.

"So, we're going to start you out on three days of individual therapy with me, everyday you'll go to group therapy and then you'll have a day doing art therapy. We believe this will be the best chance to help you, Tom. Do you understand?" I nodded. I understood everything he was saying but it felt like it was all happening in slow motion.

"Why did you say a couple of days?" I asked him to expect him to come up with some rubbish.

"Honestly, I didn't think I could get you here if I told you the truth, and I am facing some backlash of my own because of it. Tom I shouldn't have lied, and I apologise for that. I just thought it was the only way to get you where you needed to be. I didn't want to call the police and detain you." Dr Sanford looked down at his hands, at that moment he looked like a patient. He looked tense and sad at the same time.

"What do you mean you're getting backlash?" I asked him. I looked at the way that Dr Sanford's eyebrows frowned and for the first time in ages I realised how old he looked. I don't mean to sound rude but it's insane how he looks 30 and 50 at the same time. His face looked fine until you got to his eyes and then they just looked tired, like he hadn't slept in days. Of course, I'd never say anything like that to his face because it's rude.

"I shouldn't really talk about it with my patients" Dr Sanford told me, but I was persistent, telling him that seeing as it had to do with me then the least, he could do was tell me. That because he lied to me the least, he could do was tell me what was happening. I told him I wouldn't tell another person and that if I did, he was more than welcome to increase my stay at The Cotswolds. He laughed and told me he wouldn't do that, but it seemed to work. "My boss isn't happy. As part of my oath, I shouldn't lie to a patient for my own gain or for someone else's gain, I just shouldn't lie. They found out that I lied and now are finding the correct punishment for my behaviour. I'd get told off if they found out I was telling you, so please don't." Dr Sanford seemed down, he was not lying he was telling me, a mental patient, his problems.

"I don't suppose there's a way that I could help, to explain that because you knew me you knew I wouldn't go anywhere near the hospital if you wanted me to stay. That there was no other option for my wellbeing other than to lie."

He told me he didn't want to get me involved. That it wouldn't be fair on me. That it may end up escalating. I didn't understand what he meant but he was adamant, so I wasn't going to question him any further.

Our session started right after; I knew it had started because he asked me again how I was feeling. I told him, "I feel fine, I don't feel any different."

He looked at me, picked up his pen and held it up to his mouth.

"How do you feel about being back at The Cotswolds Hospital?"

I looked at him. I thought about what I wanted from being here and the answer was simple, I didn't want to come back and become a lifer. "I'm annoyed. I'm annoyed at you for lying to me. I'm annoyed at mum for allowing me to come back without hesitation...but I'm annoyed most at myself." I looked at my hands which were intertwined together.

"Why's that?" he asked knowing that I had thoughts running through my mind.

"I'm annoyed because...because I didn't want to come back and if I worked harder during my therapy and worked harder at home then I wouldn't be here. If I had the right motive, I wouldn't be worried about becoming a lifer" Dr Sanford looked at me confused. "A lifer is in The Cotswolds Hospital for most of their life, like John. I didn't want to be like him. Be John 2.0" Dr. Sanford remained quiet for a moment

"I don't think you're going to be a lifer" he said while air quoting lifer then continued "I think you've hit a hurdle and you just need some help getting over the hurdle, and sure more hurdles will come in life, but you'll be more prepared, you'll see the hurdle coming and be able to react correctly. You'll be able to take on the hurdle a lot easier because you've practised." Dr. Sanford dropped his pen lightly onto the table, but in a victorious way. I imagine him thinking of something like 'Damn Doc you give the best advice'. I could imagine him secretly hi-fiving himself under the desk. I wondered if he just thought of that or if he had a list of quotes to use on different people. Depending on their circumstances. Like he would have one for a teen who had anxiety and another for a 40-year-old with schizophrenia. I wonder if they came to him at night and he would quickly grab his pen and paper to write it down to remember.

"What are you thinking about?" He softly asked me, and I suddenly shot back into reality. Dr. Sanford was looking at me, his pen and pad were shut, which was a surprise, and he had the strangest look on his face.

"Sorry?"

"You zoned out for a minute, what were you thinking about?" He repeated. I wondered whether I should be honest with him and tell him I was thinking about him or if that would be too weird. I knew it would be weird, but I honestly didn't know what else to say, "It occurred to me that I literally have no idea about you."

Dr Sanford moved in his chair, I could tell he was taken back and maybe a bit uncomfortable.

"I've known you for half a year, I've seen you a minimum of once a week and I don't know anything about you." I sat back on the sofa and crossed my legs as if I was now becoming the counsellor.

"What would you like to know?" He asked. "You said you weren't married but, do you have kids?"

"One."

"What's their name?"

"Scarlett."

"How old is she?"

"She would be seven this year, but she passed when she was 4."

"Oh, sorry to hear that doc"

"Thank you, Tom. Do you have any more questions?"

"I do but I feel like I killed the vibe with the question."

"It's been four years; I've done my mourning. Next question?"

"What's your favourite movie?"

"UP."

"It's a good movie."

"It is."

"Do you live around here? Don't worry I'm not a stalker."

"I live on the outskirts of town"

"Keeping it vague, I like it. If you could be anywhere, where would you go?"

It took him a while to answer, it looked like he was thinking about it and then wondering whether he should say it. "Anywhere Scarlett is." and with that the session was over. Dr Sanford asked me to keep patient-doctor confidentiality and not tell anyone about his life, which seemed like a stupid statement because I wasn't going to anyway.

When I left Dr Sanford's I headed straight to the breakroom, I didn't want to stay any longer in my room. I had only spent two days there, but it was driving me around the bend. Dr Sanford told the nurses they no longer needed to keep an eye on me 24/7, so I was allowed to go to the break room by myself. In the breakroom there was an array of different people, there were some young adults who had only just hit 18 and then there were 70-year-olds, but they all seemed to fit in. The older people were in the armchairs reading the newspaper mumbling to themselves, now and then shouting bloody murder to someone who wasn't there. Then there were the depressed kids who were all huddled in the corner playing a game. It was easy to spot the depressed, they wore as much black as possible and always had long sleeves. There was only one person who stood out from them and that was a girl dressed in green and pink. she had dark brown hair and glasses, she looked completely normal, but she wasn't because she had been admitted. She was just as invested in the game as the others playing but brought her eyeline up just enough for us both to look at each other. I quickly walked over to the empty chair and watched TV.

"You."

"Oi, you."

"Oi, kiddie."

I ignored everything that was being said because they could have been talking about somebody who was not there, I didn't automatically think that someone was talking to me.

"Oy, Zac Efron wannabe." I looked around to see who this voice was and who they were talking about. I turned to see the same girl staring right at me, "there we go, wanna join?" I looked at her disgusted, but I stood up and walked over to the table.

"I'm not trying to be Zac Efron." I scoffed but this girl started laughing, "yeah you do, look at the hair."

I looked at her and touched my hair, it was in a quiff. "Look boys have three hairstyles; Zac Efron as you call it, bald or Troy Bolton from high school musical. There are no other hairstyles for guys." I looked at her and took a seat that had been placed down for me.

"Dreadlocks?" she asked, and I now laughed

"I don't think white people look good in dreadlocks" I said. Suddenly it was quiet around the table and someone sitting opposite me was staring at me with the biggest dreadlocks I had ever seen "except you, you look good... You look good" I told him, which I think helped because he smiled and continued with the game.

Close one. The last thing I needed was a patient punching me because I said I didn't like his dreads. We got ourselves together and started a new game, one that I could join in on. We decided on playing rummy, easy enough game but the nurse had to remind us that we couldn't play with money, I didn't know if it was to let me know or to remind everyone else.

"Mike used to try to make everyone gamble, we got away with it a couple of times, but the nurse caught us out, so now he reminds us of every time. Do you gamble...umm... What's your name?" She asked.

"Tom" I responded

"I'm Grace. Do you gamble?" She asked. I shook my head, I had never been a massive gambler, in fact I was the opposite, I liked to stay safe.

"What are you in for?" She asked me but I didn't answer, I didn't want everyone to know. "We'll find out in group therapy anyway." She spoke and then continued playing the game. We all played silently with the occasional shout or scream from Mike.

When it got to dinnertime I wasn't at all hungry, I was used to food being at 7pm maybe 8pm but here it was at 5:30pm on the dot. You got half an hour to eat and if you were a person who didn't have an eating disorder, once that half hour was up, you could pick up your trays and put them on the trolleys. It was like primary school all over again. The nurses would even remind us of when we had five minutes left. It felt weird being back, It was only when I was eating dinner that I realised I was back.

Grace practically begged me to sit next to her at dinner, so I had no choice but to. Grace was chatty, she's incredibly chatty and you wouldn't think there was anything wrong with her until you looked into her eyes. She had this amazing laugh, but her eyes always looked glossy. They didn't look like they were there, it was like her body was in the room, but her soul was in another building. She could laugh and laugh but it seemed forced. It was strange she would say something funny; I would laugh, she would laugh and then all of a sudden, she'd be straight faced. I knew that there was obviously something wrong with her because she too was in the hospital with me, that didn't need to be made any clearer. I knew I shouldn't, but I wanted to help her, I wanted her to feel better, I wanted to protect her. I didn't know if that was a good thing or not. I didn't know if that meant my OCD was getting better or worse. I used to be protective with the girls, but this felt different. It's not like my brain was telling me to do it otherwise she'll hurt herself or I'll hurt her. It was different, I felt a sudden electric pulse and now and then my heart would flutter when she spoke to me.

TV time was about the only time Grace would be quiet, but she would only be quiet if we were watching something she too enjoyed. After dinner the first thing we watched was a David Attenborough documentary, it was the one where the penguins were being chased by the whales. I thought it was strange that they put a documentary on like that in a place like this. I thought it would have made the mental patients even more mental. Grace sat there with her legs up to her chin, holding herself. She looked on in amazement, she was engulfed in watching the entire documentary, but I was too busy watching her. Eventually I told her I was going to bed, but she didn't even register that I was there, that I had said anything. She continued staring at the tv screen in awe.

I stood up and walked over to my room, the door was now always kept open so that the nurses could see what I was always doing. The only privacy I got was in my bathroom, but the nurses still had a key that would unlock the door if I tried anything. Not that I could try anything because the whole wing of the hospital was suicide proof. The curtains were made from a material that would easily break with too much pressure, there weren't any proper doorknobs, they were all slanted, the bed was made of a similar material to the blue mats you had in school, and the windows had an outer layer of unbreakable plastic. It was the first time that I properly took in my room, I didn't realise how little they took away.

I led on my bed overhearing the other patients chatting to each other and sometimes themselves, when I suddenly felt a hand on mine, I opened my eyes to find Grace knelt next to me just staring into my eyes.

"Wh..what are you doing?" I asked her, shocked to find her in my room.

"I wanted to come and do this" and without saying anything else she grabbed my head and kissed me. I have to say the kiss was uncomfortable and her lips were rather cold, but it was nice. She let go a couple of seconds later and then walked out of the room. I remained still, not knowing what to do. I know most guys would jump out of bed, go find her and then continue where we left off, but I wasn't that kind of guy. I simply laid in bed and fell asleep.

I woke suddenly to the nurses yelling, it was early morning, and the sun was blinding my eyes. I jumped out of bed with a sudden urge of energy. Grace, I needed to find Grace. I got out of bed, changed my clothes and walked down the corridors to the TV room. Grace was already there with John and Mike playing another game of rummy. Before I could even ask if I could sit, Grace pulled a chair out next to her, patted it and smiled at me. I sat straight down; I wasn't going to question it. She reshuffled the cards and put some in front of me. We started playing and a couple of cards in, I asked, "Can we talk about last night?" I wanted to know what happened and why it happened.

"I won," she answered, holding down her cards. Everyone groaned and put their cards out.

"We've only just started" "How could you win?" Mike and John moaned.

"I'm just really good," She answered. I looked at Grace. She always wore skinny jeans, a top and some long cardigan. She looked great. She was great. I couldn't believe that she kissed me last night.

"Grace, can I talk to you?" I asked again and this time she heard me. I knew she heard me because she rolled her eyes back and then stood up.

"Come on then," she answered and started walking away. I jumped up and started following her. She stopped in a corner of the ward that was without cameras, I wondered if she was going to kiss me again. I couldn't stop thinking about kissing her.

"Can we talk about last night?" I asked.

"Oh yeah sorry about that" she answered, which confused me because it seemed like she wanted it more than me.

"Why are you sorry? It's nothing to apologise for" I looked at Grace, who was now looking at the floor. She looked embarrassed.

"Look, don't worry about it. Forget I said anything" I told her and started walking away. Did I do something to her? Did I say something last night that she didn't like? I was confused. I walked into the TV room, but no one was there. That was when it hit me that it was group therapy.

When I got to the hall everyone was already in their seats, there was one empty seat, which happened to be right next to Grace so I walked over and sat down. "Thanks for joining us, Tom," Dr. Jonathon said. Dr. Jonathon was a doctor, but he was training to become what Dr Sanford was, he wanted to become an individual CBT doctor. I knew this because Grace told me she had him as her main psychiatrist.

"So, this week we're going to be talking about self-image. What do you perceive yourself as? What would you like to perceive yourself as? Does anyone want to start?" He asked but nobody answered. "Okay, how about we let the newbie start? What about you Tom?"

I could feel everyone's eyes on me, I looked around the room, "umm...I don't know" I answered knowing it wouldn't be good enough.

"What do you think of yourself as?" He asked, changing the subject slightly.

"A failure." I answered knowing it sounded pathetic.

"Why do you feel like a failure?" He asked.

"Because I should have been the man of the house, the one looking after the girls and helping mum with money but instead I'm here." I bowed my head and saw that most of the other patients had done the same.

"Does anyone else here feel the same as Tom?" Dr. Jonathon then asked. I looked around the hall to see multiple people had put their hands up including Grace. I looked at her and smiled and she returned a smile to me.

When group therapy was over it was time for lunch, so far, the food wasn't that great so I thought that lunchtime would be better. I mean how could someone mess up on sandwiches, it was literally the easiest food to make. However, when I looked at it, I realised that somehow, there was a wrong way to make a sandwich. It looked like they had left the sandwich on the side for too long and the whole sandwich was mushy. I had the choice of tuna or cucumber and cheese. I didn't fancy getting food poisoning from lukewarm tuna, so I opted for the cheese and cucumber. While I was slowly biting into the soggy mush, I listened to Grace talk about Star Trek and the latest movie coming out. I had no idea what she was talking about because despite being nerdy, I didn't watch Star Trek. I preferred Doctor Who or Harry Potter, which I know was science fiction, but it was different.

Grace wouldn't stop talking about how Star Trek was better than Star Wars, but I didn't want to start an argument with her. I decided to nod along and agree with her.

* * *

Grace was different from everyone else; she was kind, funny and talkative. God was she talkative, but it was nice. I didn't feel like I had to find a conversation to have with her; everything just came naturally. We could go on talking about shows for ages and then all of a sudden change the subject, she was amazing, she was also hiding something. We had done three group therapies so far and she hadn't spoken in any of them, she hadn't said anything. The first time, when I was forced to speak, I just thought she didn't want to talk but I started thinking that she was one of the patients that became mute when therapy started. It made me wonder why she was here, of course anytime I asked her about it she would change the subject. I assumed she was a self-harmer because she always wore long sleeves, but there was never one reason as to why someone was sent here, so there was more. I didn't want to ask too many questions and for her to get pissed off at me, I would never want her to be pissed off at me. I started really liking her.

I asked about her in Dr. Sanford's therapy session but of course he couldn't tell me anything.

"You're here to get better Tom, focus on that," is what he would tell me when I bought it up. My second proper therapy session with Dr Sanford didn't seem to go anywhere, it went around in a lot of circles, and I don't know if it was these pills finally kicking in but I felt like I didn't need to be there. Most of our sessions went like this;

"How are you doing?" Doc asked

"I'm fine."

"How are you settling in?"

"I'm doing good, I'm spending a lot of time with Grace."

"So, you two are friends?"

"Yes, why is she here?" I did know he couldn't answer but I thought I'd give it a whirl.

That's when he said "You know I can't tell you that Tom. Anyway, you should be focusing on your own therapy."

"Okay."

"Dr. Johnson says you opened up in group therapy. Well done. How did that make you feel?"

I looked at Dr Sanford and realised that he asked a lot of open questions. Questions that required more than a one-word answer. "What was it like sharing to strangers?" He asked again, I thought it was best to answer before he wrote down that I was avoiding questions.

"Good. It felt good to know I wasn't alone."

"I think that's half of the solution is realising that there are other people going through the same thing." Dr Sanford paused for a moment "Have you had any intrusive thoughts?" This took me a moment to answer because if truth be told I didn't think I had. At that moment all I seemed to be thinking about was Grace.

"No, I don't think so, maybe the meds are working." I looked at Dr Sanford who seemed pleased. "I just wanted you to be aware that the new medication increase may cause psychosis, it's incredibly rare however I did want to mention it as increased stress can sometimes be the cause." Dr Sanford told me, which I was fine with. I had never experienced delusions, I had never seen anything that shouldn't be there, so I wasn't concerned about it.

Our sessions ended bang on one hour, I never like to stay later and intrude on another patient's therapy time. I knew some people think Dr Sanford was a saviour from above, but he was just a regular guy, I didn't seem to be improving but I was definitely not getting worse. I think these meds were making me feel weird because I just didn't feel anything. I thought the tablets were supposed to help but all they did was make me feel numb. I knew typical SSRIs were supposed to do that, but I had never had this side effect before.

I remember when Dr Sanford first told me that I needed to go onto antidepressants. I told him "But I'm not depressed" and he told me, "SSRIs aren't just for people who suffer from depression they also help those who suffer from anxiety disorders such as OCD, they help boost the Serotonin levels in your body." He then went on to explain what they were, what it meant and the side effects. I was obviously put off at first and I would always struggle taking them. I would often put up a fight with the nurses and they almost always threatened to inject me with the drugs. I never believed them because I thought that was what you saw in movies and read in books but then one day it happened. I was kicking off, I was adamant I wasn't going to take my pill, I tried crumpling it up in the paper pill holder, I tried putting it in my cheeks, I tried the lot, and the nurses were not happy. I started arguing with them accusing them of poisoning me and keeping me here under my free will. Eventually they got tired of my crap, wrestled me to the floor and injected me. It was horrible, I had never felt so humiliated in my entire life, not only did I kick off on them for no reasons and accuse them of things that I

144

knew weren't true, but I was also then tackled to the ground like a terrorist. Once they injected me with my drugs, they put me into an isolation ward. I was left by myself for two days to calm down. I mean it would have only been the day if I hadn't tried attacking the nurses when they were trying to give me my food.

* * *

Grace and I were getting on really well but there hadn't been another kiss since that night. I wondered whether she regretted it but she was still talking to me, so I guessed it was a good sign.

"What do you think would win a whale or a hundred penguins?" She asked me while watching another documentary programme.

"Well it depends, can the penguins go to land? Do they need to stop for food? Are the penguins all in cahoots and know they're attacking the whale? Can the whale go deep under the seas?" I asked so many questions that Grace turned, looked at me dead in the eyes and then simply replied, "you ruined it". I didn't know if she was being serious, but I laughed anyway. It felt kind of good to annoy Grace so much that she stopped talking. It was a rare moment, so I felt more victorious when it did happen.

Grace left halfway through the documentary to go to her therapy session, it was boring without her, playing rummy wasn't the same because there was no-one to stop Mike and John from cheating and then trying to take each other's cards. I gave up after the second game because they were too busy playing against each other. I stood up and walked down the hall. I had never really explored the hospital before, I was always too busy trying to get out. I went from one end of the hall to the other, looking into the rooms but not being too nosey. Most of the rooms were empty as the patients were in the tv room or in therapy. I continued walking down some stairs and into our 'garden', it wasn't much of a garden, and it was fenced off completely from the outside world. I looked around, there was no way anyone could get out. I walked back inside when a nurse came up to me "You shouldn't be down here by yourself" she moaned. "I didn't know" I told her and walked back upstairs. Okay I did know that I wasn't allowed in the garden by myself but seeing as there was no issue of me getting out, I didn't know what her issue was.

I got back upstairs and found Grace back at the TV, she was curled into a ball and her shoulders were moving. She was crying. I didn't need to hear the sniffling or see the tears to know she was crying. It was obvious. I went and sat next to her on the sofa, without even thinking about it I pulled her into a hug, and she let me. I didn't say anything, I stayed quiet until she was ready to talk. I didn't want to force anything out of her. After about ten minutes of crying, Grace sat up, looked me straight in the eyes and then kissed me again. I pulled her away and looked into her eyes, they weren't the same ones as I had looked into on our first kiss, they were darker, sadder and that wasn't just an observation because she had been crying. I mean her eyes were bloodshot and they had started going puffy from her rubbing them, but she looked different. She felt different. I pulled away and a smile grew on her face. "I've wanted to do that since you got here" she let out while grinning.

"Do you mean since our first kiss?" I asked her chuckling away, but she didn't chuckle. In fact, her face got incredibly serious incredibly fast. "What do you mean?" She asked.

My mind started racing at 100mph, I remembered her coming into my room, I remembered her hand on mine and her moving closer to kiss me. I remembered all of that, so why didn't she? I started to wonder if she had forgotten the moment. She must have forgotten it; she must have but why? Why would she forget it? I stood up from the couch staring at her.

"Come on you know what I mean" but she shook her head. "The other night you came into my room and kissed me, then left."

Grace looked concerned for a moment and stood up from the sofa, slowly backing away from me.

"I didn't come into your room the other night; I don't know what you're on about." she said agitated. I was confused. It was definitely her; she probably didn't want to get into trouble for being in a boy's room.

"Why are you lying? I was there!" I asked her suddenly enraged; I couldn't believe she would lie to me over something so mundane

"I'M NOT LYING. IT DIDN'T HAPPEN." Grace shouted which happened to gain the attention of the nurses who were now running over trying to diffuse the situation. I looked at Grace and she had this confusion and fear in her eyes.

"Why are you lying? YOU WERE THERE." I may have OCD, but I was not stupid or crazy.

"Tom, calm down." one of the nurses shushed me but I was angry. I was the kind of angry that filled in the pit of the stomach. I pushed past the nurses and ran out to the garden. I needed to breathe, I needed fresh air.

When I was in the garden I paced back and forth by the fence.

I know I'm not crazy. I know I'm not crazy. I know I'm not crazy. I didn't imagine her kissing me. I'm not psychotic.

"Tom, what's going on?" One of the nurses asked but I was too busy thinking. Thinking about that night, I went through it in my mind making sure that I remembered every detail and Grace was real. I couldn't remember every small detail, but I know it was her.

"Tom, calm down." I heard the nurse tell me, but I didn't listen, I was still pacing the same two metres back and forth. I walked two metres, stopped, turned, walked two metres, stopped, turned, etc. My brain felt like it was on fire. "Tom, you need to calm down."

"SHUT UP!" I screamed at the nurse who jumped from my reaction. "Just leave me alone. I need to be on my own." I told her but she didn't leave, she stood by the door. I tried to tune her out, but it became difficult, I could feel her judging eyes on me. I could hear her think the words 'freak' and 'crazy'

"I'm not crazy." I told her, hoping that would keep her mind quiet.

"I don't think you're crazy, Tom."

Which made me laugh, I mean really laugh but something about my laugh changed, it was bitter. It was a bitter, evil laugh, I walked up to her and looked her straight into the eyes.

"DON'T LIE TO ME. I KNOW WHAT YOU'RE THINKING." I screamed, right into her face. She was scared I could see it in her eyes and only moments later when two more nurses came out, I realised she pressed her panic button. She thought she was in danger, she thought I was going to hurt her. She thought I was crazy.

What am I?

Who am I turning into?

That monster that I feel in the pit of my stomach is growing inside.

I can't do it.

* * *

I woke up to find the same nurse by my door. I looked at her and she looked back, this time there was something different about her. She looked friendly but she also looked wary.

"I'm sorry." I mumbled, not sure if she even heard me.

"It's okay, Tom." She said simply, and then went back to looking at her phone. I tried to sit up, but I couldn't, I tried to remember what happened after the nurses showed up, but it was still blurry. I remembered Dr. Sanford's face, but I didn't remember anything else.

"What happened?" I asked the nurse, but she didn't respond. "Did I hurt anyone?" I asked her, which seemed to get her to answer.

"No, you didn't" she told me but somehow, I didn't believe her. I had never been like this before; I didn't know what was happening to me. "What's your name?" I asked her, realising I didn't know it. "It's Maisie." she told me, and that was the end of our conversation.

Dr. Sanford came into my room about an hour later, I was just able to sit up properly. I could tell he was coming when Nurse Maisie stood up and left the room unaccompanied for two minutes. When he came in, I bowed my head in shame. It felt like I was getting told off by my mum.

"Hello Tom." I looked up for a moment and the bruise on his eye was barely visible, but I could tell this was not going to be a good check-in by his unusual lower voice.

"How are you feeling?" He asked me and I scoffed.

"How do you think I feel?" Dr. Sanford took the chair that Maisie was sitting in and placed it directly in the middle of the room. I positioned myself so that I was able to see him and be comfortable.

"Can we talk about what happened?" Dr Sanford asked and despite my urge to forget what happened I found myself nodding in agreement.

"I spoke to Grace, and she told me that you started being erratic when you mentioned the other day with her." I held my head down, I felt so embarrassed that she thought of me as a mental case "I don't know why she lied to me." I told him, sounding weak.

Dr Sanford shuffled his chair, he was uncomfortable "why don't you tell me what happened the other day." I closed my eyes and tried to remember it, but with the drugs it's a bit fuzzy. "I was led in bed trying to sleep, she came into my room and kissed me. She smiled and left." I looked at Dr Sanford who was writing notes down. He flicked through his notes and stopped at a page "can I tell you what Grace said happened that night?" I nodded, not sure if I wanted to hear it.

"So, Grace says after everyone went to bed, she couldn't sleep so she went for a walk. She found you in your room and you were just staring at her, smiling. She said she felt uncomfortable so went over to the reception desk and sat with the nurse for a while, and when she felt better, she went to bed."

I looked at Dr Sanford, I couldn't believe that Grace would say something like that. "She's lying." I took a breath, trying to contain myself.

"She was there, I saw her, I felt her. She was there. She's lying." I told him. Dr Sanford crossed his legs and looked at me.

"We have security cameras, so I thought I'd check just to see whether or not she did come into your room." Dr Sanford stopped for a moment, he looked at me with sadness, such sadness and maybe a little bit of pity. "Tom, Grace is telling the truth."

"How..How...How could I have..seen her in my room?" My head was spinning, I was trying to remember that night and now everything just seemed fuzzy.

"Tom, I need you to breathe."

But I couldn't breathe, not when I had imagined Grace, not when I imagined kissing her.

"Why?...Why would I imagine that?" I was trying to talk but my lack of oxygen was making it difficult.

"Tom name three things you see." Dr Sanford wasn't helping. Three things I see, what if he didn't see them, what if I was imagining everything? I tried to stand up, but my legs buckled, and I found myself on the floor screaming. I felt Dr Sanford's hands wrapped around my shoulder "Tom, I need you to breathe. C'mon three things you see." But I couldn't name three things I saw because my eyes were messing with me.

"LEAVE ME ALONE." I shouted and despite Dr Sanford standing and walking away he didn't leave the room, he just stood above me repeating, "Tom breathe, you need to breathe."

I tried to gulp big breaths of air, but it didn't seem to be helping.

I don't remember how I calmed down but about thirty minutes later I did, Dr Sanford was still in my room.

"I'm crazy, certified crazy," I mumbled, letting out a small laugh in disbelief.

"You're not crazy, Tom."

I looked at him in anger, "then why did I imagine someone who wasn't there?!"

Dr Sanford looked at me like the gears in his brain were working overtime trying to find an answer. "As I mentioned in a previous session psychosis can sometimes happen with the increased medication and added stress, I think this is what happened, which is a good thing, it means it could be a one off. You're not the only one I've seen to experience this in similar situations." Dr Sanford thought letting me know I wasn't alone was going to help but my brain went to something different.

"What if it's not a one off?" I asked. I didn't want to experience this for the rest of my life.

"If it was a recurrence, it could be something that comes with extreme stress..."

"...or if I fixate on someone?"

"I'm unsure to be honest, Fixation is a common symptom with your OCD which could then take effect when the psychosis comes around, but I don't a hundred percent know."

I thought I could be screwed forever. I could wake up one day thinking it was all normal and nothing was. I could fixate on someone and see them everywhere instead of thinking I see them everywhere. How could I live a normal life if that happens?

"Talk to me Tom, I'm here to talk. What are your thoughts?"

I looked at Dr Sanford and a single tear rolled down my face. "What if I can't lead a normal life anymore? What if I like someone and start seeing them everywhere and then one day they notice and leave?

What if I become too much and the fixations start getting worse? What if I can't have a normal job anymore?" All these questions. All the burning questions in my mind.

"Tom, you have never experienced hallucinations before, I believe that it's simply a blip but that doesn't mean that it may never happen again in your life. Substance abuse can definitely interfere and have a negative impact." I nodded in agreement; it was easier to agree with him. I didn't want to keep causing a scene and I was honestly exhausted from it all.

"I'm tired." I told Dr Sanford.

"I'll leave you to go for a nap, but you'll need to be up for dinner. It's not helpful that you're also not eating properly." He told me and left. Nurse Maisie walked in, moved the chair to the door and sat down in it. I pushed myself onto the bed, not even bothering to bring the blanket over me and I fell into a deep sleep. A nice, deep, peaceful sleep.

* * *

I was woken up by Maisie's voice, "Tom, it's dinnertime. I can bring you something here if you don't want to go into the dining room?" I got up and rubbed my eyes. "No, I'll go" I told her while standing up and stretching. Maisie and I walked down the hall together, her steps three behind mine. I walked into the dining room and for a split second everyone stared. Most people turned their heads back, but Grace's table stared at me like I had done something illegal. I picked up a tray of food and sat down by myself. I don't want to scare her any more than she already was, especially of me. I looked at my food, it looked to be Sausage and mash with a brownie for dessert. I started eating it too hungry to care about how I was shovelling it in my mouth and then I

153

realised Grace was still looking at me. I kept my head down and started slowly cutting up my food. Maisie had gotten herself a tray and had sat two chairs down from me. I pretended to ignore her as it was more embarrassing to think of her as a dog tamer. I was minding my own business when a tray slammed on the table, before looking up I cursed to myself. I assumed it was someone from Grace's table wanting to start something on me.

I looked up slowly and surprisingly saw Grace. I looked at her and she looked at me for a moment. She then continued eating her dinner.

"I'm sorry" I said, but all she did was smile and continue eating. I looked over at Maisie who was minding her own business "Maisie" I whispered, and she looked up and smiled, I pointed towards Grace and whispered, "do you see her?" Maisie smiled and nodded. I had to be sure.

"I'm definitely real" she answered as she put some mash into her mouth. "Why are you sitting here?" I asked.

"I wanted to make sure you were okay." She answered and then went back to her food. I didn't talk anymore and surprisingly neither did she. I didn't know what was worse, her constantly talking or not talking at all.

After dinner, Maisie escorted me back to my room. I think she thought it might be a good idea to stay in my room tonight seeing as I caused such a ruckus earlier. I thought that it was also a good idea. I laid on my bed not knowing what to do. I stood up and walked over to the door where Maisie was sitting.

"I'm bored." I said and Maisie laughed.

"Would you like to go outside for a bit?" she asked but I didn't want to do that. I didn't know what I wanted to do, all I knew was I was bored and wanted something to do but walking was not it.

"Can we chat?" I asked her like it was the stupidest question, but it took her by surprise "sure but I have to remind you I'm not a psychologist."

"That's okay, I just want a normal conversation. Being in here you don't get normal conversations. You get 'oh what drugs are you on' or 'hey that person isn't real' or 'how are you doing today on a scale of one to ten?' I've had enough of that chat."

"What do you want to talk about then?"

"What's the day today?" I asked her but she shuffled in her chair. "Look I know I'm going to be here longer than I wanted, and I've accepted it. I'm not going to go all Hulk on you for it." She looked down at her phone and turned it in my direction. I looked at the date 20th, that means I had been here almost a whole week. Mum should be visiting tomorrow according to Maisie's phone.

I quickly glanced at the background; it was of a child which I assumed was Maisie's. But something wasn't quite right, the baby was small and a greyish colour.

"What's their name?" I asked and Maisie quickly put the phone in between her lap. "Zeke," she told me "Zeke?" I questioned and she chuckled.

"Zeke. Ezekiel would have been his full name" I realised now from the photo that Maisie had lost this child.

"How old? Before, you know" I wondered if it was over the line.

"He was 8 months old when we found out he passed. Extremely late in the pregnancy and I only found out because I kept getting excruciating pains. I thought I was going into labour."

I looked down at the floor. "I'm sorry for your loss."

There was nothing worse than losing a child, and there was no name for it either. I could never imagine being a woman and having to go through that. I mean I get guys would be devastated over the loss of their child; I would be devastated but I would never know the pain that a woman would go through. I mean they change their whole life for their child and then out of nowhere it's over.

OH
MY
GOD

Is that what mum felt with me? Did she go to bed thinking she's going to lose me? What would happen if I ever left her? She wouldn't cope. She would feel exactly like Maisie felt. I suddenly felt immense guilt for putting mum through everything I did, I wanted to get out to help mum. I wanted to be healthy this time and to really be healthy. I wanted to get better, start a new job and live a new life. I wanted to be the best version of myself. I could do this. I could get better. I could lead a normal life without OCD getting in my way.

First, I needed to come up with steps in my recovery, things that I needed to do to get better. Whose help I needed to make me better, I mean except from Dr Sanford and Mum. I needed to write everything down. I asked Maisie for a pen and pencil, and she came back within a minute or two with a piece of paper and a pen that didn't have any plastic on. I started writing everything down. Everything I needed and wanted.

What I wanted from life:
A stable job
A family (eventually)

For the girls to grow up not screwed up
For me to find happiness
For mum to live her life

How I go about getting my goals:
Getting out of The Cotswolds Hospital
Doing the work and getting better
Finding a healthy way to express my
thoughts and feelings
To stop my OCD from telling me
what to do
See a therapist (an ongoing one)
Too look for a better job, one that suits
me and my life

Who do I need to get better:
Dr Sanford (and when the time comes
another therapist)
Mum (I know she's supportive, I need
that to continue)
Me (I need my old me to come back, I
need my brain to focus long enough to
make myself better)
Mikey? (I'm undecided, his friendship
means the most but if he is negative for
me then it's not a good idea)

I wrote down everything I needed, wanted and I was adamant I was going to do it in order to become the best version of myself. At the bottom of the paper, I made sure to write some words on encouragement from my favourite shows or movies

"The way I see it, every life is a pile of good things and bad things. The good things don't always soften the bad things, but vice versa, the bad things don't always spoil the good things and make them unimportant." - Doctor Who Series 5 Episode 10

"Happiness can be found, even in the darkest of times, if one only remembers to turn on the light." - Albus Dumbledore Harry Potter and the Prisoner of Azkaban

"No one has a perfect life. Everybody has something that he wishes was not the way it is" - Stan Lee

I tried to think of a few more quotes but my mind was blank, and my eyes were heavy. I felt like a lot had happened in such a short amount of time. I put the pen and paper down on my desk and lay back on my bed. I saw Maisie get up and walk over to the pen and paper, she quickly glanced at the paper but picked up the pen and walked away. I had no intention of using the pen as a weapon, but it was still a good choice she made. She was doing what she had to.

* * *

"VISITING DAY" Grace shouted from across the tables. I chose to sit on my own at breakfast as I wanted to go through my list again. Grace was incredibly pumped to be seeing her family. I think only Grace and I could share this enthusiasm, everyone else was groaning. From what I knew from group therapy the majority of the people ended up here because of their parents, their parents didn't know what else to do so had them sectioned. I thought that they were just angry at their parents because from what they have told me the parents didn't seem like bad people, they just seemed stuck as to what to do. They were the kind of parents like mum but with a lot more money, these kids here would get whatever they wanted whenever they wanted.

Mum came in just after breakfast, she wasn't allowed to bring the girls as Dr Sanford wanted to talk to mum afterwards, and she didn't want to leave the girls unattended. I laughed and told her, "you could leave them here, nothing bad would happen to them with a room full of crazies." Mum laughed. It was nice knowing I was able to make her laugh again.

"How are you doing?" she asked. I didn't want to tell her about everything that had happened, about me freaking out twice and ending up being sedated. I didn't want to tell her about the negative thoughts that came.

"I had a revelation of sorts last night, I wrote down what I need to do to get better, who I need and how I'm going to go about getting better. It was very helpful" I told her, smiling.

"That's great honey how is your therapy going?" she asked me, basically glossing over the fact that my revelation was because of therapy.

"Well, I mean seeing as I had my revelation, I'd say it's going well." I told her smiling again and despite her smiling back I knew something wasn't right. She wasn't her usual self. "What's going on?" I asked her

"Nothing, have you done anything fun?"
I looked at her confused. Is mum high?

"Mum, what's happened?" I asked her "Tell me" I edged forward in my seat.

"Your work called me, they said because of your illness and how much time you've had off and not being able to work full-time that they couldn't keep you on anymore."

I looked down at the floor, I finally realised what was happening. Since I had been back in hospital work had been giving me sick pay but now, they had let me go there was only one wage coming into the house.

"I didn't like the job anyway. It will be easier to find a new job now." I told her and smiled, she smiled back, and this time it was a proper smile. Did she think I was going to be affected by this news? I mean, would I have reacted differently beforehand? Would I have fallen into a pit and thought I was useless, so useless I couldn't keep a job? But in this moment, I laughed, I laughed because of how I thought mum would react and the fact that I thought she would be furious but all she wanted was for me not to have a breakdown over it.

"How are the girls?" I asked, seeing as they weren't here to tell me everything that they had gotten up to.

"They are good, as mischievous as normal. Callie is currently obsessed with Scooby Doo, so now I have the song in my head. All day everyday" mum laughed.

"I think that's my fault" I laughed back. When it was time for mum to see Dr. Sanford, she pulled me into a massive hug. I missed mum's hugs; I wish I could hug her more often without her asking me what's wrong.

I missed the hugs you get as a child, not the ones you get when you're hurt or scared but the random ones. The ones where mum would be doing something, and she would randomly swing you around and hug you. I want to make it clear I don't want mum to swing me around and hug me, I just wanted the random hugs. The ones that showed she still loved me without saying she loved me. Words can be deceptive.

Nurse Maisie told me to wait outside Dr Sanford's office with mum. When he came out mum stood up and shook his hand. He told me to wait outside and that he'd call me in, in a couple of minutes. I sat outside wondering if I could hear them talking. I wondered what they're talking about? I wondered if he was telling her about my meltdown, about me going loony and seeing something that wasn't there. I bet mum was crying and wondering what she did wrong. A couple of moments passed, and the door opened. Dr Sanford was waving his hand, a sign to come in. I walked into the room and looked at mum, her nose was red, and her eyes were bloodshot. He had told her everything.

"Tom, your mother and I have been having a chat. She knows about what happened with Grace and I've talked to her about the likelihood of it happening again."

I nodded, I mean I knew that she would find out, I was still living at home so they would have to tell her.

"I've also spoken to her about your panic attacks. I think it's vital for your mum to know everything in case anything like this happens when you're at home." Dr. Sanford goes on about my mood and how he had changed the meds so that my moods stabilised and hopefully the hallucinations didn't happen again. "Tom, I don't think you're a danger to yourself or others anymore, however I do need to consult the team. I'm hoping they'll all agree with me and then this time next week you could be out of here. Obviously, you'll continue therapy with me, but you'll be able to go home."

I couldn't believe it; I mean it was only yesterday when I had my major breakdown. "But what about yesterday? I went mad." I asked, confused. Because there was no way we could beat around the bush; I did go mad.

Dr. Sanford smiled for a moment. "Tom, I genuinely believe that what you experienced was because of several different factors. I don't think that you're going to experience another psychotic episode and if you do there are certain factors that both your mum and you can look for."

He started explaining about the different signs of me having a psychotic episode and the reason as to why he believed I wouldn't have another. I told him that believing, and happenings were too different things, mum told me to stop being rude, but Dr. Sanford laughed. He told me that even when I first came here, I didn't have any psychotic episodes, he said that he believed it was a blip. That I exhausted myself out and therefore my brain went into hellfire. I'm not 100% sure but he said that with therapy and the right guidance I didn't need to worry, which was the worst thing to say to someone whose OCD is all worrying about health.

I looked at mum, she was taking everything in, she was nodding, agreeing and now and then pitching in with questions. As Dr Sanford was talking mum looked between me and the Doc, she looked tired. She looked sad but she also looked hopeful. She believed this was my last blip, so I wanted to show her it was. At one point she held my hand, I thought of doing my usual swipe away, the one that a 24-year-old son would do to his mother, but I didn't. It was nice to have her there, it was nice knowing I had the support. I thought back to the other patients and how some of them didn't have anyone. Out of all the patients Grace and I were the only ones excited to see our parents.

Once Dr. Sanford was finished, he asked if either mum or I had any more questions. I shook my head; I was feeling too tired from sitting through this meeting let alone thinking of any more questions. Dr. Sanford stood up which was a sign for mum and me too as well. "Tom, give me a day and I should have a final answer for you regarding your last day." I nodded and mum thanked him for everything he had done. We headed out and down to the reception area. I stopped and looked at mum who seemed to be welling up again.

"Are you okay mum?" I asked.

She looked at me and grinned, "Yeah, I'm just worried about you that's all. I just want you to be happy. That's all I want is for you to be happy." I felt guilty for letting myself get this bad again even though I didn't know I was getting bad again. "I'm going to try this time properly. I'm not going to rush everything. I'm going to get better at my own pace rather than the expectational pace." I told her and I think that was enough for her to hear. Mum started bawling her eyes out but smiling at the same time "I'm so proud of you, Tom" she cried and pulled me into another massive hug.

Mum and I must have been hugging for an awkwardly long time because even one of the nurses walked over to see if we're okay. We let go and I noticed a damp patch on my t-shirt, I didn't care because it showed that mum did. It showed that she loved me, and she wanted the old Tom back.

Not the one who had crippling OCD, not even teen Tom who stopped everything to help the family, she wanted the funny Tom back, the loving Tom back and the happy Tom back. She knew that he wouldn't come straight away but she was willing to wait and work with me to help me become who I wanted to be and to live my life to the fullest.

Chapter Six

It had been five days since mum visited and was Grace's last day at the Cotswolds Hospital, she was going to go live with her grandma for a bit as her parents were re-doing her bedroom. I always wondered why Grace was in here, she never properly spoke out in group therapy. She would talk about her past but not about the reason she was in here in the first place.

On her last full day, we were sat playing rummy, it seemed to be a daily routine that stuck. John and Mike were talking about the birds and how because the season was changing the birds would start flying west. Grace was shuffling the deck of cards for a new game.

"What are you going to do without me here?" she asked.

"Continue therapy and get out myself" I chuckled. I thought Grace would find it funny, but I felt like I had touched a nerve. She changed the subject quickly.

"I can't wait to see Grandma; she has the nicest bedroom there is and I know she's going to treat me to the best treats that there are."

I nodded along "Why aren't you going home?" I asked, I knew they were redecorating but I didn't know why.

"My parents think it will be good for me to have a fresh start when I'm out." I looked at Grace who was still shuffling the cards.

"Grace, can I ask you a question?" She knew what I was going to ask.

"I tried to commit suicide, I umm... Slashed my arms in my room, that's why my parents are redecorating. I remember when I woke up in hospital the first thing I thought was, why? Like why did my mum forget her sunglasses and make dad drive back home? If she had just bought the sunglasses while she was there, then I would be dead. They wouldn't have known until grandma found me the following day. The Doc thinks I have borderline personality disorder, which would explain a lot to be honest. Unfortunately, it's a personality disorder, I'm never going to be cured of it, I just have to deal with it, to live with it, and it's exhausting. Every day I have to try to live, and it gets tiring." She stopped shuffling the cards and put her head down. I could tell how big of a step it was, but I didn't want her to feel uncomfortable.

"I have OCD, my brain tells me my twin sisters are going to die unless I wrap them in bubble wrap and protect them at all costs AND I imagined you kissed me when you didn't." I told her, which made her smile.

"There are crazier people out there than you," I laughed. I mean it wasn't the best speech in the world, but it helped her, she gave me a smile and continued shuffling.

We must have played rummy more than six times; it was all we wanted to play. I felt like despite how happy and excited Grace was to leave and go home, she was nervous. Everything she was doing she was prolonging the inevitable from happening. She wanted to go home but she didn't want to go home and for things to be different. She wanted the same life that she had before she came to the loony bin. She knew that her bedroom door would remain slightly open for the near future, she knew her parents would be constantly asking if she was okay, and she knew her friends may be careful with what they said around her. She didn't want that to change, she wanted things to go back to normal. I knew Grace wanted to go home and she wanted to live her life, but I think she was worried about what would happen the next time. I didn't have to ask her anything, I didn't need her to tell me her thoughts and feelings because I had been in her shoes. I knew how she was feeling. I was the same when I first left The Cotswolds Hospital. I looked at Grace and pulled her into a hug "It will be okay", she didn't say anything she just hugged me back, squeezing me. I could tell this wasn't my imagination, this was real, I could feel the emotions running off her.

Grace didn't want to leave the next morning, but I managed to convince her it was for the best.

"You have the world at your feet right now and I know how scary it is. I know what it's like to be leaving here and not know if it's for the best but stick with it. Take each day at a time and you will find your version of happiness."

Grace smiled and a tear fell down her cheek "I'm not scared," she said, then pecked me on the cheek. I held my hand up against my cheek and it went warm. I smiled and before I knew it her parents were walking her out of the hospital and into the car. I walked over to the bay window that looked out onto the car park and waited for her to look up, but she didn't.

And like that another patient left The Cotswolds Hospital and next it was my turn.

* * *

The ward wasn't the same without her, it was quiet, John and Mike's playful banter was just bickering without her here. I no longer played rummy, I didn't discuss Star Trek or Star Wars, in fact I hardly spoke at all. Dr Sanford must have noticed the difference in me because he asked in our session if I was okay.

"Yeah, I'm good," I said, but he wasn't happy.

"Some of the nurses have noticed that you've become quieter than usual. Is there a reason?" He asked and I mean sure Grace was the reason, we got along so well.

"Well, I only got along with Grace, and she's left so there's no-one else to talk to" I told him.

"What about John or Mike?" He asked but I just shrugged.

"I never really spoke to them, I hung out with Grace who hung out with them. It's not the same without her" I then realised how pathetic I sounded. I mean I was a grown adult; I shouldn't have missed someone like we were five years olds.

Dr Sanford didn't see it like that though. "She had a big impact on you, losing anyone whether they've passed away or not can be difficult. In fact, sometimes it's harder losing someone who's still alive because you know that you could be in contact with them, and you just aren't." I thought for a moment, and he was right.

"At least if they were dead, I wouldn't have to think about whether I would see them again" I told him. I knew exactly what he was on about, it was a different kind of grief. It was grief without death. It was the same feeling I had when Mikey told me he didn't want to see me again.

"Other than Grace, how have you been feeling?" Dr Sanford asked.

"I've been fine I guess," which prompted him to ask, "you guess?"

I looked down at the floor. "I don't feel anything, Doc. Like apart from how I'm feeling with Grace, I have no other feelings. It's strange." I always wondered what it would be like to have no feelings and I think if I took away the fact that I missed Grace then yeah, I would say now was that time where I understood.

"Do you feel depressed?" Doc asked.

"No, I don't know how to explain it, but I feel nothing, like my emotion is a straight line at the moment, like if it was a graph, it would be a straight line on the axis, it isn't hitting negative but it's not hitting positives either. Does that make sense?" I asked Dr Sanford because the only way I could explain this was by using Maths.

"I understand. Sometimes that's the effect of being on the SSRI's that you are on. A feeling of flatness.

Not depressed. Not happy, just in the middle," he paused for a moment then continued talking. "Hopefully it should not last too long but if it lasts longer than two weeks then we'll need to think about changing your meds or dosage."

I nodded and agreed. I'd rather not change meds again and have God knows what side effects. I didn't want to change and see more imaginary people, but I also wanted to feel something. I chuckled to myself because I thought about how ridiculous the situation was. Most people my age were worried about their relationships, whether their partner loves them, if they were out cheating on them, or if they were worried about if they were going to get the promotion in their new job. It was funny how my worry was if my meds would keep me from having hallucinations or if I was never going to feel anything again. I mean I did have the normal problems as well like I wondered if Mikey and Sammy would ever talk to me again. I wondered how I was going to find a job that worked around life at home, but those seemed trivial compared to the problems in my mind.

Dr. Sanford had given me the good news that I would be allowed out sometime early next week, he said it would probably be Tuesday, but he told me that I needed to work hard to keep it up. He said, "the rest of the team weren't too sure, seeing as you had come back. So, we came up with a happy medium. You'll be released early next week but, in the meantime, you will participate in every therapy. Once you're out you will continue doing two days of therapy a week for a minimum of three months with myself, and then I will help you find a suitable Psychiatrist that will help you while you return to some form of normality. I know you would like to find a job; however, I think it's best to meet with your new psychiatrist first and then they can decide if you're ready for it."

I felt like I was a child again, but I knew that I wanted to live my life right, and that I couldn't do that if I was going to half-ass the treatment and then come back six months later. "How do you feel about that?" He asked.

"I just want to get better and to lead a normal life. I want the same problems that any guy my age would have."

Dr. Sanford smiled, and I returned the smile.

I was so worked up with Grace leaving and Dr. Sanford telling me I was leaving next week that I had completely forgotten it was visiting day, that was until two balls of energy ran into the room and jumped on top of me, making me lose my balance and fall over.

"TOM! I missed you" Callie screamed, ignoring the multiple faces that were now staring at us. I pushed the girls off me and stood up.

"I see both of you haven't changed" I ruffled their hair, which Elise did not like one bit, but Callie didn't bat an eyelid. Mum walked in after the girls.

"Hey look who it is." she shouted and turned her body to reveal Mikey standing in the doorway like a figure of my imagination.

"Uh...H...hey Tom" he stuttered, but I didn't say anything. I couldn't say anything, I was completely stunned to see that he was still alive, let alone had decided to visit me. We all sat down on a round table, Elise and Callie were asking me all the questions under the sun, they had managed to ask me what I had eaten for every single meal, every single day since I had gotten there and then they would "ooh" or "eww" depending on what I told them. I looked at mum who looked visibly uncomfortable and Mikey who did as well, but his facial expressions were giving off more constipated vibes.

"So, how's grandma and grandad?" I asked mum.

"Yeah, they're good, it's easier with the girls in school." Then it fell silent, the girls were in their own little

169

world playing together, Mikey and I were in some sort of staring competition. Both of us were wondering who would talk to who first.

Mum stood up first. "I think you boys need to chat, come on girls give Tom a hug" The girls stood up and hugged me one at a time and as Callie was hugging me, she whispered, "I miss and cherish you" I looked at her confused but smiled and told her the same. Mum gave me a quick hug and told Mikey she would wait in the car for him. We both sat opposite each other wondering who was going to speak. After a while Mikey gave in.

"I'm sorry bro." Is all he could get out.

"Where have you been?" I asked. I was less annoyed about him shouting and screaming at me at the hospital and was more annoyed that he hadn't bothered with me since.

"Once they let me out, I, uh, I was just sleeping on the streets. I managed to get myself a flat share outside the village for cheap and I start a new job next week so that's good." He told me becoming quieter the more he spoke, knowing that I wasn't on about that.

"I felt like shit for what I did okay, I am sorry about the hospital, about blaming you." Mikey finally said, and I laughed.

"I'm not annoyed about that Mikey, you weren't in the right headspace, I get it okay" I gestured around and continued, "trust me, I get it, but you didn't have to ignore me, I had no-one Mikey. I couldn't find you anywhere, or Sammy. I thought I had lost you; you could have been dead, and I wouldn't have known." I looked at Mikey who had his head down. I stopped talking and just stared at him, when he brought his head up, I could see that he was crying.

"I thought you hated me, I thought you would be disgusted that you gave me an opportunity and I screwed it up." I dropped my attention from Mikey because I realised that that was exactly what I thought everyone

170

thought of me when I returned to the ward. "Our minds are our worst enemies. I never thought that I just wanted you to be okay." I told him.

When it was time for Mikey to leave, he grabbed me in the biggest hug we'd ever had. Mikey wasn't a touchy-feely friend; he didn't hug or give you a kiss on the cheek or do anything like that. He was the complete opposite so seeing him like that made me feel sorry for him. I hugged him back tighter than usual.

"Don't drift man, I'm here" I told him. I mean a psychologically scarred man who had been in a hospital twice probably isn't the most stable to be giving advice, but I could tell he needed me in that moment, and I needed him back.

* * *

Dr Sanford called me into his office just after Mikey had gone. I'm guessing mum spoke to him about Mikey and he asked how I was.

"I feel better knowing that we're just two screwed up guys who misunderstood our own signs." I told him, the words rolling off my tongue like I was a poet.

"Have you ever thought about writing, Tom?" Dr. Sanford asked me like he hadn't given me a notepad to write my feelings in.

"I have the notebook" I told him "I don't mean that kind of writing, I mean fiction writing. Like writing a book. I think you would be great at writing; you have a knack for words you just need to put them in the right place" and before I could say anything else he was listing off a ton of writers who suffer from mental health disorders.

"Most artists suffer from mental health disorders; they find writing from a place of pain helps to get their creative juices flowing"
Note: I hope Dr Sanford never says creative juices again.

"Artists write beauty when they're in pain because it helps to verbalise or talk about something that nobody

171

else can see or feel or think." Dr. Sanford told me about how there was an artist that went to The Cotswolds when he first started being a psychiatrist, how this artist was burdened with abuse and pain but found beauty in painting. Apparently, this person was now a famous artist but of course he couldn't tell me who it was due to patient confidentiality.

I didn't believe him. I thought Dr Sanford was talking a load of baloney. He didn't know anyone famous. I didn't know anyone from the area that was famous, like ever, so there was no way that he would know anyone famous. I knew that he was trying to help me, that he was wanting me to bring out my more creative side which before dad left was great. I used to write all the time; I couldn't draw well but my writing was amazing. I would write stories of fictional planets and wars, they used to win short story competitions in school, and I was even in the paper at one point but when dad left, I didn't have time and my hobby got chucked aside. However, I knew I would need a hobby while I was still at home, especially if Dr. Sanford wanted me to stop smoking so I suppose I could give it a try. What was the worst that could happen?

When I left Doc's office, I headed straight to my room, picked up the notepad that he had given me from this visit, and headed to reception. "Can I have a pen please?" I asked Nurse Maisie, she handed me a pen, like a proper pen with the plastic on and everything. I looked at her for a second holding the pen up so we could both see it clearly. "I can trust you to not use it as a weapon, right?" She asked knowing that was my question.

"Yeah, I don't think I'm going to go Hulk Hogan and try to use this pen as a makeshift shiv." I told her and walked over to a free table. I started jotting down ideas that I had in my head. I had a method in creating my stories: I would write down lots of different ideas and then see which I preferred, or I could put them together into one story. Some Ideas would be binned out because they

172

were terrible and some would be worked on until they were better, but writing notes was the best way for me to start a story.

Now and then when I was really bored in school, I would make a story using my random ideas. Once I made a story up about a cowboy who got abducted by aliens that all looked exactly like the Actor, John Hurt. Like there were 50 John Hurt Alien look-alikes and the character had to escape, which he did using a water slide that sled all the way down to earth. However, the aliens followed him, and he had to create a forcefield with single pieces of uncooked spaghetti to keep the aliens out.

Yeah, strange, but that's how bored I was in History that I came up with bizarre stories rather than listen about Pioneers in America. I never understood why we were forced to do American History in a British School, there weren't Americans at the school, the history teacher wasn't American, and the school wasn't built by American's or anything like that, but we had to do it. I remembered our teacher asking us if we wanted to do American history or medicine in time. Majority of people chose medicine in time in our class, but the other class must have chosen American History because that's what we got stuck with. I would often ask my teacher why we couldn't study British History, seeing as we were in England and the majority of our great grandparents would have fought in World War 2. Everyone was interested in that but we were told that it wasn't part of the exam questions so we couldn't. I failed History, apparently, I was two points away from getting a C, but I didn't mind. I only took History because I had to, I didn't want to do it, I didn't like it, but it was History or Geography, and let's just say that I wouldn't be able to tell you where most Cities in the UK were, let alone talk about rock formation and how cliffs were formed.

* * *

"So, what's the plan when you leave?" Dr. Thomas asked in group therapy. I looked around at the blank faces that were staring at me.

"I don't know" I told him, because I hadn't thought of it. "Basically, what I would do here but outside and with different people" I joked. I hadn't thought about leaving because I didn't want to get my hopes up. "What's the first thing you're going to do?" John asked.

"Probably get a burger" I smirked, and a few people laughed. I wasn't lying, I was really hungry, the food wasn't the best so I ate very little in fear that I would throw up otherwise.

"What kind of burger?" John asked and I had to think for a second.

"BBQ Burger with Mac N' Cheese in the burger. It's amazing you have to try it" I told John who looked like he was going to dribble from his mouth being so wide open.

"Okay getting back onto the subject, how do you think you're prepared?" Dr. Thomas asked , bringing the attention back to the matter in hand.

"I will be seeing Dr. Sanford outside of the hospital, mum is being supportive, and the girls are, well, the girls so they don't change at all. I just need to process the emotions and feelings I get and work on correcting them." I told Dr Thomas and he smiled.

"Sounds good. Can anyone offer any suggestions to Tom if he feels those emotions? What can he do?" He asked and I looked around to see people scratching their heads.

"Umm, maybe do something you enjoy, I like drawing so maybe draw. Or scribble if you're angry." A quiet voice rose from the silence, it was a kiddie that was sitting next to Dr. Thomas, he looked completely lost and it was the first time I had seen him in group therapy.

"Good Idea, Lewis."

This would be my last group therapy however I still had an individual therapy with Dr Sanford tomorrow and our final session the hour before I left. I wasn't nervous this time. This time I was ready, I didn't have concerns like last time. I knew what I wanted my future to be, I knew that I wanted to live my life. Group therapy ended a bit sooner than it should have because no-one had anything to say, and I had done enough talking. I didn't want to make people like John jealous for leaving knowing that he wouldn't be anytime soon. I didn't think John wanted me to leave because when group therapy ended, he came up, put his hand on my shoulder and just stared at me. He used to do this to Grace all the time, apparently it was his way of showing affection. Which I think was quite sad, like either his life had been so low that he was unable to show affection because he wasn't shown it, or his brain was unable to function anything more for human interaction. I could tell he was unable to verbalise his thoughts and feelings and that was why he was in here for so long. I wondered how Dr Sanford dealt with him, I wondered what kind of therapy he used to try to get John to communicate. I would have thought he used art therapy, but I saw John's art and it was abysmal. I mean Callie or even Elise could do better by miles but maybe that was what helps John. Maybe the reason he was constantly in and out was because he was just inept. I didn't mean that in a harsh way, but he didn't seem to completely understand anything, he seemed to forget quickly but looking at him you wouldn't think there was anything wrong with him.

I assumed he was either born with something wrong or he had an injury. I knew I shouldn't judge a book by its cover but with some people I couldn't help it. From what I knew about John, which was very little, he would lose his temper and forget who he was. He loved animals and wished he could work with them but because of his anger he didn't want to end up hurting the animals.

I mean if you asked me, I would have said he reminded me of Lenny from Of Mice and Men, but he wasn't as big as Lenny and he never actually killed someone (well from what I know). I didn't think John was stupid I just think he lacked the education that I was given. I also believed him when he said he couldn't control his anger, he seemed like he genuinely didn't know what happened, and he would get so upset when he talked about what happened and how the police would tell him what he had done and how he didn't remember any of it.

He told us this story of how he was found with blood on his hands just before he came back to the Cotswolds on this occasion. He said how he had gone for a walk at night because the half-way house was too noisy, and he couldn't sleep. He explained that he went down to the river and was walking along it. He explained how it was a normal walk until he came across a group of teens who had started hurling abuse at him. He started running away because he didn't want to black out, which he ended up doing. He told us the next thing he remembered was waking up by the river again, he had been on the floor, and the grass was wet, so he didn't think about the cold feeling on his body. He wiped his hands on his clothes and started walking home.

"Obviously I was scared I did something, but it was dark, and I couldn't see myself." John told us; he then went on to explain that the police stopped him as he was coming out of the alleyway. He looked down and saw blood everywhere. He explained how he just bawled his eyes out on the coppers, and he told them to shoot him because he'd be better off dead. Once the coppers calmed him down, they arrested him but because none of the teens that saw him filed a report and because he didn't remember what happened they couldn't keep him illegally. Apparently, he was the one who suggested to come back, he felt safer if he was locked up than he did out in the open.

Every time John got close to being let go, he would go off the rails again. I noticed that when I was last here but didn't know why until he mentioned it. I didn't know if I respected him for what he did or if I was more scared of John now. It did however make me realise that John was never jealous of anyone leaving, he was jealous of them leaving him. If he could have it his way, he would keep everyone on the ward forever. He wanted to keep everyone safe in the confined Hospital Ward, safe and sound.

When we all left the hall, we were deflated, I think the ones staying were down that I was leaving. Even if they didn't speak to me, it was still one more person leaving before them. I felt deflated from talking for so long, I had never actually spoken that much in group therapy before and even though it was basic conversation I felt like I had let everything go, like I had been holding in my words but now I felt free, or at least closer to freedom.

I headed back into my room, I had one full day left but I felt the urge to start packing my very minimal bag that I had. I wasn't one of these patients that brought loads of stuff with me, I kept minimal because that was how long I wanted to be stuck in here. I thought the less I brought in the less time I would serve. I could imagine someone like John bringing in suitcases knowing that he would stay for a while. I just didn't understand it, this was my second time here and I didn't want to come back for a third. I mean I didn't want to come back at all this second time, but I believed I was ready now. I was definitely more prepared than last time, and I didn't feel scared, well except from turning into a John 2.0, but Dr Sanford believed I wouldn't so that got me through.

I put my things into my rucksack that mum had brought with her when she visited for the first time, I neatly packed them all and left out one item of clothing for tomorrow. I then made sure to check the room in case I had left anything in a mess, but the room was bare, and it wasn't like we were allowed to eat in our rooms. I walked the circumference of the room taking in every detail. I noticed the brick walls that were covered in a horrible mint green, which I assumed was supposed to make us happier but if anything, just gave me a headache. The desk was a tiny square desk that was bolted to both the floor and wall, in case you had the strength of the Hulk and ripped it off one, you then had another to go. The bolts were glued shut so there was no way you could undo them (like you could undo them without a wrench anyway), and it was painted white to match the chair and floor (a disguise you could say), the wardrobe had no doors and the pole was again bolted into the wardrobe, the wardrobe was some sort of wood metal hybrid, which you wouldn't be able to move or break. The bed too was bolted to the floor, it was one of those beds that you couldn't see under because it had the weird wood/metal under the bed. It was a basic room, and you could see an old piece of tape that was stuck on the walls from where someone had stuck photos or posters.

Rule #1 in a mental hospital - you don't get blue tack because you can swallow it and suffocate or hide blades. You obviously don't get nails, paperclips, staplers, or anything that has a pointed edge. We got scissors but they were the plastic ones that you used in year two that wouldn't even cut up paper correctly.

In the corner of the room, I noticed something that I hadn't noticed for my whole stay. It looked like pen marks, I got closer and noticed that initials had been scratched into the walls, lots of initials, there must have been a good 15 initials, how did I never see this before? I looked around to see if there was anything that I could use to put my initials in with, a bit of plastic hidden by the desk, a pen or pencil. Anything, but there was no luck. I wanted to put my initials; I couldn't explain why but I just wanted to. I headed out into the hall and down to the reception desk, Nurse Maisie was sitting there.

"Hey Tom, how can I help?" I look at her and smile.

"Do you have anything sharp?"

"Why do you want something sharp?" She asked before thinking about what the best way to go about this conversation would be.

"Oh...oh no it's not what you think, people have scratched their initials into the wall of my room and I wanted to do it as well as a final hurrah" I told her, and I didn't know if it was the innocence on my face, the manners I used or the fact that I then proceeded to beg her for 10 solid minutes, that made her reluctantly agree

"I have to watch you though."

We both headed down the corridor and we headed into my room, which soon would no longer be my room. I headed straight to the corner. Maisie was right behind me making sure she had the pen in her eyes at all times. I started scratching my name into the wall "I didn't realise people did this" Maisie spoke, I turned around and she had this sudden look of innocence about her. To her this wall was full of all the people that the hospital had kept in this room, it was her old patients, it was the people with clinical depression, OCD, personality disorders, schizophrenia but no matter what our illnesses were, we were all in the same boat. We had a similarity, and some of those people might have gone on to lead glorious lives and some may have walked out of here and stepped into traffic.

Not only were their names carved into the wall but their stories, the stories of the innocent who were dealt a cruel hand and told to deal with it by so many until they arrived here. I wondered if Maisie remembered any of them?

"Do you recognise any names?" I asked her
"Most of them."

179

"Do you know what happened to them after they left?" I asked her, she looked down and nodded.

"One is now a very successful singer, one owns their own company, two work in shops and a few of them passed away." She explained. I handed the pen back to her, stood up and hugged her. I didn't know why, but it felt like the right thing to do, it felt like at that moment Nurse Maisie needed it. She didn't hug back; I didn't think she was allowed to. We walked out of my room and Maisie went back to the nurse's desk. The other nurse that was there asked if she was alright and she just nodded and smiled.

It made me wonder how the nurses and doctors didn't get attached to people, how they did not get attached to even just one person. I couldn't keep my professionalism if I worked in this job, it would be too much for me. I was not one of these people who could easily switch off emotions, there would be a patient crying and I would end up crying with them. I wore my emotions on my sleeve (I believe that was the expression people use). I tried to be as open as possible with people, I believe that was why my OCD got so bad because I didn't see it as a problem, I didn't understand that my emotions and feelings and anxiety were all linked.

I headed into the tv room, Monsters Inc was playing, since Grace left there were no longer documentaries on TV. It was a kid show and films, I thought the nurses were scared to change it to anything else in case we got ideas from shows or movies. Not that Monsters INC was any better, the opening was about monsters creeping up on kids and scaring the crap out of them for the monster's entertainment. I sat there for a bit but gave up when one of the patients started screaming at Sully. I didn't know why; I didn't stop to find out. I headed into my room, I looked at the scratchings, how old the others were, some by years, some by months and then I looked at how new and fresh mine were.

Someone had to have noticed the initials and just never told anyone. It looked like a memorial wall. I wondered what would happen if I asked Dr Sanford about the initials, I mean if they weren't his patients anymore, I'm sure he was able to talk about them. I wanted to hear about the survivors, the ones who beat the odds and came out okay. I wanted to be them, I wanted to be able to tell my story like the last person told theirs.

* * *

My last full day was pretty uneventful, I thought something interesting might have happened, like it was the last day of camp, and we were going to eat cake and dance but then I realised that this wasn't camp. I know that nothing major would happen, it was a psychiatric ward. It's not like they would celebrate, like "hey congratulations on getting out the nut house" no. It wasn't like that at all. I would celebrate in a year, I thought if I was still out of here by this time next year I would celebrate then.

At dinner time we all sat in the dining hall, for the majority of the time people ate in silence. There were a few girls arguing in the corner, crying because they didn't want to eat the full fat yoghurt that had been left on their table. I didn't have any problem with eating, I would eat whatever you gave me but the food in this place wasn't the best, so I couldn't imagine being forced to eat the food here. I remembered Grace telling me that the majority of the girls that had Anorexia or Bulimia actually loved food and that was the issue. They loved food and eating but the little voice in their head would tell them not to eat, they would tell them how fattening the food was, and that was why they stopped eating. When Grace put it like that, I understood what they were going through, it was like they stopped being able to do something they loved. That made sense to me.

As I was eating my concoction of vegetable curry (the safest option), I noticed the same boy from group therapy this morning, Lewis. I watched him from my table, he walked over to the E.D. table and took a seat. He was wearing a red jumper that had the words "suck it" in big bold white writing. He sat on the table but didn't touch the food. He had to be new, I couldn't have not noticed him this entire time. I mean I knew he was quiet and small, but I would have still noticed a whole other human being. In group therapy I was always trying to look anywhere but at Dr Thomas. If you looked at him, he would pick on you. I looked at Lewis who wasn't eating anything despite the nurses trying to get him to eat. I knew what would happen, I had seen it happen so many times, he would refuse to eat until the doctors and nurses became worried about his weight, he would then be sectioned under 63 of the mental health act. It would allow nurses and doctors to force feed him, that included with a tube, and from what I know at group therapy, tube feeding is the worst.

Note: According to research 69% of people who have eating disorders also have OCD. Fascinating. I asked Dr Sanford a while back and he googled it for me. He of course asked me why I needed to know the information and I told him that he could clearly see I had no eating problems.

I wondered what went through their minds. I thought about it often. I thought about what other people with mental disorders thought of, or what they were going through or what their voices were telling them. I remembered when I had my first ever counselling session. It was with a guy named Dr. Williams; he was amazing. Mum thought it would be good for me to see someone after Dad walked out because she thought it might have traumatised me. She was right but it wouldn't show until years later. Dr. Williams was great; he would ask me about the girl's, and he remembered the girl's names and how old they were, and he never looked at a book or notepad when I was with him. He had his whole attention on me, it was great. He was great but mum didn't have enough money to keep me with him, so I had to go to a public counsellor. Dr. Williams helped me, and it wasn't like I was being counselled, he was like a friend, he talked to me about his family, his kids and his wife and his history of depression but he didn't do it too much. He did it at the exact right time that I needed to hear it and that meant a lot.

Dr Williams taught me about the "void" as he called it. He said the void was something that would come and go and each time it did, it would get slightly bigger. It might not visit for a month but when it did, it got bigger and worse, and scarier than before. He told me how the void would hit at any moment and sometimes you'd think it would go and then it would all of a sudden come back. He told me how most people's voids are depression, but everyone has their own void and their own meaning and feeling for the void. He told me how despite how hard it could be for some people, that some people welcomed it with open arms because deep down it was a comfort, they knew what to expect and they were prepared every time. He would tell me that sometimes, some people would want the void to come because they thought that was what they deserved. They thought they deserved the void. It was their punishment for merely existing. I always remembered what Dr Williams would say. I remembered his words of wisdom and how he didn't patronise me or talk down to me. He spoke to me like I spoke to him, we had mutual respect.

* * *

I tried sleeping on the final night, but do you think I could sleep? Of course not, it was strange. I was ready to leave, like really ready this time but as I was twisting and turning and trying to fall asleep, my body just

183

wouldn't get comfortable. It was like I was already getting used to my bed at home. My body was preparing for the transition back. I guessed that was a good thing. I mean I didn't feel this last time, so that was different. That was good.

I gave up trying to sleep, I could have walked down to the nurse's station and asked the night nurse if I could have a sleeping tablet but, in all honesty, I wanted to savour the last night at the hospital, I wanted to remember everything. I saw things differently now, I didn't know at what moment it happened, but it just happened one day. Maybe the meds started working or maybe something Dr Sanford or mum said made me think differently. I wasn't sure of the exact reason, or even when it happened, I just knew that I felt different compared to when I came in, I felt more positive.

Whenever the flashlight shone into my room, I would close my eyes pretending to be asleep, the light would only be kept on there for a second or two before darkness hit the room again. I opened my eyes when the nurse left, thinking about everything that I was going to do when I got out. I wanted to take the girls to the park, I wanted to allow them to play on the swings and the monkey bars and not have to worry about them getting germs from the playground. I wanted to see Mikey and to catch up on everything that had happened since we both weren't talking. I wanted to find a new job, one that fit both my life and my family's life as well because even though I was not the girl's dad, and even though I didn't have to protect them or look after them as much as I did. I wanted to. I had always wanted to do it; it was never a question to me. Nobody ever asked me if I was okay with this life and that was because nobody had to ask me, I always loved looking after the girls. They were my family, and I would never love anyone as much as I loved them.

And anyway, I was still their brother, I still loved them and as they got older, I thought about becoming more brotherly and annoying the hell out of them. I thought about getting into a fight with them (I'll allow them to win a couple of times), I thought about walking into their room, knocking stuff about and then walking out without saying a word. I thought about eating their food that they left in the fridge, and I thought about purposely being an idiot because they still needed to know what it was like to live with an older brother. Then when I finished with all that, I will still have their back if someone bullies them or upset them. I would get protective when they wanted to start dating and I wanted to interrogate the person to make them know who the boss was and to not mess with my girls. I would be that brother one day but for now. For now, I was happy being me.

* * *

I must have dozed off at some point because I woke up to Nurse Maisie calling my name.

"Tom, you slept in. It's time to see Dr. Sanford." She shouted from the doorway. It was the day, and I was ready, I just had to answer Dr. Sanford's stupidly long questions first.

I walked down to Dr Sanford's room, but Dr. Sanford wasn't there, no-one was. I thought I was in the wrong room, so I walked outside, checked the sign on the door and then walked back in. It was the right room; I was just early. I sat on the sofa, twiddling my thumbs hoping that he wasn't going to be too late. I wanted to get out. I wanted to go home. My mind wondered, Dr Sanford's book was on the desk, I could be nosey and look. I could see what he wrote about me. I shouldn't, what if he was watching. What if it was a trick and he was watching me right now? No, he wouldn't put cameras in the office just to spy on me or for anyone, surely that was breaking patient/doctor confidentiality.

I stood up and walked outside again, still nobody was around. I walked over to the desk, and realised it was the first time I had ever been behind his desk. It looked weird from this angle, his seat was old, the leather was rubbing off in the most used areas. The desk was simple, it had two drawers on either side which both had locks on, and his desk was empty. He had pieces of paper perfectly lined on top of each other and a pencil holder that had two pencils and a fountain pen in. His notepad was open, but the page was empty. I brought my hand down and touched the book, I paused for a moment wondering whether I wanted to read what Dr Sanford got out of the lessons.

Before I could turn a page Dr. Sanford pushed the door open, he looked up from the book to me and straightened his back.

"I just wanted to know what you wrote down in our sessions." I told Dr. Sanford expecting him to punish me, to tell me I wasn't ready to leave, and he wanted me to stay longer but he didn't, he simply lifted his arm pointing to the book, "be my guest." He sat on the sofa. I looked at him in disbelief.

"Wait really? I can look?" I asked, completely stunned.

"Of course, I've never stopped my patients from reading my notes. Wouldn't really be fair if I did that."

I sat in his chair, which wasn't very comfortable and flicked through to the first page of his notes. They went right back to when I first got put into the hospital.

Thomas Peter Johnston
Aged: 23
Nationality: British
Height: 6 Foot 4 Inches
Weight: 147 Pounds
Diagnosis: Obsessive Compulsive Disorder and
Depression - commonly linked together

Notes: When Tom first came to Cotswolds Hospital, he found it hard to understand that his OCD was serious, he was adamant that he was protecting his sisters from anything and everything. He was highly paranoid that his sisters were going to die if he didn't clean everything thoroughly and check everything was off. According to Tom's mum (Maeve Johnston) he would have to follow every procedure 13 times before he was able to do anything with the girls. Maeve mentioned that she first started noticing Tom do it at 22 when he spent 30 minutes in the bathroom and when he came out, he told her that he was washing his hands. When Maeve asked to see his hands, he became angry.

Maeve has explained that Tom will often smoke Marijuana, having 4 to 5 spliffs a day. She believed it helped him and that when he was smoking was the only time, he was calm. When he was sober, he would show high anxiety levels including shaking legs, biting nails, excessive cleaning, and counting. Anything he did, he would have to do 13 times, if he was interrupted, he would have to do it again 13 times to make sure it was correct. Maeve told me the worst it got was when it took him 4 hours to leave the house because he wanted to be helpful and clean, apparently Tom went through 3 bottles of different cleaning products.

Tom was unstable when brought into A+E and wasn't fully cooperating, he had to be sedated for Nurses to be able to examine him. When they examined him, they found that his hands were badly injured by excessive washing and constant cleaning fluid contact. They also noticed faint scars on his thighs which they believed were from self-harm but when asked Tom denied having self-harmed.

I believe with intensive therapy and medications Tom will be able to go back to normality, however the process will have to be slow as Tom does not yet believe that he is suffering from a mental health disorder. He has

*been sectioned under Section 4 of the mental Health act
and won't be released until I fully believe that he is able to
deal with his Obsessive thoughts properly. I believe once
the obsessive thoughts are under control then the
depression will become easier to handle with medication.*

* * *

I put down the notes and looked at Dr. Sanford.
"I don't quite remember it that way, why?" I said.
"You were very fragile the first time you got here
Tom. You were very unstable, apparently when they
brought you into the hospital you couldn't speak
coherently. You were repeating yourself and didn't know
where you were. Your OCD had been in control of you
for so long that after a while you became exhausted.
From what I was told you hadn't slept for four days, you
kept washing yourself believing you were contaminated,
your mother was terrified when she found you burning
your clothes outside, so she called for an ambulance."

I looked at Dr Sanford who was still sitting on the
sofa, he had changed his position but was still facing me.
"I don't remember coming in, even now I don't
remember it, but my mind is better now. Why can't I
remember?" I asked him.
"Sometimes a traumatic event for a human can
lead to dissociation, which can often lead to memory loss.
Your mind was in a fragile state when you came in and
therefore before you became better your mind could have
easily forgotten things." I understood that Dr Sanford was
trying to explain it to me in the best way possible, but I
felt like a child at that moment. Like how could my 22-
year-old brain forget something so big?
"But it was such a big thing, how could I
forget?" I asked him. Dr Sanford looked at me for a
moment, rearranged his positioning and then spoke.
"It's hard to explain. It's all about the chemicals
in your brain and how certain chemical imbalances can
cause memory loss, depression, anxiety and many other

mental health problems. Also, the lack of sleep you had prior to coming in had an effect, your body was close to shutting down so memory loss, temporary or permanent could easily happen."

I was pretty good at science, and I had done quite a bit of research on depression and what caused it, so I understood the basics of chemical imbalances. I just never thought I would be someone who got it. I never thought my brain would suffer from imbalances. "Did you know some scientists explain that the higher IQ you have the more likely you are to suffer from a mental health disorder" I told Dr. Sanford.

"It didn't necessarily mean that you can't be stupid and not suffer from mental health, but it was something to do with phycological overexcitability. Basically, people with a higher IQ were more likely to overanalyse every situation they were given which caused problems like anxiety and in some cases OCD." I then told Dr Sanford who smiled at me. "That is very true, a lot of research has been shown to prove that intelligent people are 10% more likely to suffer from mental health problems."

I remembered reading the article online, I was researching OCD and depression on one of my sleepless nights and I remembered finding the article. It went through all the different reasons how intelligence and mental health disorders were connected. Obviously, I didn't believe I was the intelligence side, but I didn't think I was the stupid side either, I was in the middle. I wasn't stupid but I wasn't intelligent, I was half and half.

"You do a lot of research?" Dr. Sanford asked.

"Yes. It helps me understand more if I research." I always loved researching things, I loved seeing the small details that most people missed because they were concerned about the big picture. I liked watching behind the scenes of movies, whereas people would prefer the movies themselves or I liked to know what ingredients were in the meal whereas people just wanted to eat the food.

"I feel like I see things differently from other people" I spoke aloud. I hadn't realised until now that I was still sitting in Dr Sanford's seat, so I stood up and gestured for him to sit down. He smirked, stood from the sofa and sat in his chair, "I quite liked the sofa, I would get one, but I think it would be unprofessional." He spoke and I chuckled. I sat on the sofa, and it was automatically much more comfortable.

"Why do you think you see things differently?" He asked me once he got comfortable and opened a new page of the notepad.

I looked at him and then looked down at my hands, I didn't know what to say.

"I don't know, in school people would talk about things in a way that I never did. Mum always said I was just older than my years, she called me an old man in a child's body, and that never really changed. I can't form an opinion until I answer all the questions I have in my head. I like things to be very simple, so I ask a lot of questions so that nothing gets confused. I don't know if that makes sense." I told him.

"Of course, it makes sense, for some people they find things out along the way and they're happy with that, for some people they must know everything as soon as they meet someone to better engage that person. There's nothing wrong with it, actually it saves a lot of time." Dr Sanford told me and smiled.

Dr. Sanford started rearranging his paperwork and I knew when he did that it meant this session was going to become more serious and he was going to start asking the final questions. It felt like I was in a quest, and this was the final battle, this was the decision if I was going to win or not. Just like a game, even if you fail the first time, all it teaches you is how not to do it the next time. Losing isn't a bad thing, it means you get to make mistakes and learn from them. I knew what I did wrong the last time I was here, last time Dr Sanford asked me the questions. I knew now that I lied on a lot of the questions. I knew that and this time I wouldn't lie because all it would do would keep me from getting better.

"Serious time?" I asked Dr. Sanford, smirking at him, he gave me a small nod and then started his questioning.

"How do you feel from when you first came here?" He asked.

I thought for a moment "I feel different, not in a good or bad way, I don't feel healed, but I feel more prepared and more able to deal with bad things happening."

Dr Sanford wrote down some notes and then looked back at me "Do you intend to hurt yourselves or others?" I shook my head; I don't think I've ever wanted to hurt anyone except dad but I'm over that now. "Do you have any intrusive thoughts you can't shake off?" He asked me and again I shook my head.

"Not since the new meds" I told him, he wrote it down and smiled.

"Do you feel ready to leave Cotswolds Hospital?" He asked me and for a second, I thought about it, I did feel more ready, but I didn't think I would ever be 100% ready.

"I don't think it's as easy as a yes or no. I mean yes, I feel ready now, and I feel a lot better, and I definitely feel more prepared, and I know what I'm doing but I also don't think I'd ever be truly ready to leave here. This isn't real-life, this isn't the real world. For some people like John, this is all they're used to so this is their normal but my normal out there is different. To answer your question, I feel ready to leave and to take it one step at a time, with support from my family, friends and you, Doc." I told him. Once he finished writing he looked up and smiled at me

191

"Well done, Tom. I think you're ready to go."

* * *

I was so excited to find out that I could finally leave, it wasn't just a thought or a potential thing to happen, it was real and this time I was taking my recovery seriously. Mum deserved that, the girls deserved that, and I deserved that.

Dr. Sanford told me that he was going to call my mum to come in, he wanted to have a meeting about me leaving and tale-tell signs of me getting bad again, but he used fancy words to make it sound less daunting. I went to my room and picked up my bag, I looked at the wall that had all of the initials on and after a minute or two of staying in the moment and allowing myself to realise everything that was happening, I left.

I headed down into the tv room but there wasn't anyone in there, surprisingly the whole ward seemed to be quieter than usual. I headed down to the nurse's station where Nurse Maisie was sitting.

"Where is everyone?" I asked her, she looked up to me, smiling.

"They're in group therapy."

"What day is it?" I asked her pretty sure I knew that it was Thursday.

"It's Thursday" she replied, which made me wonder why everyone was in group therapy at this time. It was too early for group therapy unless they changed it so I would have left when they came out but that didn't make sense because they wouldn't change all of it for one person.

"Who died?" I asked chuckling and despite Nurse Maisie having a sense of humour she just looked at me, an eyebrow raised.

"It was a joke" I responded and then walked away.

I wonder if someone did die, I mean from experience I knew that when someone killed themselves then a group therapy session was called to go through emotions and feelings etc. Maybe it was John, I mean I could normally hear him every morning with his screams or cries but not this morning, I think that was why I slept in. He was my personal alarm clock.

I tried to think about something else, about leaving and living my life and getting better but all I could think about was who died. So of course, when Dr. Sanford invited me and mum into his office that was the first thing I asked.

"Did someone here off themselves last night?" I asked Dr Sanford, mum hit my leg and sharply whispered "Thomas." But Dr. Sanford saw it and smiled

"No, someone here didn't off themselves." He said putting the word off in quotation marks.

"I'm here to talk about your release Tom." I took that as my queue to stay quiet. I still wasn't sure that Dr. Sanford was telling the truth, it was the way he said 'here' like he was putting emphasis on it. I wondered if an old patient died but soon got pulled away from my distracting thoughts by Dr Sanford starting the conversation.

"I believe that Tom is ready to go home, I think with continuous counselling from myself, with the new medication and dosage and with the same support from home, he'll be more of himself in no time." Dr. Sanford told my mother who looked different from when I last saw her, she looked more tired but when she looked at me it seemed to float away. Mum grabbed my hand and squeezed it. I allowed her to do it. I missed her affection,

I missed her so much, even if she did annoy me sometimes.

"Thank you, Doctor," mum answered and looked at me.

"Do you feel ready this time?" She asked, I nodded.

"I feel so much better than last time Mum" and I was telling the truth. I wasn't lying to anyone, not to Dr Sanford, not to mum and not to myself. I lied before and it got me back here so there was no point in lying again.

"Okay so here's the deal you'll come to see me once a week for a minimum of six weeks, if I believe you have improved more, I will refer you to our outpatient's therapist, Dr Goodall, who will then continue therapy with you. I'll give him all the information and notes that I have so he'll be educated. Of course, once you get to outpatient therapy it's your decision whether you continue therapy or not, you may even decide that seeing a therapist once a month is sufficient enough for you but once you get to that point then you can start living your more normal life you wanted." Dr Sanford stopped and looked at me.

"Do you feel ready?" he asked me, I looked at him and smiled, "Yes."

Chapter Seven

Freedom. It wasn't what I expected, sure it was fun. The first couple of days Mikey came to see me, we watched movies and cooked new foods but once the initial buzz of coming out of the hospital died down it was just like before. There wasn't a massive difference, except the girls had again grown in both knowledge and size. Every mealtime since I had been released, they did this stupid thing where they would say what they were grateful for. As annoying as it was, it became catchy and despite how embarrassing it was, both mum and I joined in. It was nice to have something as a family even if it was by saying something we were grateful for.

It first started when they visited me at the hospital and then on my first day home when they said it at dinner time. Mum later explained to me that one day they came home from school, and during Religious Education they had to explain what they were grateful for, the girls had put their family. Mum explained that they came home and since then always said it. She told me they said it so much to start off with that mum had to ban them from saying it except at dinnertime. She told me that it was the most religious she ever felt, I thought it was quite funny. Some families might sit around the table and say a prayer if they were religious or they might talk about football or extracurriculars but for the girls this was more important than anything else, this was the priority.

My first meal back Elise told us she was grateful that the doctor let me go and Callie was grateful that I could now read bedtime stories because apparently mum was terrible.

"I don't do the voice" mum whispered to me.

"Your turn" Elise shouted to mum.

"I'm grateful to have my family all together." She looked at me and smiled, I smiled back.

"Tom your go!" Elise shouted to me.

I thought about it for a second. "I'm grateful for you two nutcases" I told them while laughing and patting Elise on her head. "And of course, I'm grateful to you mum, you've been amazing while I've been going through all this stuff. Truly amazing" I smiled, and tears rolled down mum's face. She patted my back and stood up "finished girls?" She asked, and the twins screamed, "yes". They both got up from their chairs and ran into the living room.

I chuckled. "At least they haven't changed too much". Mum was at the sink washing her dishes, she had her back to me, but I could tell she was crying, I took the plates over to the side.

"Are you okay mum?"

"Yeah, I'm just glad you're home" she told me. I patted her on the back.

"Want any help?" I asked but she shook her head.

"Be with your sisters they missed you loads."

I walked into the living room and the girls were squabbling over what to watch.

"I wanted to watch CBBC." "I want to watch Cbeebies." The girls screamed at each other.

"Woah, I think CBBC is a bit too old for you girls, your only 6" I chuckled and switched over to Cbeebies where postman pat was on.

"Wow Postman Pat has changed in recent years; I do not remember him looking like this." I remembered small bits of Postman Pat, he used to be mainly two dimensional and he would go around delivering mail and get out of trouble, but Postman Pat changed it looked like he had had Botox and a nose surgery. He was not the man I remembered.

"I want to sit next to Tom." "No, I do." The girls squabbled.

"Woah you can both sit next to me; the sofa is big enough for both of you." I suggested.

"Why are you both arguing with each other?" I asked them, they seemed different than what I remembered, they both looked down, staying silent.

"Well, what happened between you two?" "Elise thought it was my fault that you went back to the hospital."

"And Callie thought it was mine." they both answered almost in unison. I got off the sofa and kneeled on the floor so I could look at them.

"I need you girls to understand something, me being in the hospital was nobody's fault. I had to go back into the hospital as I needed to let my mind rest. You know when you're feeling poorly, and you stay in bed all day to rest."

The girls both nodded their head.

"Well, that's what it was like for me but with my illness you can't see it, I don't show any symptoms outside, it's all inside. It's all in my head." I told the girls. I knew they were only six and they didn't need to know anything but the last thing I wanted was for them to blame themselves.

"Promise me, you know it's not your fault." They both put their heads down. "We promise.'" I took my hand and raised their chins, making sure they looked at me. "Is that why you keep saying what you're grateful for?"

They both nodded their heads, it made sense now. Despite the age difference we were very similar.

"Girls, I love you more than anything and I promise you have nothing to worry about ."

The girls both looked at each other and then me.

"Okay." they sniffled.

"Anyway, you two are best friends, there's no need to argue. Hug and make up, please."

They gave each other a massive hug and said sorry to the other and we all continued watching the new and updated Postman Pat.

* * *

The girls were still grateful for me although tonight they were grateful for me giving them cheese sticks when mum said they couldn't have them which got me into trouble, but it was worth it. I then proceeded to say I was grateful for Elise's honesty. This stupid little tradition became something that I started enjoying, it gave us time to talk to each other and say positive things. It made us all a little more honest with each other, even if it got me into trouble. Even mum was starting to like it I could tell. She never told me, but she didn't need to, I could tell she was happier.

"They're really good at talking now." I commented to mum.

"Yeah, they're really good. The schools have been helping them a lot, apparently, they have the

learning age of 8-year-olds which I thought was brilliant."
Mum smiled. I always knew the girls were special, and it
wasn't just because I was their sibling and undoubtedly
biased but also because it was obvious, at two they were
talking and communicating like they were four, they were
always more mature especially Elise. Elise had this
intelligence about her that I hadn't seen before, and
Callie's competitiveness allowed her to remain at a similar
pace.

"You were the same, " mum added as I helped
her dry the dishes.

"Well, let's hope they don't get what I have" I
sighed.

"You know it doesn't define you, right?" Mum
asked and for a moment I had to think about it because to
me my OCD did define me, it said everything for me.

"Sure." I answered. "Unless you count the not
sleeping or the constant fear. Of course, if not defining
me includes not being able to hold a handrail without the
urge to wash my hands until they bleed, or every time the
girls want to play in the playground I can't go because I
wouldn't let them on the slide or on the swings. My
OCD docs define me, it's the reason I am the way I am,
and nothing is going to change that."

Mum had stopped washing up and was now facing
me, the tea-towel on her shoulder and her hands on my
arms. "Sure, OCD stops you from doing things, it's
something that I can't understand because I don't have it.
It's something that I only research to better understand but I
will never get it. However, I know one thing. It doesn't
define you. You're Tom, the boy who stepped up and
looked after his sisters even though he wasn't asked too.
He's the one who at six years old fell down the stairs because
he was so excited to see his grandparents and had

to spend three weeks with a cast on. He's the one who made me laugh when I felt like crying. That's you Tom, that's what defines you. Your OCD is something you're battling but it doesn't define you. And even if it did, that's not a bad thing. You're able to not only live a life like other people, but also battle something that is in your head, that other people can't physically see and your kicking ass. You need to give yourself more credit than you do."

Mum pulled me into a hug, and it was the first time in ages that I felt human connection. I felt something from that hug, and it was nice. For that moment I didn't think about the germs or diseases I could catch, I just thought about how long she was going to hug me for and if it could last longer.

"I will always love you, remember that." Mum told me.

"Even if I was a murderer?" I asked her, pulling away from the hug before I began to cry.

"Well, that would be a difficult one, it would depend on the reason for killing, like if you killed someone because they hurt family, I'd still love you but if it was just hundreds of people for no reason, I don't think so. Although I don't think I'd ever not love you, I could be angry and disappointed with you and maybe even hate you but my heart, my soul would still carry that love." She chuckled.

Mum and I spoke for a while until Elise came downstairs asking me to read them a book. When I sat down in their room, they informed me they wanted me to read something new, so I went into my room and picked a book from my selection.

"Right girls, I think you're both ready for my favourite book series of all time, this is called Harry Potter and the Philosopher's Stone."

They both got excited, they had only ever seen bits of the first movie because mum thought it would be too scary for them to watch. I wasn't impressed but I listened to what she said, I didn't want to disagree. However, I feel like now is the right time to read the book to them, I mean the first book came out when I was their age.

"Settle down girls because you're going to be engrossed in the magical journey of Harry Potter."

Both girls led down in their bed and squirmed around until they were comfortable. I opened the book and started reading. I didn't stop until I found myself dozing off. I looked up at the girls who were fast asleep and wondered how long I had been reading to myself.

"Oh, I didn't realise you were still in here." Mum whispered as she peeped her head round the door.

"Yeah, I don't know when they fell asleep, what's the time anyway?" I asked in a hushed tone.

"Well, it's 9:30pm so they've probably been asleep for an hour." Mum told me, I stood up from the chair bringing the book with me, I didn't want the girls destroying it, as I left the room I looked back once more. The girls were both fast asleep.

"I can't believe I was reading to myself for an hour. " I laughed quietly to mum as we stood outside the girl's room.

"It's nice to see you so peaceful." Mum smiled. "Goodnight, Tom." She kissed me on the cheek.

"Goodnight, mum."

I looked around my room, it was bare. My room was always bare, I didn't like things on my wall or cluttered over my desk so I kept very little, I always felt the more stuff I had in my room the more my mind would be cluttered, so I got rid of the clutter. Of course, it didn't work, well not completely. It felt similar to being at the hospital, like it was mine but also not, and I didn't know why but I quite liked that. It was the same feeling of how you tend to sleep better when you're on holiday. My room was my own escape and that was why no-one was allowed in my room, even the girls. I didn't have photos hanging up on the wall, I didn't have lots of clothes lying around. I had what I liked to call a hotel room. It was basic but it was functional, it did exactly what I wanted for a bedroom. It allowed me to sleep. The only thing I had on my walls was one maths poster that mum bought me when I turned 18. She believed I was going to go to university to do a Maths Degree, unfortunately that didn't happen, but I didn't want to get rid of the poster.

I still didn't want to, it's not like I was ever going to become a maths teacher or a scientist but maybe I could do something more creative. I enjoyed writing. Maybe I could write a book. Maybe I could write a book about my OCD, or maybe the hard reality of OCD might put people off. So many people think OCD was just cleaning and liking things in a straight line, they always used the expression "I'm so OCD" whenever they were about to say something that they liked to do revolving cleaning or organising. THAT'S NOT OCD. I got sick and tired of having to explain to people that they didn't have OCD just because they liked their pencils to be aligned. I had to explain to people that that was fine until you were doing those things because your brain was telling you, you have to. That something terrible was going to happen unless you did that compulsion. People didn't seem to get it. They thought it was cool and edgy to have a mental illness, but they didn't realise that there was a difference between being depressed and having depression. It didn't make them cool, or quirky or edgy having a mental health disorder. They were making it look bad for everyone else, for the ones who genuinely struggled to live with it, day in, day out. They made it look like a trend on social media, which made it harder to be taken seriously.

* * *

I abruptly woke up to the sound of the girls stomping down the stairs and screaming. It took me a moment or two to realise that I had fallen asleep on my chair and not in my bed. I looked around on my desk, but I couldn't recall what I was doing before I fell asleep. I stood up slowly still staring at my desk hoping for the memory to come back but it didn't, last night was a blur. I got myself together and headed downstairs, it had been a week since I left the ward and my next session with Dr. Sanford was at 11am.

When I walked into the kitchen the girls were chewing on their toast, jam smeared across their faces. "Nom..Nom..Nom" the girls chomped away.

"You two are such noisy eaters" I laughed.

"Hey mum" I smiled. Mum smiled back; she was too busy making the girls lunches to talk. I looked around at the kitchen and it was messier than usual, mum must have been up for most of the night as well. Her laptop opened with the wire plugged in, the coffee cup left next to it and the two dirty plates in the sink suggested she'd gotten up early to do some work.

"Mum, you need to slow down, you're going to end up killing yourself."

Mum looked at me with a stern expression.

"You know what I mean" I added. "Can't you ask work for a day off, maybe we could all go to the Lookout, the girls haven't been there for ages. It would be nice for them if we all went out together." I looked at mum who had dark bags under her eyes and a coffee stain on her pyjama top.

"I'll ask."

I went over to the kitchen table, picked up the mug and put it into the sink. I then shut down mum's laptop and put it in her bag ready for work.

"Hey mum," I shouted out just as she left the kitchen, she groaned and walked back.

"What?" she asked.

"No, nothing," I answered, mum already looked tired enough without me having her worried about my new memory loss.

"No. What is it?" Mum asked looking both concerned and tired at the same time.

"I don't want you to worry or anything and I'm fine, honestly, I feel great but this morning I woke up and I had slept on my chair, which isn't unlikely, but I don't remember how I got to my desk last night. The last thing I remember is sitting on my bed and that's it." I told her.

"Sometimes memory loss happens with new medication. You're seeing Dr Sanford today, right?" She asked and I nodded my head.

"Ask him, I'm sure it's just a side effect of the meds, talking of, you haven't had them this morning." She stopped talking, walked over to my box of meds and unpicked everyone. Since I got home mum had been watching me take my meds, no matter how often I told her that I would take them, I think she just wanted to make sure.

In the short period I had been home, the girls decided to decorate my medicine box, they placed as many stickers around the box as possible. There were fairies and princesses, there were stars and hearts all over it, and I loved it. When they first showed me what they did mum wasn't too impressed, but I couldn't stop smiling over it. It was a reminder as to why I took the pills. I wasn't just doing this for me, I was doing it for them, so they could have their brother around.

It didn't take long for mum to get ready, and because my appointment was in the morning both mum and I walked the girls to School. On the school walk, Elise told me how she had two boyfriends, one was in her class and one in Callies class. She told me how she was thinking of breaking up with them because she didn't love them anymore. I laughed and told her that she was too young to be in love and she definitely shouldn't have one boyfriend let alone two. I looked at mum who was too busy holding in her laughs to agree with me. Callie then explained that she didn't love any boys and just wanted to play hopscotch but had no-one to play with, this made me feel sad for her. Knowing that Callie was so young and yet kids were being mean to her. Callie walked ahead but I held Elise back for a second.

"Hey, I need you to do me a big favour?" I asked Elise whose attention was all on me. "I need you to play with Callie, she seems sad, and we don't want her to be sad, do we?"

Elise shook her head. "No, she's my best friend" she told me and skipped off to catch up with Callie. Mum hugged both the girl's goodbye and walked over to me.

"It's a good thing they're twins, they'll always have a best friend" I said.

I left mum at the bus stop, mum had work at home today so she didn't need to go into work but thought it would be nice for us all to walk to the school together.

"I love you." Mum told me, and I repeated it back to her. I got onto the bus and sat at the front, knowing that the front of the bus was normally cleaner than the back. It helped me to use the techniques I used with Dr Sanford. The bi-weekly task of pressing the button and holding onto the bar while controlling the impulsions were made easier with the new medication I was taking. It didn't feel like a whole monster was inside of me screaming; it felt more like a small niggle. When it was time to get off at the hospital I pressed the button, stood up just as the bus was pulling in and held onto the handle, I waited for the bus to stop all the way before making my way to the front, thanking the driver and then getting off. Once I stepped off the bus, I looked down at my hands. They felt dirty, it's like I could see the germs on them, and the thoughts came;

You need to wash them. What if you get germs? What if you give them to your sister?

As the thoughts came, I took a deep breath and walked inside. The thoughts were still there but I distracted myself, I looked at the Coffee shop and focused on the people, I looked at the family whose kids were asleep across the chairs and the parents were holding hands. I looked at the elderly couple who were laughing and joking. I looked at the woman who was silently crying by herself. I looked at all these different people who were at the hospital for a number of different reasons and suddenly I didn't feel so alone. I didn't feel so scared. The thoughts subsided and in that moment, I felt like my problems were so trivial. I felt a bit embarrassed.

I headed to Dr. Sanford's office, I knew the hospital's layout so well I could recall it with my eyes shut. When I got to Dr Sanford's office I waited outside, I was 20 minutes early as I always was, so I knew that he was still going to be with his previous patient. It must have been only 10 minutes later when his door opened but no patient came out.

"Early as always, Tom," he remarked. "My mother always says it's better to be 20 minutes early than five minutes late." I smiled and walked in. I took a seat in my usual. "So, I took the bus today" I told him just after he took a seat.

"Oh, really? how did that go?"

"It was difficult, but I did what we did in the training, I pushed the button and held onto the handle."

"That's great news Tom, that's a massive step, but you don't seem so happy about it?"

It took me a second to realise that no I wasn't.

"Because it's so trivial, like there are people out there with Cancer, there are kids out there dying of illnesses and they're braver than I am. I can't touch a handle without thoughts in my head but a six-year-old kid is able to go through chemotherapy and lose their hair. I just feel weak, something so small that is an everyday thing and shouldn't concern me whatsoever, takes over my life. I feel weak."

Dr. Sanford looked at me for a moment "Just because your pain is different it doesn't make it invalid. Just because someone in this hospital is suffering something physically worse than you, it doesn't mean that your pain is void. You are allowed to feel the way you do despite worse going on in this world. Your pain is still valid, Tom." I looked at Dr. Sanford, but my eyes began to water, and my voice became scratchy. "Real men don't

207

feel like this" I told him "I'm not a man, I'm weak."
Clearing my throat to avoid crying.

"Fuck that." Dr. Sanford declared which shocked
me. "If real men don't have feelings or emotions then I'm
not a real man. Real men feel things just like women and
they talk about it just like women. This ideation of men
not being able to talk is exactly why male suicide is the
highest cause of death in men in their 40's." Dr. Sanford
stopped for a moment and took a deep breath; I could
tell that he had told this to a lot of men. "The Real men
that you're talking about is old news, real men are just
men. You could be a feminine man and still be a man. If
you identify as a man, you're a man. It's as simple as that.
You need to stop torturing yourself, you won't recover if
you don't."

I didn't know what to say. It was the first time
that Dr Sanford had ever swore, he seemed genuinely
upset about what I said so I changed the topic quickly.

"I think my meds caused memory loss; well, my
mum thinks it could be the meds. I don't remember
going to sleep last night and I woke up in my chair, not
in my bed."

Dr. Sanford looked down at his notes. "Yes. A
side effect of your medication is memory loss, it's not
massively common however it should subside in the next
couple of weeks. Let me know if it keeps happening
though as we may need to change your medication again
or at the least change the dosage." The last thing I wanted
was for my medication to change again, I didn't want the
side effects that I had from my other one, I didn't want to
hallucinate again but I didn't want to keep getting memory
loss. I guess I would have to wait and see.

"Tom, you're making great progress, you should
be really proud of yourself. This time, what almost a year

ago now you first came in and you were completely different. Your vocalisation of your feelings and emotions has improved massively and because of that it's allowed you to start getting better. Just keep at it and you never know this time next year you might have that life that you wanted" Dr. Sanford smiled.

"How's home life?" He asked.

"It's okay, I asked mum to take a day off so that we could spend the day as a family, she said she was going to ask, so that's good." Dr Sanford looked at me. "It seems you're not the only one who changed recently, it seems like your mum is spending less time working."

"Not really, I don't think she's sleeping properly so she gets up and works instead. I asked her to take a day off specifically so she could relax for one day, without that she works six days a week." I always felt guilty for mum having to work so much, I knew that she would never tell me that I was the reason she worked so much but it was hard not to feel guilty whether I had an illness or not.

"I always feel guilty, I know that mum didn't care. I know that she just wants me to get better but it's hard to not feel completely guilty knowing that if I was okay then she wouldn't have to work so much because I'd give her another income." The mention of my mum caused tears to roll down my face. Dr. Sanford passed me some tissues.

"You know Tom, guilt is something everyone feels, it's a natural emotion, but it's what we do with our guilt that defines us. What do you think your mum would want you to do with it? Do you think she would want you to continually feel the guilt and let it slowly eat away at you or do you think she would want you to use it for your own benefit? To use it as your strength to heal, to let yourself heal?"

I looked down at my feet, I suddenly felt 18 again. I felt like I did the day I woke up and dad had disappeared in the night. The day mum told me he'd gone and wasn't coming back. I felt that same pain again.

"You're good." I laugh with tears running down my face. I picked up a tissue.

"I know what mum would want but I can't just change my mindset."

Without hesitation Dr Sanford answered, "you don't have to change your mindset, sometimes you just have to ignore it, you did well today ignoring your thoughts. It's a similar process."

Dr. Sanford had a way with words, I guess 25 years of being a psychiatrist had given him a few words of wisdom, well maybe more than a few words. Our session was ending, I stood up, but Dr. Sanford asked me to sit back down.

"I don't have another patient for two hours, but I feel like I need to share some information with you." I sat down wondering what he was going to say, he seemed a lot more serious compared to five minutes ago.

"Last week when we were doing your leaving interview you asked if someone died."

I interrupted him "oh god who died? Don't tell me it was John, he was different, but he was kind to everyone. It's not John, is it?"

Dr. Sanford didn't reply straight away. "I'm sorry Tom it was Grace, she took her own life."

I looked down at my hands and clenched my jaw.

"Well, it's what she wanted, we couldn't have stopped her." I told him, surprised at my own words.

"You don't mean that."

"Of course, I don't mean it but what can I say? I knew her for what, two weeks, it's not like we were best friends, I hardly knew her." I found myself getting wound up, not with Dr. Sanford but with Grace. I couldn't believe that she would do something so stupid. I thought she was going to make it. She told me she was going to try and now she's gone, am I going to end up like that?

Am I going to end up just as broken again and find no way out?

My breathing became staggered, my heart began beating faster.

"Tom, breath. Focus on three things and breath." And without hesitation I did.

I looked at the bookshelf and how half of his books were showing the spine and the other half showing the cover. I always thought it looked odd. I looked out at the window at the carpark and focused on the cars coming in and out. I looked at Dr. Sanford who had gotten from his chair and sat next to me on the sofa. I took a few deep breaths and then I was fine.

"Well done Tom you did great." Dr. Sanford smiled at me.

"Why do I keep getting panic attacks? I never experienced them until recently. Why?"

"Except the fact that you have OCD there isn't any real answer to that, Tom. There's no real scientific evidence as to why someone may experience panic attacks suddenly. I mean there's stress factors, genetic factors, other mental health factors but no definite answer."

I thought for a second before replying "So it's like having a snotty nose, sometimes it's just a snotty nose, there's no major factor for it but sometimes that snotty nose is because you have a cold. I guess it's just waiting to find out if you get the other symptoms or not."

He smiled "I couldn't have put it better myself"

Dr Sanford and I spoke for another half an hour. We spoke about how I felt despite hearing the news. He asked if I wanted to talk about anything and even asked if he wanted me to call my mum to get me. I laughed at that request, I told him I wasn't five and that I would be okay getting the bus. I told him that it might even help, with the button pressing and handle holding. I told him that I really did want to get better, and I wanted to live a more normal life, I think he knew I was telling the truth. I did get the bus home and I did press the button and hold the handle and I did continue to think about the families in the coffee shop, but I also remembered what Dr Sanford said to me and I continued to do things that my OCD would tell me not to do.

When I got home, mum asked how it was and I just hugged her.

"Bad Day?"

I nodded. "Do you remember Grace from the hospital?"

"The loud one, the one that hung out with the two guys?" I nodded again.

"Dr Sanford told me that she committed suicide last week."

Mum looked annoyed. "Why did he tell you that about another patient?" She asked.

"Because he knew we were close when we were in the ward, I got a little attached to her, so he thought I should know." I explained. "Mum he did the right thing, I would have wanted to know. Even if it wasn't her, if John had killed himself. I would have wanted to know as well." I knew I was trying to convince her, but she wasn't going to be convinced.

"Well, what if it puts you in a bad way?"

"I can't go my whole life avoiding negative things, the only way I can learn to cope is by those things happening. Like after Dr. Sanford told me he asked me if I wanted you to pick me up, I told him no and that I'd get the bus. I got the bus, ignored the intrusive thoughts and was able to take a normal journey. I wouldn't have been able to do that a couple of weeks ago" I told her and grabbed her into another hug "mum I promise I'll tell you if I start getting bad again. I don't want to go back to the ward for a third time. I don't want to end up like John."

I wasn't lying when I told mum I wanted to be more honest, I really did, I knew that that was the only way that I could move on and become better in myself was if I was honest, not only with my family but with myself as well. When I thought about it, I knew that I was getting worse last time, I knew what was happening, but I wanted to ignore it in hopes that it would go away. I guess I thought it was a blip or it wasn't like it was before, so it was okay but being honest with myself, I knew that the obsessions were coming back. I hoped they would go away, I hoped that I would be able to brush it under the rug and it would work.

I will say this, if you know something is happening, if you know and you're choosing to ignore it, don't. It won't go away; it will keep happening and it will get worse and then one day it will be too late to do something.

* * *

On Saturday I borrowed mum's car and took Mikcy and I out. We couldn't do anything major because we were both broke, so we ended up driving to the lookout and trying to get a tan. The British weather stopped us from getting an actual tan, but we enjoyed relaxing for a bit. Mikey and I didn't talk about the stuff that was going on with us, we knew the basics. He knew that I was continuing therapy and taking it slow, and I knew that he had managed to get a council flat and started getting Working Tax Credits, but we never went into detail. It was something we never did massively anyway, we weren't the kind of people to talk about our feelings and I didn't mind it. We were back to how we used to be and having that kind or normality made everything else a little bit easier.

"How's Sammy?" Hopefully now Mikey had his own place then they would start things up again.

"His dad sent him to the Army Reserve. He told him it was that or living with his dad for the rest of his life and his dad beating the homo out of him" Mikey started kicking grass on the ground.

"Oh" is all that I managed to get out.

"What his dad didn't realise, is that there's a lot of 'homos' in the army so he'll be fine." Mikey said putting the words homo in air quotes.

I felt sorry for him, Mikey and Sammy were good together, they would bicker, but they never had a proper argument. They truly loved each other and just because of Sammy's dad it was completely ruined.

"Why can't people just accept what their kids are? Why do parents feel the need to change them to how they want them to be?" I asked Mikey who shrugged.

"Do you want to get revenge?" I asked Mikey whose ears perked up.

"Always" he answered and with that we made a plan.

Revenge wasn't the answer, I knew that, but beating up a homophobic father might give us a little bit of satisfaction. I mean he did all that, he beat Sammy up all because of the fact that he loved men not women. I didn't know if it was the new meds or the fact that I hated seeing Mikey like this but I had this new lease of life and I wanted to make Mikey feel better.

"We can't just walk up to his house and beat him up. He knows a load of the police officers around here. He'd have us arrested in 10 minutes. We need to be stealthy; we need to get him when he's on his own. Make it look like a mugging or something"

"You've thought a lot about this," I laughed. I was slightly concerned he had a plan to murder him.

"I've watched a lot of movies and besides it's like the only way we won't get caught."

I nodded. Mikey was a connoisseur when it came to movies, specifically action ones so I believed him. It was kind of hard not too, I didn't have a better plan. Mikey and I decided we would do it next Saturday when Sammy's dad would be down the pub. We thought we'd wait until he was on his way home and a bit tipsy.

Mikey was thrilled about the plan, and I was until I got home, and mum asked me what Mikey and I had done for the day. I couldn't tell her that we'd planned to attack a man who attacked his son and then sent him away. Mum wouldn't understand, this man could have murdered someone, and she would always tell me that violence didn't end violence. I would normally agree with mum, but it was the way Mikey was that I had to go through with the plan. I had to. I was in too deep; I'd convinced Mikey and he wouldn't change his mind like I did.

* * *

The week leading up I did all my normal things. I took the girls to school; I went to my session with Dr. Sanford, and I helped mum around the house. It was a

215

completely normal week except for the fact that every minute of every day I was just thinking about what I was doing. I kept thinking about how stupid I was to even try to convince Mikey that this was a good idea but what could I do? If I backed out now Mikey would call me a 'pussy', he would end up going by himself and end up getting beat up not do the beating up. But what if I went and Sammy's dad got seriously injured? I mean I hated the guy, but I didn't want a prison sentence for a bit of revenge. I knew this was something that I should talk to Dr Sanford about but how could I tell him that I had planned to beat someone up without sounding like a complete mentalist.

On Friday, I took the girls to school and went straight to see Dr Sanford. It was just one day until it was going to happen, and I didn't know if I could go through with it. I entered Dr Sanford's office and sitting next to him was a man "ah Tom, this is Dr Goodall, he's the outpatient therapist on Flook Street, he's the one you'll be seeing soon" I looked at this guy, he didn't look much different from Dr Sanford except from age and a freshly shaved face. I wondered if he shaved that to meet his new patients? To make himself look more approachable? Maybe he preferred to be clean shaven. Who was I to judge, I could hardly grow a moustache let alone a full beard.

"Nice to meet you." I glanced, between Dr. Goodall and Dr. Sanford.

"Tom, why don't you take a seat?" Dr. Sanford spoke and so I did. We all sat down, Dr. Sanford and I in our usual seating positions and Dr. Goodall sat on the spare chair in the corner of the room. He looked slightly menacing, he was in the room but in the distance, it felt like I was in the room with a mob boss.

216

"So, Dr Goodall is going to sit in the room with us, he's not going to intervene, he's just a fly on the wall. Pretend he's not there." Dr Stanford said, which made me chuckle.

"He looks like a typical film villain sitting in the corner." I replied. "No offence," I quickly added

"None taken." Dr. Goodall responded. I knew that just like Dr. Sanford, Dr. Goodall just wanted to help but I didn't trust him yet. Dr. Sanford and I's relationship was all based on trust, I trusted that he knew what he was doing. I trusted that what he was saying was from experience and I trusted he knew what he was talking about. I had been seeing him for so long that I trusted he would give me the best advice and help me out to the best of his abilities, and I trusted that he would be honest with me. Dr. Goodall and I didn't have that trust, I had met him five minutes previously so of course I wasn't going to trust him.

"How have the last few days been?"

"It's been alright. I've just been at home, I've taken the girls to school for the last couple of days, with mum obviously. I don't think she still completely trusts me."

"How does that make you feel?" Dr Sanford asked.

"Annoyed." I said simply. But Dr. Sanford was waiting for more. "My issue isn't endangering the girls, it's the opposite so the simple walk to school should be fine for me but mum didn't allow me to do it. She wanted to be there, like all the time" I told him.

"Do you think maybe she's doing it less for the girls and more for herself?"

I looked at Dr. Sanford confused. "What do you mean?"

"Well do you think that maybe your mums wanting to make sure you don't end up back in hospital?" I sat there for a while wondering if Dr Sanford could be right.

"Yeah maybe, I know she's always worried about everything, it would make sense."

"Have you tried discussing it with her?" Dr. Goodall commented.

"Yeah, it wouldn't work. She would continue doing it anyway."

I thought Dr. Goodall was going to remain quiet the entire time, but it seemed that he was already wanting to get involved. I don't think Dr. Sanford was massively impressed as he gave Dr Goodall a slight glance, raised and lowered his eyebrows and then looked back at me.

"Apart from that is there anything else that's been happening this week?" He asked.

"Not really" which I thought would be a good enough answer and then we would be able to move on.

"What do you mean, not really?" He pressed.

"Well, I saw Mikey, it was nice but apart from that it's the same stuff, different day." "How did you feel seeing Mikey?"

"Yeah, it was nice, we went out for a bit, it was nice to see him."

"It's good that you are interacting with your friends again, Tom."

At the end of the session Dr. Sanford explained that from next week I would be seeing Dr. Goodall. He explained that he would still be available if I wanted to see him. "You're doing great Tom, and I know it's quite soon, but I think you're ready for outpatient." He explained that because it was a reference from him, that I wouldn't need to pay for the counselling that I would be doing sessions with Dr. Goodall until the service then became a voluntary thing that I chose to do.

"Take your time. Allow yourself to heal and you'll do brilliantly Tom." Dr Sanford smiled. Despite the news being good, I felt sad. I knew that unless I got worse again then I wouldn't see Dr. Sanford and I didn't want to get bad again.

"Do you mind waiting outside for one sec?" I asked Dr. Goodall.

"Of course," he answered and left.

"What's up Tom?" Dr Sanford asked, but before I could say anything I pulled him into a hug.

"I just wanted to say thanks. You've really helped me massively. Thank you." I answered, tears rolling down my face.

"You should be so proud of yourself Tom; you've come so far." And with that the tears came. I shook Dr Sanford's hand, wiped my tears away from my face and then headed out of the door.

"See you next week." I said to Dr. Goodall and left the hospital.

Dr Sanford was an amazing Doctor, he really did help me and, in the year, or two that I had gotten to know him, he was always honest with me, he always told me how it was, even if it didn't benefit me. Even if it might have hurt my feelings to start with. He did what was best for me. He was the dad that I didn't have when I needed one the most.

* * *

When I got home, I noticed an unfamiliar voice in the kitchen. As I headed towards the kitchen a man in his late 30's early 40's with grey hair and thick glasses was sitting on one of the dining room chairs. Mum was sitting with him laughing. When she heard the floorboard creak, she turned around and quickly got up.

"Hey Tom, how was today?" She asked, but all I could do was look at this man, he looked so familiar.

"It was good, who's this?"

"Oh, this is Charles he's an electrician." He stood up and went to shake my hand. "You're Sammy's dad."

"I'm sorry?" He said.

"You're Sammy's dad, I met you at your house." "I'm sorry kiddo, I don't have kids."

I knew I was right. I was right. "Yes, you do. You kicked Sammy out." I raised my voice.

"Tom, living room NOW." Mum murmured. I walked into the living room. "Mum, listen."

"No, you listen Tom. I know it's difficult for you, but I actually like this man. He might look like Sammy's dad, but he isn't. He said he wasn't, and I believe him."

This only infuriated me even more.

"I met him, I spoke to him, and I'll prove it." I went to walk past mum, but she held her arm up against the door.

"No, you won't."

"Fine. but I'm staying in the living room and listening closely."

I listened to them chat all day and for most of the evening, mum was laughing along to whatever he was saying, and soon my anger started to disappear because I realised that this man made my mum happy. He made her laugh like nobody else did, and that was the least she deserved for what she had to give up raising three kids by herself. Maybe I was wrong, maybe he wasn't Sammy's dad, but I knew one thing.

I had to cancel the attack on Sammy's dad/Charles just in case. I left the house slowly shutting the door on the way out. I didn't know what I was going to say to Mikey, how was I going to explain why we couldn't do it. I tried thinking of something else to tell him. Maybe that he had gone out of town or that I had to look after the girls, but I knew with both of these he would come, and check and I knew I couldn't tell him I backed out because he would go do it anyway. I had to tell him the truth. I called Mikey

"Yo Tom, whatsup?" he answered a couple of seconds later.

"Yo, mate we gotta cancel Saturday." I told him
"Wait, why?"

"I know it's gonna sound mad, but I think Sammy's dad is dating my mum."

All I heard in the background was, "oh shit," and then silence.

"Yo Mikey."

"Yeah sorry man, ummm, shit, what's your mum said? You told her, right?" He asked.

"Well, that's the problem, he's denying it. He said he doesn't have kids."

I could hear how angry Mikey was getting. "That fucker, he's a dead man walking, I'm telling you. Is he still at your house?"

I didn't know whether to tell him the truth or to lie, the last thing I needed was a fight in the front garden.

"Na he's left now, look he knows what I look like. We can't do the attack." I told him.

"No, you can't do the attack, but I still can." Mikey said and before I could ask anything he was hanging up the phone. I tried calling back, but he kept letting it go to voicemail.

I headed back inside, as I came into the door, he was standing there putting his coat on, mum was in the kitchen putting the glasses into the sink.

"I know your Sammy's dad and when mum does, you're gone. She didn't take too well to homophobic pricks."

Charles finished putting his coat on and then turned to me "Okay you got me, but listen I like you mum a lot, so that truth ain't ever getting out. I'll put you back in the ward before you've got the chance to even prove that I did what you said. So why don't you make it easy for everyone." He smirked and headed back into the kitchen

"It was so nice to see you Maeve, hopefully I'll see you soon." he said, and gave her a peck on the cheek. I walked into the living room and sat on the sofa. "Bye Tom, it was nice to meet you." Charles added, smiling and winking at me.

When he left, mum and I had an argument, I tried explaining to her that I wasn't being paranoid, I didn't mistake him, and I wasn't being over cautious. I knew that that man was Sammy's Dad, he told me it was him and that's when I told her that Mikey was out for revenge. I told her everything about the plan and that if Charles came back with any marks on his face, any bruises, scratches, anything then it was proof that Charles was Sammy's dad.

"I want you to be happy mum but not with a man like Sammy's dad. Not with that monster." I told her and stormed upstairs. Luckily the girls were out with our grandparents for the night, they were having a sleepover, I guess mum thought it was a good idea for the girls to be out when he came round for the first time.

I tried calling Mikey again and again, all through the night. I couldn't sleep, worrying about what was happening. I felt terrible knowing that he could be getting seriously injured right now but I couldn't do anything. I rang Mikey until 3am and then gave up. I knew Mikey well enough to know that he would still be going ahead with the plan and that chances were that he was already in A&E with bruises all over his body. I didn't sleep that night, not properly at least. If I wasn't thinking about Mikey, I was thinking about what Charles said to me, about having the power to send me back. I imagined being stuck in there forever like John. I must have fallen asleep for a few hours because I had a dream, where I was old and grey and still in the ward. It felt like a nightmare, and it felt like I was stuck in between doing what was right and doing what was easy.

Chapter Eight

"So how did you feel?" Dr. Goodall asked. I sat in silence. I didn't know what to say, what could I say?

"I don't know." I told him because I didn't.

"Okay are you angry at him for what he did?" I was, yes. "I guess, but at the same time it's not my life." I answered.

"Not directly no, it isn't but he is part of your life, which means that it does affect yours." Dr. Goodall wrote something down in his journal and looked back at me.

"Tom, I know you don't trust me as much as you did Dr. Sanford but if this is to work you need to work with me."

I looked down at the ground. "Okay, okay. Yes, I'm angry, I told him not to go and he went anyway and now he's in hospital because of something I planned in the first place. So yes, I'm pissed off at Mikey but I'm ashamed of myself. I'm normally the one that can control everything, I'm the sensible one. I knew it was a bad idea and I told him anyway. He's in the hospital because of me."

Dr. Goodall suggested upping my medication due to the stressful events that took place however I refused.

"I want to feel this, I don't want this to go away. I need to remember the domino effect of my actions, of my words. I need to work through this without adding medication."

Dr. Goodall sighed. "Okay it's your choice, I think it might be the wrong choice but it's your decision. Just know that if you think you're getting bad again, we can revaluate." He pulled out a business card. "Here's my number, you can call no matter what the time is, I'm here Tom." I took the card from him and put it into my pocket.

"Thanks" I whispered.

I left Dr Goodall's office feeling the same way I did when I entered his office. I knew it was only our first meeting and that I should give him time, but it was so hard when I was used to Dr Sanford. I mean if I would have known that Mikey would end up in hospital, I would have told Dr Sanford, maybe he could have helped me or told someone about me. I shouldn't have suggested going to Sammy's house. I knew even if I pulled out that Mikey would have gone, and I did nothing to stop him. I bet Charles didn't even have a scratch on him, he wouldn't have given Mikey the chance to move a step forward let alone take a swing at him. Of course, Charles lied to the police as well, I mean he knew half of them, so it wasn't hard to convince them.

From what I knew Charles told the police that Mikey was acting drunk, trying to fight him, Charles told him to leave several times, but Mikey didn't, and then Mikey started hitting him. Charles then defended himself, hit him twice and then ran inside to call the police but by the time he looked outside the police were already there. That was it, no court case, no jail sentence, not even community service. Nothing. And he had beat Mikey to a pulp.

So, while Mikey was in the hospital with a tube in his mouth, after the doctors had to do numerous tests to make sure he had no internal bleeding, Charles walked free and was about to go on a date with my mother. My mother who still didn't believe me. I told her to ask him about what happened, but he acted like he had no idea what I was talking about, and when I pushed him on it with mum in the room, he made a joke about it probably being the voices again. I didn't know how to react, I was annoyed that he would make a comment like that regardless, but I was angry that mum didn't say anything. She didn't stick up for me, she didn't say "oh Charles that's a bit far." She didn't say anything, she just sat there. I couldn't believe what I was seeing. The mum who had been there for me for so long now stood there while someone made a tasteless joke about my OCD. All this anger was boiling up inside of me and I knew that I couldn't do anything, I was defenceless. Sure, I could have fought and fought but where would it have gotten me? I'd probably end up back in the hospital myself but not in the ICU like Mikey, I would have been seeing Dr. Sanford again. If Charles had his own way, he'd get rid of me in a heartbeat, I was a threat to him, and he didn't like it. I was the only thing stopping him from having my mum.

I tried staying away from my house as often as I could, Charles spent more time in the house with mum and I didn't want to be there. I would often take the girls to school and then go for a walk; I would often walk around the local village seeing if there was anything interesting going on, but I was 24 so the most interesting thing I saw happening was a police car outside of the coffee shop. I did try to stay and listen to what was happening but there was a very aggressive lady being dragged out in handcuffs by two police officers. Despite the officer's strength they seemed to be struggling to hold on to her. I looked into the coffee shop and saw two girls, both seemed distressed, and I thought it was probably best to leave before my gawking became rude or creepy. I walked to the shops but had no money to buy anything, so I just looked around.

By the time I had walked around the village it was time for the girls to be picked up. I headed back to the school and collected them both. I'd already told mum that I would do it and she didn't seem to mind. The girls were so excited to see me they both ran up and wrapped their arms around me, which caused me to stumble and hit the concrete floor. They were clearly very excited to see me so I didn't mind them tackling me to the ground, in fact they would make great rugby players if they wanted to. "Are you girls ready to go home?" I asked them and they both jumped up and down with joy shouting, "YES! YES! YES!" Which made me chuckle. The girls held onto each one of my hands and we walked home, they both swung their hands creating an out of sync Mexican wave. The girls proceeded to tell me about school and how Callie was picked for Show & Tell next week. She told me she didn't know what to do so I suggested showing the class all the books they drew and wrote during the summer holidays. She liked that idea and couldn't wait to get home to go through them all.

When we got home, Charles had left, and mum was in the kitchen making Early Dinner for the girls. She was humming away and only stopped when the girls ran up and hugged her from behind.

"Hi girls, how was school?"

They repeated the same things that they told me but with more excitement.

"Umm, Tom, I need you to stay in with the girls tonight, I'm going out." she told me

"Well, I was going to go see Mikey, see if he's woken up yet. Can't your date with Charles wait?" I asked her, pinching a chip from the oven tray, and leaning against the kitchen counters.

"It's not a date with Charles, I'm..umm..I'm meeting a lawyer to talk about changing my name back."

I looked at her in horror. "Wait what? Change your name? As in your last name?" I asked her, completely shocked that she'd ever think of it. I knew she hated my dad, but she always said she wasn't fussed, that it didn't mean anything to her, it was just a silly last name.

"Yeah, I think it's been long enough now and I'm ready to move on,"

227

"with Charles. You're moving on with Charles, aren't you?" I asked, knowing what the answer would be but not wanting to hear it.

"We're taking it slow but we both agreed it would be a good idea for me to change my name back to my maiden name and to actually file for divorce."

I couldn't believe what I was hearing "Oh so because Charles thought it was a great idea, you thought you would do it! I can't believe you! You've been seeing him less than three months and you're already doing whatever he says!" I raised my voice, but mum stayed a little too calm.

"Tom, I know this is hard for you, but I really like him. You need to let go of the fact that you think he's Sammy's dad, he isn't. He showed me his driving licence, he didn't have the same last name as Sammy." I was fuming, I was so angry I think even mum could see the steam coming out of my ears.

"There could be an easy explanation for the last name! It's him mum and the fact that you don't believe me or you're refusing too is infuriating. I tell you what, I'll stay as far out of your love life as possible but when he hurts you, and he undoubtedly will, given his track record, don't come crying to me because I won't be here." I walked away. I picked up my bag and jacket and walked out the house, I couldn't think, I was just so angry. Mum hadn't had a proper relationship since dad left six years ago and now in two months had gotten with an absolutely revolting bloke who was clearly lying about his identity and wanted to rush into things, Charles smelt of trouble but how could I make her believe me?

I could easily follow him around and photograph it and show mum but that was called stalking and I knew Charles would call the police on me and have me committed, for good. I just didn't know what to do except wait and hope he messed up somehow. Mum had to stay home now anyway, she couldn't go out with the girls and my grandparents were both busy, so she had no choice but to stay home. She would just have to re-book for a time when the girls were at school, she would have to book time off. I wasn't looking after the girls, not for this.

I just... I just couldn't sit by and watch my mum choose another shit guy who was only interested in ripping her heart out. I didn't know how mum could ever trust a bloke again after dad.

I didn't know what to do. I walked around for a while trying to calm down, but I couldn't help myself, I walked up to Sammy's house and as I went to knock on the door it opened and stood there was Charles with a big grin across his face.

"Hello Thomas, why don't you come in?" He smirked.

"No, I'm alright, you could be a murderer, and in all honesty that wouldn't surprise me." I told him grinding my teeth against each other.

"Thomas don't be silly. I'm not going to hurt you, I can't have two young people outside my house in one week, people might get the wrong impression." He spoke, waving his arm into his house. I didn't know whether it was the adrenaline or my own stupidity, but I entered.

"I need you to stop seeing my mum." I told him sternly.

"Thomas..."

"STOP calling me Thomas. You have no right to even say my name with what you did to Sammy." My voice was stern and serious, but my fists were clenched and shaking. He put his hands up as if admitting defeat but then said,

"Whose Sammy?" he chuckled.

"She's not here you don't have to pretend." I told him and automatically his attitude adjusted.

"Fine, but she already doesn't believe you, and she's already siding with me so how long do you think it's going to be until she believes everything I say?" His words were like a viper's bite, infecting my whole body, making my anger grow by the second.

"She won't believe you, one day you'll slip up and she'll see the real you." I said but he laughed.

"I've been pretty successful so far, Sammy's mum wasn't the first one either, I can be incredibly charming."

He spoke, adding a Cheshire cat size smile and at that moment I realised, Charles wasn't Sammy's Dad, he was his stepdad.

"Wait, why did Sammy always come over then? If Sammy wasn't yours, why did you let him stay?" I asked. Charles, he squinted his eyes for a second and then let off another one of his incredibly annoying grins.

"He wouldn't like anyone knowing this, but his mother is a junkie, she loves ruining her life with shots of Heroin or just about anything else. He stayed with me because it was better than that, but now the little shit has gone back. He's probably injecting as we speak, she was always a stupid slut."

"Why did you get with her in the first place?" I asked.

"At first it was by accident, we met in a bar, she got me a drink and we talked. Turns out her parents left her mega-rich after they died, and I thought she'd only waste it on drugs, so I thought I'd help myself out." As he was telling me, I couldn't believe what I was hearing, my face must have been giving it away because he then added. "Oh, what like you would be any different?"

"Yeah, literally everything you do, I would do the opposite way," I shouted, and he moved closer.

"Oh congratulations, you're one of them ethical people."

"Why are you with my mum then?"

"Oh, yeah no I actually like her, she's one of the rare women I meet that I do like. God knows how long it will last though, I mean you're cramping my style with this whole Sammy thing, and that Mikey kid... What a faggot"

He laughed. I couldn't speak at all; my whole body was burning with rage. "Aww what's up Tommy? Are you upset with me? You millennials are getting butt hurt by every joke that comes along."

I couldn't breathe let alone form a sentence. I knew what was happening and I had two options, I could control it and continue fighting or I could leave and avoid the potential embarrassment.

"Haha you youngens, so upset by everything, you didn't get OCB or whatever it's called back in my time, you dealt with it like a man you didn't go to therapy unless you were proper mental."

The more he was talking the harder I found it to control myself, my heart was pounding 100 times faster than was humanly possible.

I left before I could lash out, ignoring the taunts that Charles was bellowing behind me. I managed to drag myself to the nearby woods, where I leaned against an old oak tree and tried to steady my breathing. I used the same technique that I was taught by Dr Sanford, it helped but not massively, until I heard branches break beside me. I jumped a mile landing in the mud and looked around to see Sammy stood there, looking just as shocked to see me. I looked at him, his clothes were dirty, and his hair was scruffy.

"You scared the living daylights out of me." He finally said.

"Ditto."

"What are you doing out here?" He asked.

"Charles is seeing my mum; I went over to try stop him." I knew it sounded stupid, but I didn't realise how stupid it sounded until Sammy started laughing.

"Oh yeah? how is that working out?" He chuckled.

"I didn't really get round to asking properly, I had a panic attack and left." I told him feeling completely embarrassed.

"He's a dick, he knew I was gay before my mum did, before they broke up and he always said to me, if I ever find you doing that gay shit in my house you're dead, and well he wasn't completely wrong." Sammy confided.

"I didn't know that." I added, realising Sammy and I had never talked to each other about anything except Mikey.

"Yeah, we're not friends so why would I?" He answered, the truth stung, but he wasn't wrong.

"What happened? Mikey's been dying to see you."

"I was staying with my mum, but she overdosed and ended up in hospital so now I'm just trying to find somewhere to stay each night." I felt bad for Sammy, I knew I couldn't do much, mum was already incredibly angry at me she wouldn't allow me to have someone over, especially when that person's stepdad was going out with my mum, and she wouldn't believe me.

"Have you seen Mikey recently?"

"Come on let's go," I said and we both headed to the hospital.

I told Sammy in detail what had happened, I asked him if he had been to Mikey's new flat, and he said once but Mikey was off with him, so he didn't stay long. I told him about the plan and how I figured out that he was seeing my mum and then went there to try and get him to leave her. Sammy told me that no matter what happened he would do whatever he liked, he told me that at first Sammy had hesitations about Charles, but Charles told him that he loved Sammy's mum and would do anything for her until he allowed her to take drugs and then left when she needed him the most.

"He's like a cancer, at first you don't notice the small things, or you shrug them off thinking it's a one-time thing but then it gets worse and worse until he's infected the whole body and there's nothing left of that person." I didn't know what to say, Sammy and I had never been mates, we always only ever got along for Mikey's sake but damn I'd be lying if I didn't want to give him a massive hug right now.

"I'm sorry, I've never really made it easy for us to be mates. I'm sorry about that." I told him and he patted me on the shoulder.

"It's alright" he answered, and we continued walking in silence.

* * *

By the time we got to the hospital mum was already waiting in the car park, her hand was on her hip, and she looked pissed. I mean really pissed, I tried to look into the car to see if Charles was in there, but I couldn't see inside.

"He's in room 25, go to level 3, turn right and it's straight down the hall, a nurse should let you in. I'll meet you up there." I told Sammy and headed to meet mum at the car.

"What's going on with you?" Mum raised her voice.

"I went to see Charles earlier; I was angry at him for what he did with Sammy, but he said that he really liked you. I'm not going to get involved in your relationship mum." It felt like with each word I was swallowing glass.

"Thank you, that's very mature of you."

"But believe me when I say he is trouble. If he, sorry when, hurts you I will kick the living shit out of him." I added.

"Tom!" Mum gasped.

"I'm serious, one day he will show his true nature, and I won't let him do to you what he did to Sammy's mum."

Mum looked at me with raised eyebrows, which was all she could do because there was nothing more to say. She wasn't going to start an argument outside of a hospital, and she was never going to convince me that Charles was decent.

"Now I'm going to see Mikey." I told her. I was still fuming.

"Of course, and you're right Tom, about the name change. I think it's best to wait. I shouldn't change something because of a man, I should do it for myself."

"Okay."

I walked into Mikey's room about 20 minutes after Sammy, I could tell that they had been having a heart to heart as Mikey quickly coughed and wiped his face when he saw me. Mikey wasn't one to show emotion, but I could tell Sammy meant a lot to him, and if Sammy was the only person that made Mikey show his softer side then he was good for Mikey.

"Hey, how are you feeling?" I asked him as I walked into the room and stood at the foot of his bed.

"Yeah, I'm good" he answered but it was obvious he was still in discomfort.

"I'm sorry man, I shouldn't have suggested it." I told him but Mikey put his hand up.

"Mate, you told me not to, but I still did it, it's on me. It's just your mum's treated me like a son so many times, she treats me nicer than my own mum. So, when you said that he was seeing her I just saw red. I got angry thinking he'd do to her what he did to Sammy and me." I could see Mikey's eyes filling with tears.

I hated seeing Mikey like this, not the beaten-up part of him, Mikey was a tough cookie. I've seen him beat up loads of times but to see him upset, that was completely different. He didn't show his emotions at all when he was upset, he hid it thinking it was unmanly. I remembered asking him once why he didn't cry and he looked me dead in the eyes and said, "my family already think I'm a pussy for being gay, I don't want to prove it to them by being a wuss and crying."

I tried explaining to him that it was not more or less manly for crying but he didn't care, he was stuck with his parents' words in his head, and it was hard to change that.

I didn't stay long, I told Mikey that when he was feeling better to pop round, I told him that we would do it when the dick (Charles if that isn't obvious by now) wasn't there. I left Sammy and Mikey to talk everything through, they hadn't seen each other in so long that they had a lot to catch up on. Despite everything that happened I left the hospital feeling good, I mean if I hadn't confronted Charles and had a panic attack and then ran into the woods, I wouldn't have jumped into Sammy. We wouldn't have ended up in the hospital. Then they wouldn't be semi-back together. I felt like that one small choice led to this cascade of other things happening. I always thought like that when my OCD was bad, but I always saw it in a negative connotation, like doing one thing would lead to another worse thing but this time it was different. This time it wasn't a negative thing.

Chapter Nine

It's been about two months since Sammy, and I visited Mikey in hospital. He got sent home about three weeks after our visit. The doctor suggested that Mikey tried counselling, but Mikey didn't want to. He said he wasn't that kind of person, and I could understand that. He wasn't a massive fan of talking so for him I didn't think it would help either. Mikey was discharged with strict instructions not to do too much heavy work. I laughed at the thought of it, I hadn't seen Mikey do a hard day's work his whole life so that wasn't going to be hard to miss out on. Sammy moved in with Mikey as soon as Mikey was discharged, he used the excuse that he was going to look after him but two months later and he was still there. I was happy for him, for both of them, they seemed to be doing a lot better. I saw Mikey a couple of times and he seemed to be more of his usual self. I thought I'd never miss his sarcastic responses and slightly offensive jokes, but it was refreshing to hear, it meant things were starting to balance back out.

I was doing okay; I had been seeing Dr. Goodall every Friday for the last eight Fridays, we had been talking through my past, talking about things with my dad and how he left affected me, I knew that I spoke to Dr. Sanford about all that but Dr. Goodall wanted to go through it as well. He wanted to see if I missed out on anything or if talking about it helped me in a different way. It was Dr. Goodall's idea, and I went along with it. I was trying to stay more open minded when it came to therapy. I came to realise that with a new Doc it meant having to repeat things so that he could hear them. He wasn't a bad doctor, he was good, but he wasn't Dr. Sanford. Dr. Sanford was great, and I was sad about not having my therapy with him, but I realised it was a good sign. It meant that I was getting better, and I was able to control myself more.

Dr. Goodall told me that if I kept going to therapy and kept taking my meds then I could be cleared fit to go back to work. Obviously, I would have to find a job first seeing as my old job let me go. Mum told me that their reasoning was that I was off for too long in a short amount of time and they needed the member of staff. They said there were no hard feelings, but I didn't think they knew how to deal with me. They always gave me the easy jobs hoping I wouldn't go mad and have a breakdown in front of them. When I came back the first time they would scuttle away like mice when seeing a rat. I was a rat to them, I was someone they were scared or unsure of, they didn't want to get to know me enough to know the difference between my mental illness and my personality. They assumed my mental illness was my personality, that I was one of these quirky kids that would go around with a badge saying "oh look at me, I have OCD" but it wasn't like that, and they didn't take enough time to stop and talk to me. What I realised was that they didn't deserve me there, they didn't take the time to understand me and find out what I was good at, and for that, they didn't deserve me.

I spent weeks looking for jobs, I went onto a job website but the only things available were 48 hours plus or doing things I had no experience in. Mum suggested I tried writing blogs, she told me how good I was at writing and how much I enjoyed it but there wasn't any money in writing blogs, not unless I became one of those famous ones. Mum told me to write stories, to do a collection of children's stories and put them into one book. I liked that idea; I knew that I wouldn't make enough money and I knew I'd have to find a publisher but writing stories seemed like a great way to spend my day instead of spending it doing housework or watching tv. I remembered telling mum that I would start it that night and I ran up the stairs into my room. The excited writing phase lasted probably three days and then that excitement turned into frustration when the words no longer flowed out of me as easily as they had the previous days. I still continued writing but with a lack of words mixed with a lot of procrastination it was near impossible to write more than a few sentences.

The girls on the other hand loved my stories. I had written about four short stories in total and that was all they wanted me to read. I always brought in the Harry Potter books but they insisted on one of my own. At least I had two fans of my work and it was the only two fans that I needed. Callie would often tell me to tell her a new story and as I told her one from the top of my head she would go "no I want a new written story" which I had to inform her that I didn't have. I always planned on writing more stories, but I just never get around to it. I always ended up binge watching TV shows.

* * *

When I saw Dr. Goodall next, he asked me how I was getting on.

"Yeah, I'm doing good, not much has happened this week, there's not much to say really."

Dr. Goodall shuffled in his seat, "how do you feel about Charles staying over?"

When mum and I had the discussion at the hospital I thought it would be over with but they kept seeing each other, he would come round when the girls were at school, I would stay in my room, or I would go see Mikey, so I didn't have the chance to bump into him. I stayed out of her relationship, for as much as I could, until a week ago when Charles stayed the night. The girls were at our grandparents so mum thought it might be nice to have him round, to make a night of it. They went out for some food, so I thought it might be nice to relax at home and watch some films. They came back a couple of hours later.

I watched to the end of the movie and then went to head upstairs but mum had other plans, she cornered me in the hallway. "Why don't you come watch another movie with us? We'll watch whatever you want."

"Mum, I told you, you could do whatever you want with him, but I wasn't going to get involved."

I could see the sadness in her eyes. "You don't have to be friends Tom; I just want to spend time with both of you. You can pick out the movie." Mum looked at me and I sighed, "fine, but I'm having a smoke first." I told her and headed outside. Normally mum would be annoyed but I think she was just pleased that I said I would sit down with them for two hours. I went outside and lit up my spliff, I always had one saved in my baccy tin in case of emergencies. I started taking drags and very quickly felt the effects. I hadn't smoked in so long that by the first half I was already woozy. I dabbed out the rest of it and placed it back in my baccy tin for later.

When I headed back in, I sat down the furthest away from Charles, I could see he was looking at me, but I didn't want to give him the satisfaction of looking in his direction. I wanted to pretend he wasn't there at all. I picked up the TV remote and went onto Netflix, I knew what I wanted to watch. Spiderman but the original with Toby Maguire.

"We're watching a kid's film." Charles scoffed.

"Mum and I watched Spiderman all the time when I was younger, it's my favourite film. And it's not a 'kids' film." I snaped back.

Mum looked at Charles. "Don't be rude, it's a good movie."

I was taken back by the fact that mum had sided with me. I could see the rage in Charles' face as he realised that mum didn't take his side. I couldn't help but smirk knowing that he hadn't taken my mum's voice just yet.

The movie itself was as brilliant as the first day mum and I watched it in Cinema, the childhood nostalgia came back, and I was blown away by how good the CGI was despite it being an early 2000's movie. The company was a 5/10, Charles made snide remarks now and then, but I could see mum jab him in the side and shush him, which made me smile each time. I have to say at the end of the movie I felt better, I didn't like Charles more or even want to be in the same room as him again but seeing how mum stuck up for me and stood her ground, it made it easier to know. It was like I knew she would be able to stick up for herself and wouldn't let him walk all over her. I would still be weary; I would still check up on her and I would always put myself in the firing line if it was between her or me, but it felt like she might do okay. I obviously didn't tell her any of this when she joined me out in the kitchen. I just told her, "it's your life mum, I don't need to like him, in a couple of years I'll have moved out anyway, but if he ever touches you or the girls I need to know."

After the movie Charles spent the night, mum thought it would be a good idea. I couldn't sleep that night, knowing what he had done to Sammy and Mikey, I couldn't simply sleep. I stayed awake until I heard mum get up at seven and then I dozed off. I probably had about two hours sleep when the girls came home and woke me up with their screaming and shouting. I could tell Charles was still there because the girls were explaining what they did at grandma and grandpa's while also asking him several questions. They asked him who he was, why he was here, if he was mum's boyfriend, if they had kissed.

I got dressed and headed downstairs, the girls saw me and came screaming and shouting then telling me what they did last night.

"We went to the cinema! We watched the Peppa Pig Movie! Then we had ice cream!" The girls screamed and shouted, I just stood there half-asleep, nodding my head and pretending to sound incredibly interested in what they were saying. I looked in the front room and Charles was sitting on the Sofa with a cup of coffee in one hand and his phone in the other. I headed into the kitchen and the two little munchkins joined me, continuing to tell me about their night. They stopped when mum pulled out bowls of cereal and placed them on the dining table.

"Oh, thank god, they're quiet" I sighed, rubbing my eyes.

"You look exhausted" mum said.

"I am, I didn't sleep much last night."

"Oh no, are you okay?"

She was worried that I was having side effects from the med's or that they had stopped working and I was getting bad again.

"I'm fine mum, honest, in fact I haven't felt this good for a while." I told her and I wasn't lying, despite the devil dating my mother, I was feeling pretty good. Mikey and I had made up and we were friends like the last couple of months didn't happen, and I had gained a friendship with Sammy.

Mum smiled at me; I think she knew I was doing better. "Okay well try and get some rest" she added, handing me my medication and a glass of water.

"I'm going to go to Mikey's, it will probably be easier than here" I told her, taking the glass, quickly swallowing the pills and putting the empty glass in the sink.

"Okay but can you be home at six tonight? Charles and I are going on a date, I need you to look after the girls." I nodded and waved goodbye, kissing the girl's forehead as they were finishing their cereal. I headed out into the landing and as I was putting my shoes on, I looked into the living room. Charles was sitting there with his phone in his hand but this time he was looking at me. I glared back for a second and then continued putting on my shoes. I could see he was still staring but I didn't want to give him the satisfaction of staring back at him again. I left the house quite quickly feeling myself getting irritated by the eyes burning at the back of my head.

Mikey's new flat wasn't too far away from mine, it was slightly further than his parents' house but in the opposite direction. The walk wasn't too bad. It was nice and scenic for most of it, passing a few houses and a graveyard, but it was nice and quiet. It was a warm winter's day, and I'd left the house in only a jacket, but I didn't mind. Soon enough I had arrived at Mikeys, I still found it weird coming to his flat, I was so used to meeting with him at the park. After Mikey came out of the hospital, he gave me the spare key. He told me to use it whenever I wanted, he said the only rule was to message him before I was coming so he knew to expect me. I would have never just walked into his home anyway, I wasn't that kind of person, my mother had taught me better than to just walk into somebody else's home. I rang the doorbell and then put my key into the lock, it opened, and I heard Mikey shout, "come on in Tom."

"Here you go mate," was the first thing he said to me as he passed me a spliff. I knew I shouldn't have taken it; I was trying to quit; I knew how bad it was for my mental health, but I couldn't resist. I took the spliff and sat next to him on the sofa.

"Where's Sammy?" I asked.

"Oh, he's got a new job, he started last week." "What about you?" I asked.

"What about me?"

"You got a job yet?" I spoke as I exhaled and passed it back to Mikey.

"Na, I don't think I'm a working person." which made me laugh.

"Nobodies a working person Mikey, we work cause we have to, for money."

This comment wasn't unsurprising coming from Mikey, but it did annoy me. I thought to myself, how could he not care about going out and making hard, honest money? I would die to be able to make some decent money rather than the £70 a week the government gave me. I always knew that Mikey was lazy, I just didn't realise that he cared so little that he didn't even want to get a part time job. I mean four hours a day for five days is better than nothing, but I couldn't say that to Mikey. He didn't care, he really was too lazy to get up off the sofa, I was surprised he hadn't started peeing in bottles instead of getting up to go to the toilet.

I didn't remember falling asleep, but I must have because the next thing I knew I was waking up to Sammy coming into the flat, I couldn't believe that I had slept for that entire time. I sat up on the sofa, throwing off the blanket that Mikey must have put on me when I was sleeping.

"Hey Tom," Sammy shouted as he entered the kitchen.

"Hey," I answered, folding the blanket up and putting it on the side of the sofa. Sammy came into the living room and sat on the single chair that they had, Mikey was in the kitchen cooking something spicy from the smell of it. I never knew he could cook but I guessed Mikey was the stereotypical stay at home mum while Sammy was the working dad.

"How was work?" I asked Sammy, still half asleep.

"Yeah, it was good, thanks" Sammy replied.

"Charles stayed the night. Is that why you're here?" He asked.

"Yeah, I couldn't sleep," I told him, and he nodded. I think he knew what I was hinting at but didn't ask me any more questions.

"Tom, are you staying for tea? I'm doing fajitas." Mikey shouted from the kitchen.

"No thanks" I shouted back. I looked at the time, 4:30pm. I had to be home soon to look after the girls. "Actually, I should probably head off. I gotta babysit tonight." I told them both. I grabbed my shoes, said goodbye to Mikey in the kitchen and waved to Sammy as I went past the living room and left the flat.

Heading home the atmosphere felt a bit different, there was a slight chill that kept hitting me from the back and the sky was becoming darker and darker every minute I was walking. I passed the graveyard and looked at it, there was a family in there huddled around a grave. I wondered what they were doing, whether they were simply cutting the grass and putting fresh flowers down or if they were mourning at the recent loss of their family member. I walked past not wanting to stop in case it was disrespectful, or they thought I was being rude but remembering what I saw. I thought about how my family would have reacted if I had died, how mum would have coped with the girls without me. I had to quickly shake that thought out of my head, I couldn't think about things like that. It wouldn't help.

I got home with plenty of time to spare, mum had already given the girls dinner and had left some money out on the side.

"Treat yourself to a takeaway," she told me as she left for her date night with Charles. I always felt bad for taking her money, but she basically shoved it into my pocket making sure I couldn't give it back.

The girls wanted to watch Finding Dory, but I told them, "if we're watching a kids movie, it's going to be Finding Nemo, the original story." The girls moaned and groaned but in the end I won. I ordered a pizza and shared most of it with them. By the time the movie ended the girls had fallen asleep. I carefully picked each one of the girls up and took them upstairs to bed.

I stayed downstairs waiting for mum to come in, it was past midnight when she returned by herself.

"Oh, I didn't think you'd still be up" she whispered walking into the front room.

"I wanted to wait up for you," I told her, looking around for Charles.

"Where is he then?" I asked.

"Uh, he's gone home. We had a few too many and things got heated." Mum came in from the front room dripping wet from the rain, making it hard for me to tell if she had been crying.

"Are you okay? He didn't hurt you, did he?" I asked her, my voice raised slightly but mum shook her head.

"No, but I couldn't shake off what you told me about Sammy, so I did some digging... a lot of digging, and umm... I'm so sorry..." Mum started crying and for a second I stood in the living room not knowing what to do. "... I should have believed you straight away, but I didn't and I'm really sorry."

I walked over to mum; I didn't know what to say. I felt like turning around and shouting "I KNEW IT. I WAS RIGHT. I'M ALWAYS RIGHT." but it was neither the time nor the place. So, I stood in front of mum, gave her my most sympathetic smile and hugged her.

After 20 minutes of hugging, apologising and reassuring mum broke free from my grasp.

"Do you want a drink or anything? I mean we're both up now. How about my famous hot chocolate, you always loved them." I asked.

"As much as I would love one right now, I think I might just go to bed. It's been a long day." Mum ran her hand through her hair. She looked exhausted. She gave me a kiss on the cheek and walked upstairs to bed.

I stood in the middle of the room trying to make sure that what had happened was real. I knew mum would come to her senses; she always did but I thought Charles would have taken her to the dark side. I thought I'd end up like Sammy.

* * *

When I woke up the next day, I had a spring in my step. It was Friday, which meant therapy and I knew I wanted to talk to the Doc about what had happened. I walked into Dr. Goodall's office two hours later.

"Good morning, Tom, you're walking like you mean business." He joked and I nodded, "yeah I know what I want to talk about today." I told him. Dr Goodall opened his notepad and looked at me.

"Go ahead."

"My mum and Charles split up, and I couldn't be happier. They had an argument about Sammy and how Charles was lying. I don't know the exact details, but they broke up." I stopped talking and looked at Dr. Goodall trying to figure out what he was thinking. He wrote in his notepad for a few moments and then looked up at me

"Okay that's what you wanted, wasn't it? So why are you bringing it up in session?" He asked me.

"I know that Charles wasn't a good person, it was nothing to do with my OCD thinking he was a bad man. He was an outright, horrible tosser, but what if I think every man my mum dates is horrible. What if my mum can't ever date anyone because I start thinking guys with mullets are bad people. Or what if a guy who dates my mum doesn't like animals and I think he's a psychopath. I'm worried that my mum won't be able to date or have a life because I'm always going to have those negative thoughts."

For a moment Dr Goodall stared at me, he didn't write in his notepad, he just spent a moment looking at me.

"It's a difficult one isn't it, figuring out what's an intrusive thought and what's a normal, protective thought. I think the difference with Charles is that you had evidence, you had Sammy's word and you had no reason to believe he would lie about something like that. With that evidence and with Charles' confession you knew that Charles was a dangerous man. So, if your mum dates again, do the same."

"Wait, you mean I should interrogate every man that dates my mum?" I chuckled.

"Within reason, yes. It's completely normal for people to want to interrogate potential dates of family members. Most dad's do it with their daughters."

"Oh, that's good, I thought I was going mad again," I laughed, but Dr Goodall remained straight faced.

"No Tom, I don't think you're going mad again, in fact I think you're ready to go back to work, if you think you are." When he said that I couldn't help but open my mouth in shock. I didn't know what to say, I had always assumed I was going to be sticking to the same routine for another couple of months.

"You've been an outpatient now for over two months, and you're doing really well. You're always going to have setbacks but today has just proved that you know how to correctly respond to them. You're doing great Tom. I think you're ready but only you can know if you're ready. Are you?" He asked and for a moment I was stuck, I didn't know the answer. I did feel ready, but I felt that last time and only lasted a month.

"I guess there's only one way to find out." I answered and with that Dr Goodall was filling out my back to work sheets. He told me that he still wanted to see me every Friday especially for the first two months and then once a month from then on unless I wanted to increase or decrease it. I was happy with the plan, and I left Dr Goodalls office feeling a hundred stone lighter. I was allowed to get a job.

Chapter Ten

Charles had been calling and texting mum, but she had been ignoring him, she didn't even like me mentioning his name. I think she was just embarrassed with everything that happened and for how long she went without believing me. I think she thought my OCD was bad, but I know something must have happened for her to finally switch and trust what I was saying. A couple of days after they split up, Mum told me that Charles had been leaving horrible messages on her phone, so with the remaining money in my savings I bought her a new sim card. I wouldn't let Charles hurt my mum like he had Sammy's.

* * *

As soon as Dr Goodall cleared me fit for work, I started looking for a new job. Finding a job was harder than it needed to be. Majority of the jobs that seemed interesting to me wanted experience and a degree. I never understood why jobs needed you to have a bachelor's degree, and five years' experience. I mean how can you get experience if they don't give you a job. I was not doing five years of free labour either. I wanted to find a job that was only 32 hours long, one that I could progress into if I wanted, one that would allow me to do my writing on the side, and one that I enjoyed, but nothing was coming up and the jobs I applied for I never heard back.

In the end I started applying for part-time jobs as well, ones that I could go to and still be able to look after the girls, see Mikey and go to therapy. Something was better than nothing.

It was only when I was walking through my local village and went into a coffee shop to get a drink that I noticed they were hiring.

"Hi, um, what do you need to apply for a job here?" I asked the lady at the counter.

"Oh, you don't need experience, we just want someone who's happy to serve customers and do overtime when needed." She answered. I smiled and thanked her for the coffee and headed outside. I looked at the sign on the window of the shop, they were wanting someone for 16 hours a week and someone for 30 hours a week.

I didn't have much to lose, so I went home and emailed the owner my CV. She got back to me the next day offering me an interview on Monday after. I was quite excited; it wasn't something I planned to do but it was better than nothing and I was learning how to make different kinds of coffee. I told mum about my interview, and she was ecstatic.

When Monday came round, I was feeling quite nervous, I had never had a proper interview before, I'd only ever worked at the DIY shop and with that it wasn't even an interview, I just filled in forms and got the job. I wanted the job, so I got my best suit out. I hadn't worn it since school, but I thought it must have still fitted me. I was very wrong; it was tiny and at that moment I began panicking.

"I have nothing to wear," I told mum, frustrated that I hadn't thought about it earlier.

"I have just the thing," mum answered, she walked into her room and then moments later came back with a suit.

"Whose is that?" I asked her, wondering if Charles left it in mum's wardrobe

"It was your dad's wedding suit." she told me and held it up. I didn't know what to think, I mean I hate my dad and mum loaves him, but mum held it like it was the most sentimental thing.

"Why have you still got it?" I asked her, taking it from her grasp.

"I thought you might want to wear it on your wedding day, I kept it just in case. It also reminds me of you." She told me, taking it back off me and holding it against my body, measuring it from the eye.

"What?" I asked her, confused by what she had just said.

"What do you mean it reminds you of me?" I asked her again.

"I found out I was having a boy the day before my wedding. I was so happy when I found out, even happier than marrying your dad. I knew that I was going to call you Thomas, after my grandad. I thought if you were a girl, I'd call you Callie." She told me, now sitting on the edge of the bed.

"Where did Elise come from then?"

"The girls are named after my two school best friends. Callie was my primary school friend, she passed away when we were both 12 and Elise was my best friend until 18 when she moved to New Zealand." I had never heard mum talk about her friends, I didn't know that she had any if I was honest.

"I wanted you to wear this, not for your dad but for me." She told me and then handed me the suit. I looked at it for a moment.

"Thank you" I smiled and walked into my room.

I tried on the suit, and it was almost a perfect match, I took off the blazer because I thought it might be too dressy for an interview at a coffee shop and I changed the bow tie to a normal tie. I headed downstairs and went to mum in the kitchen.

"Where's the blazer?" she asked.

"It was too formal for an interview at a coffee shop, mum"

She chuckled "fair enough" she replied. She walked over to me and looked me up and down.

"You're very handsome."

"I better go."

"Good luck, knock 'em dead."

I was glad to be walking to the interview, the nerves needed to leave my body and exercise was a great way to do it. The weather wasn't so nice, but I didn't mind, the breeze made sure I didn't sweat before the interview. I got to the coffee shop with 20 minutes to spare. I headed up to the barista.

"Hi, I'm here for an interview with Sophie." I told the guy, he politely told me to sit down and wait, so I did.

I must have only waited for 10 minutes when Sophie came out to greet me, she was of average build with blonde hair and a massive smile on her face.

"Hi, I'm Sophie, I'm the manager of this coffee shop." She took me to the back of the shop; we entered a small room that had a computer and two chairs. "Please take a seat" so I did.

"So, this is going to be a chilled interview, I don't have a lot of questions, but I'll tell you more about the shop. Is that okay?" She smiled and continued talking "So, at the moment we have two full-timers, I'm one of them and Maddie is our other full-timer but we are looking for someone to join in just so there's added help. We also have three part-timers' currently and we're looking for someone to fill another part-time position. It gets quite busy in the morning and around lunchtime so it's nice to have the help. What position were you thinking of?"

"Well, I was thinking about the part time position just because I can't work Fridays at the moment." I told her and she wrote something down in her notepad "well we can do it where one of your day's off is a Friday. We can definitely arrange that if full-time hours are something you wanted to do."

"Sounds perfect." I agreed, excited at the prospect of going back into full time work.

"So, question time, what's your favourite season and why?"

"I like Autumn, I like that it's still warm in the day but at night you need a jacket. I like how the leaves fall and create piles and how they crunch under your feet. My sisters love jumping in the piles." I told her and

Sophie smiled at me, "it's a good season." Sophie asked me a few other random questions, I think she wanted someone to work with her who had a personality rather than experience. At the end of the questioning, she turned to me, "well Tom, I have two other people I'm interviewing but I really like you, I think you'd get along great here. You don't have to answer, it's only to write on my paperwork but what is the reason you can't work Fridays? You don't have to answer if it's personal reasons."

I thought for a moment, I didn't know whether to be honest. I didn't want her to be put off giving me a job because I had mental health issues, but I also didn't want a repeat of my old job, where they found out and then were weird to me. I thought if I was at least honest now then, it would save me from any pain in the future.

"Umm, yeah I see a therapist on Fridays." I told her. I waited to see what her reaction would be, but it didn't change.

"Okay, if it helps, so do I." she told me and smiled. I smiled back, I didn't know what else to say, I didn't have anything else to say. I'd told her the truth and she was okay with it, and she admitted she too saw a therapist. This went from a job I needed to make money to a job I wanted to be in. I knew Sophie wasn't going to judge me. It felt good knowing that someone wasn't going to judge me.

At the end of the interview, she escorted me out of the office, I looked around, there wasn't much of a back space, there were some lockers and a table and chair but that was about it.

"This is the backroom; I know it's not much but there is a back garden just through there." she pointed to the emergency door. She showed me the front again, showed me the coffee machine and let me know that the guy who I spoke to was called George.

"He makes a mean cappuccino," she told me, and I laughed. It seemed like a nice place to work. Nice and friendly, I could see myself fitting in here.

"If you get the job, you'll work with George for a day, me for two days and you'll work two full days with Maddie. She's great, she's always working, offering to do overtime. She has a bit of a dark humour and doesn't take any crap from anyone, but she's a good kid. So, what do you think?" She asked.

"it's nice, it's really nice and George seems happy to work here, which is good." I could imagine myself working here but I couldn't get my hopes up. She mentioned two other people were going for the job and if they were also a suitable match, they could get it instead of me. I didn't want to get my hopes up. I thanked Sophie for the interview, and she told me she'd get back to me Friday after my therapy session.

I left feeling good. I left feeling like I had done something. For the first time in months, I went somewhere with the intention of doing something and it felt good. I mean even if I didn't get the job, at least I tried, I put on a suit, went to an interview, told them about going to therapy and even had a laugh. It was the most I'd done in ages, and I felt good.

* * *

It was 11:06am when Sophie called, I remember it because I looked at my phone as it rang, I let it ring three times and then I answered it.

"Hi Tom, it's Sophie from the coffee shop." "Hi Sophie, how are you?"

"Yeah, all good thank you, I was calling about the job interview. You were amazing, you seemed to have a real bubbly personality." Oh no! They always say things like that just before they turn around and say we don't want you. People tried to be nice, before letting you down. "I just wanted to offer you the full-time position."

What? I couldn't believe it! She offered me the job!

"Oh wow, yes thank you, I'll take it" I laughed, I couldn't contain my happiness. I was walking around my room in circles trying to contain my excitement of being offered a job.

"Actually, we decided to only hire you, the other two weren't best matches for the company but we think you will be. Are you able to start Monday?" She asked and it took me a couple of seconds to recognise what she was saying.

"Yes! Yes, of course I can." I answered, my smile as big as my face.

"Okay great, bring your national insurance number, bank details and wear something comfortable but smart, a lot of staff wear black jeans and a plain t-shirt. We don't have a proper work uniform." she told me. She then congratulated me on the job and told me she'd see me Monday. I was so excited I didn't know what to do.

I eventually walked downstairs and saw mum waiting in the kitchen for me, her eyes were wide open.

"Well?"

"I got the job!"

"Well done! I'm so proud of you." She exclaimed.

"I start Monday" I told her, and she smiled at me. I knew she was happy. I was happy and I knew, despite not having a clue what I was on about, the girls would be happy as well.

Epilogue

And that brings me up to date, tomorrow I will start my new job and start my new life. A new chapter some may say. Sure, I'm nervous, like most people are when they start something new but I'm ready. I know I can do it. If there's something I learned in the last year, it's that life is never straight forward. Sure, you'll have brief intervals of calm and quiet and normal but then something happens, and it can be chaotic and stressful, and you can wish it didn't happen, but it did, and you need to embrace it. You need to cherish every moment you get, even if it's bad because there is beauty everywhere, you just need to look for it.

I have the rest of my life so I'm going to live it. I'm going to live a whole new life. One that's full of happiness and exploration and lots of questions. I might even take on Grace's 100 question game.

Will I like the job?
Will I make new friends?
Will I fall in love one day?
Will I go abroad?
Will I visit loads of places?
Will the girls be happy?
Will they ever suffer through anything that I have?

Having questions is good, it means you care, and I do. I care about the girls; I care about Mikey and Sammy. I care a lot about my mum and now and then I even care about myself. Just like everyone else in my life,

I deserve to be happy too. So, I'm going to live my life and I'm going to do it correctly. I'm going to do it positively. I'm going to make friends with everyone I come across and fall in love in the most ridiculous circumstances. I won't let my OCD define me; I won't let it take over. Not this time. No, this time I'm in control.

I'm Thomas Peter Johnston and only I can control my life.

About the Author

Amber R Cotterell is a Bristol born author. She's always had a keen interest in writing and at 10 years old her first ever piece was published as part of a collection of poems by people in the UK called "A guiding light". Her second published piece of work was a short story that was submitted when she was 14 that was inserted into a book called "A twist in the tale". Reading was always a great escape for Amber, and she soon found that mental health wasn't written about nearly as much as it should be. She decided to write a book that she wanted to read and in 2021 "With Love Maddie" was published.

Amber has now created the Coffee Shop Collective, a trilogy of books that focus on 3 main characters and their struggles with mental health. Tom suffers with OCD, Maddie suffers from Anxiety, and Sophie suffers with PTSD. All incredibly serious mental health disorders. Each character has their own battle to face, all while working together in the same coffee shop. The Coffee Shop Collective is all about encouraging people to talk about mental health as well as learning to be kinder to those around us, as we never know who may be struggling.

Printed in Great Britain
by Amazon

12386950R00150